Tara's Touch

by

Carla Brice-Talley

Carla Brice-Talley   *Tara's Touch*

Copyright © 2019 Carla Brice-Talley. All rights reserved.

This is a work of fiction. Any resemblance to actual individuals, events, or locations is purely coincidental.

No portion of this work, in part or in the whole, may be copied, duplicated, transmitted, or otherwise distributed in any form without the written permission of the author.

ISBN-13: 978-1-947373-15-0

ISBN-10: 1-947373-15-3

Submitted to the Library of Congress

Set in Cambria 12 point

Printed in the United States of America

First Edition

Lexingford Publishing LLC
Los Angeles   Hong Kong   San Francisco   New York
www.lexingfordpublishingllc.com

Dedication

- *To my husband, Darren, who helped build my confidence by listening to excerpts late at night and affirmed my dream to become a published author.*
- *To my children, Adam and Zoe, who encouraged me with their excitement and assertions never to give up.*
- *To both my sisters, in particular to my little sister, Kimberly, who carved out time from her very busy schedule to read my manuscript.*
- *Finally, to my parents, Willie James Brice and Kaylin Brice, whose leadership, guidance, correction and affection directly contributed to who I am today.*

Chapter 1

"Are you scared?" The nurse asked her.

The woman looked kind enough, but Tara already had her fill of people who looked kind, spoke kindly and even expressed concern. However, when she really needed the kindness to be more than words, it was never there.

She shook her head in response to the question, but did not speak. Tara had made up in her mind that she was going to limit the words that came from her mouth. She did not owe anyone extended explanations or thanks. Her number one goal was to have her baby and find a way to escape the claws of the system that had engulfed her most of her life.

"Well, don't be scared, sweetheart," the nice, chubby-looking, blonde-haired lady responded. "It is going to be fine. People have babies every day. And you –well--you are young. Your body is strong. You and the baby are doing just fine. "

Tara did not respond. She could feel her child moving inside her. Her baby was strong. Her baby was like her and, even though she had limited prenatal care, she knew it was a boy. A boy who would grow into a great man. However, she had a lot of work to do to get him to where he needed to be.

"The doctor is going to stop in shortly." The woman checked the vitals of Mommy and baby one more time. She seemed satisfied with the heart rates. She then put her hands gently about Tara's ankles again and squeezed lightly before leaving the room.

Tara had been so deep in thought she had not realized that someone else had called to the nurse. The emergency room was really busy that afternoon. The folks were preparing her for transfer to the maternity ward. Tara could hear doctors and others talking about gunshot wounds, knife stabbings and strange, unrecognizable ailments. While she could hear people panicking around her, it was more like background noise except for one case that stood out to her.

An older gentleman had shortness of breath. He caught her attention because he looked like someone's dad. She chuckled to herself. He was a tall mocha-colored black man with a big stomach, but strong and chiseled arms. Was that her dad? Someone told her that her father had worked construction. He would probably be that age at this time and he would probably look like that. It would be ironic if this man currently fighting for his life was the man she had never met.

Just then the baby kicked her and she felt a sharp pain. "Right," she said aloud. "Keep focused. I don't have time to think about foolish things right now."

Tara decided not to make a big deal about the pain she was feeling. She waited patiently. It was not long before a short man in green scrubs came into the area assigned to her. He mumbled something to her. Another person lifted the divider and walked toward her. They carefully took the baby monitor and before she knew it, she was moving along the off-white, sterile smelling halls of the hospital. As they passed by the area where the black man had been taken, she thought she heard the clear, alarming sound of a flat-line. Tara hoped they would be able to get his heart beating again, but she did not think it was likely.

"So, sorry you passed Daddy," she thought as her soon-to-be-born child kicked her again.

Chapter 2

Now Tara had to look at another white lady. This one had glasses, brown hair and a suit that Tara knew had been purchased second hand. In fact, it looked like the suit she had looked at and admired a few days ago. Tara did not have enough money to purchase the $20 suit at the thrift store and it would not have fit her anyway in her condition. The other thing Tara noticed about her was that her fingernails were bitten down like nubs and her knuckles were red. It was either her job or her home life that had this woman nervous. Was this nervous woman there to give her advice?

"We have many options," the nervous woman was saying to her. "I don't know what your plans are, but in your current state--no place to stay, no job and no family--we won't be able to let the baby go with you. I spoke with the hospital administration. You can stay here for two days, but this is a hospital, not a temporary shelter. So we'll need to secure housing for you somewhere. How old are you?"

Tara closed her eyes. She was imagining the home she would eventually make for her son. Yes. He was a boy. He was born seven pounds and four ounces. Tara had already held him in her arms and she had pumped milk for him. Was this lady seriously telling her she was not going to take her child with her? Of course she was. That is how they are trained, she thought. They are trained to convince young mothers like her that they don't have the ability or power to take care of their children. Yet God had given her body power to conceive. Her body was powerful enough to deliver the child without complication. If all that was possible, what was food? Just then she put her hands on her sore breasts. They were heavy with milk.

Maybe her mother had been fooled into giving her up. She would never know.

I got food for him, too, she thought. Tara knew if she was to escape out of this place with her child, she was going to have to play the game.

Just then she took her rich-toned voice and made it a little lighter. She even allowed a little shaking to vibrant through her voice so that the woman would not interpret her thoughts. It was important to seem weak, ignorant and eager to please. You want a scared teenager? Okay. I will give you one.

"I am sixteen."

"The child's father?"

Tara did not say anything. To her, the father of her son was a means to an end. He was the sperm that she needed, not the sperm that she wanted. It was a terrible ordeal and she did not want to remember it any longer. He slobbered over her and forced her. She heard a preacher say once that Joseph's slavery in Egypt led to him becoming the second-most powerful man in the world at the time. After the anger and frustration of being raped again subsided, she thought about it. What if she could use this awful experience for something powerful?

"Unknown," she whispered.

"You don't know who the father is or you won't say who he is?" the woman asked, in skepticism.

"He's not here and he's not coming. He is unknown."

"Okay," she said, seemingly not willing to play with that concept any longer or investigate further. "Can you read?"

"Yes."

"I am going to leave some literature with you to take a read-through. I really want you to consider adoption for your child. He is a baby and there are many well-settled, nice couples who would love a baby. Perhaps this is one of the best things you can do for him."

Arrogant, Tara thought in quiet anger. How can some strangers be better for him than the woman who bore him? Tara hid her anger wisely. They are trained to tell young girls these terrible things, she thought again. She doesn't know that Tara had already started taking care of her son. As soon as she knew she was pregnant, she handled herself in a completely different way. She avoided the dangerous shelters, looked for the best food she could find and made sure she was close to urgent care facilities or hospitals. Tara had even left the awful city of her rape. Her baby was going to have a fresh start. She did odd jobs and scraped up enough money for a one-way bus ticket. This woman would probably see that as reckless. Tara saw it as power. She was not going to be a victim any longer. Fifteen years was long enough.

Tara had already lived with some of the settled, nice people this woman talked about. They have nice homes. They have two cars. They have their own children sometimes and nice jobs. They feed you, clothe you-- even drop you off at school and ask you about your homework. However, at night the husband comes looking for rent from you. The wife does not know he has decided to obtain payment in addition to the state subsidy. The wife feels so good about her good husband and the good they are doing together. The clueless wife does not know that he takes the virginity of the helpless girls in her care as payment for eating his good food and staying in his nice home.

Tara opted for homelessness. She would rather not pay that high fee and her son was not going to land in the hands of one of these perverse men and/or women. No. She will make a home for him, but she cannot tell the nice, nervous white lady that. The social worker, still paying off her student loan dealing with case after case of pathetic individuals like Tara, cannot be bothered with a story of potential triumph. Tara decided to let her think she was doing her job. Another day of shipping a young, black, Latino, or poor white person into the system that has no mercy.

The system that is well-oiled and processes people into sub-human beings ready for the jails, welfare and public cemeteries cannot be stopped. Of course, this woman does not see it that way. She thinks it's better for Tara and her child to be separated and put in the homes of one of these "nice" people rather than to be on the mean streets.

The streets are not that bad. At least the streets are honest with you. You can prepare for hunger, pain and mistreatment in the streets.

"Thank you for the literature," Tara told her before the woman left to seek out her next case.

Chapter 3

This was her chance. After screening her for every test known to man, the nurses and doctors allowed Tara to relieve her breasts. She was told that they would give her son her milk for the first time. There he was in her arms, safe and sound. He was peaceful and fell asleep with her brown nipple in his mouth. Tara gently lifted his head, snuggled him securely in two little blankets so he could feel the warmth and security of the cloth hugging him. She made sure his air passage was clear. Then she eased out of bed.

Tara was a little sore still from the vaginal laceration she had sustained while pushing her baby out. The doctor had patched her up and she was given some aspirin for pain relief. Her nurse emphasized to her repeatedly the importance of keeping the area clean to avoid infection. She took a deep breath several times because of the stinging between her legs. Tara grabbed the squeeze bottle they had given her to squirt her vaginal area each time she used the bathroom.

Someone had done her the favor of washing the clothes she had on when she came to the emergency room the day before. She slipped into them. The pants fit a little big around the waist now. Fortunately, Tara had not gained much weight during her pregnancy. She was about fifteen pounds lighter post pregnancy. The faded jeans and V-neck yellow sweater fit her reasonably well. She was more embarrassed about the rustic-looking tennis shoes on her feet than the bagginess of her jeans. Tara pulled off the hospital bonnet and let her black curls hang about her face. It was somewhat of a messy look, but she did not have time to worry about that. She took her book bag, which never carried books. Her book bag always carried her dearest possessions. Carefully she placed Juan, her newborn baby boy, into the bag. Tara carefully tightened the straps.

Before she knew it, she was walking through the halls of the hospital. She looked like a teenager going to visit her granddad. She was careful not to take the long hall down the maternity ward. They always watched for the babies. Instead she went down the back steps and through the chaos of the emergency room. A man stopped her because he thought she dropped a twenty-dollar bill. Tara smiled and took it. It was a nice blessing, since she had no cash.

Maybe not today. But she was sure she had at some point dropped a twenty-dollar bill. In no time, she was on the street again. She dipped in the first corner to take Juan out of the book bag. She hugged him closely and placed a few kisses on his forehead.

"I am sorry for covering you like that. I just needed to get you safe. Now you are safe with me," she explained sweetly to him.

He did not respond immediately. He yawned and seemed to snuggle closer to her. In her heart, she knew he understood.

"It's okay, Mama. So glad you did not leave me in there." Tara smiled, feeling confident that she had interpreted his calm yawn correctly.

"I would never leave you," she whispered. Tara hugged him again and looked around. She could not believe it. There was a thrift store across the street. After looking both ways, she trotted across the street. Through the window, she could see the first thing she wanted to buy for Juan. They both needed it.

Tara walked into the store, noticing immediately that it smelled better than other second-hand stores she had visited before. Merchandise in the store seemed to be of good quality. A certain excitement started to bubble in her as she surveyed the simple, but sturdy stroller more closely. It was perfect for Juan. There was space to lay a newborn baby in the stroller and it could adjust as the child grew older. In addition, Tara could see that there were no visible stains on the material. She really wanted to lay her child in it.

"How much for the stroller?" she asked aloud, not looking directly at the attendant. He was a white man in his mid-thirties. When she entered the store, he did not greet her because he had not really noticed someone was in the store. He was reading something

"No price on it?" the attendant asked, a little annoyed with the interruption.

"No, sir."

He came from around the counter. He looked at the stroller. It was in decent shape. His eyes trailed over her and the baby in her arms.

"I will let you have it for twenty."

She smiled. "Sold."

Chapter 4

The first two nights they slept at the bus station. But Tara knew that was not going to do for Juan. She kept washing out his cloth diaper, but she noticed he was getting a rash. The diaper wasn't clean enough. Tara did not feel comfortable going to the women's shelter because authorities might be looking for her and Juan. Now she had to strategize and do something quickly.

She was sitting on a park bench and decided to go over to a little restaurant across the way. It was a small place with only a few tables inside. The smells of the place told the story to Tara. If she had a grandmother, her kitchen would probably smell like this place. Fried chicken, chicken fried steak, turkey wings. There were so many wonderful, savory smells and Tara realized how hungry she was. She had been filling herself with as much water as she could drink to keep her milk flowing. She would love to have a biscuit.

Tara was not the begging type, but as her stomach started to growl and the hollowness made itself more pronounced, she considered flat-out begging. However, as she thought about it, she rejected the notion. Juan could not see her beg – even as a baby.

Just then, a combination of curse words could be heard from the kitchen. The voice belonged to a woman. She hurled her swear words. Soon there was a response from a man with a very deep voice. Tara looked around. She was the only customer in the place to witness this disturbing and unprofessional display of anger.

After a few more seconds of screaming, with Juan adding his own screaming to it, the woman came stomping around the corner. "My own daddy don't talk to me like that. You must be crazy, old man. I am out of here. I quit."

She was a skinny, dark-skinned woman with muscular arms. Her short afro looked unkempt and her white uniform was stained with various food residue. Tara noticed how tight her face was. There was so much anger in the woman, it was hard to discern her features.

"Quit'n right before the lunch rush!" A big, burly black man said as he appeared from the back. "That is something that a no-good..."

Tara winced. She had been called that word before. It was frustrating to receive that type of verbal punishment or to witness it. However, she had to admit that the woman was effective in her verbal retaliation. The show made her forget how hungry she was. But she made a mental note to make sure that her son never spoke like that to women.

The lady walked past her as if she did not see her or her sweet baby. It was not long before the door swung wildly open and she disappeared. For a brief moment, one could still hear her screaming in the distance. Soon there was silence.

The man stood there for a moment looking at the door. Then he looked over in Tara's direction and shook his head. All of sudden, he seemed very calm and not upset at all. He cocked his head as though he was pondering some great question.

"Now maybe you can answer me a question." His heavy voice was rich and Tara decided instantly that she liked the tone of it. When he was not yelling, he sounded all right. "If you getting paid to work, why don't you want to do the things the man who is paying you asks you to do? I am cooking. I am doing most everything. I just ask her to clean and do a few extras,

She acts like I am asking her to do something she shouldn't do. I don't get you young folks. Ya'll don't want to work. Ya'll don't want to put time in."

"I don't mind working," she responded, sensing an opportunity. Something about him made her feel comfortable despite the anger he had just displayed with the unknown woman. He did not seem like a man who just screamed all the time.

"I bet," he laughed sarcastically. "You are too pretty and too young to do any real work." He looked her over. Tara realized he was doing an assessment of her at the same time. It was not in the nasty, uncomfortable way she had seen before. It made her want to pass the test, so she sat up and looked him squarely in the face.

"No, sir," she protested. "I need real work. I need real money, too," she added quickly.

That was obvious to him. Her clothes had a worn look to them and so did her shoes. She looked reasonably clean, but there was a rugged look to her prettiness. Where was this young woman sleeping with this baby? How were they surviving? Ultimately, he was a country boy who had been raised in the church and he knew it was his responsibility to know.

He looked from her and down to the baby in the stroller. "I suppose you do. I can't stand lazy folks. What you gonna do with the baby while you work?"

She looked around. "I will feed him and care for him. Just let me work. He won't be any trouble. I promise."

"What's your name?"

"Tara Martin."

"Well, I guess you can't be no worse than that one that just left. I will give you a try. But one sign of laziness, bad attitude, snapping your head, or sucking

your teeth and you're out of here. I am too old to put up with all this nonsense."
　"Yes, sir. What's your name?"
　"Big Mike."

Chapter 5

    Big Mike was tough. But he gave Tara a cash advance, which allowed her to get a room for a week at a motel nearby. She took a hot shower, gave Juan a good bath and slept with her son in a decently clean bed.
    Her first full day of work went surprisingly well. Breakfast was a heavy rush with business folks coming through to grab a sandwich or two. Big Mike's Dive was known for its simple, flavorful food. Most people were grabbing food to go and Juan seemed to be comforted by all the noise around him. He did not make much fuss.
    Tara had done a good job of getting him on a feeding schedule. She worked her breaks around those times. After the breakfast rush, the place was calm for a few hours. Tara followed Big Mike's lead in helping get the place ready for the lunch rush. It seemed as though she had just finished feeding Juan and gathering the last bit of salt and pepper packs when the first batch of lunch customers came through the door.
    Food service had to be fast and courteous for Big Mike to keep his edge. Tara had seen many hungry days in her life. She never thought she could get to the place where she'd get tired of looking at food. However, after serving up the last bit of hamburgers and fresh-cut fries, she could honestly say that going to bed without the taste or smell of meat would suit her just fine.
    Big Mike walked over to her as she was wiping up a spill of ketchup from a careless patron. She was so focused on ensuring the space was clean that she did not notice his looming figure. Tara jumped after a second.

He laughed with a thunderous sound. "I like you, little girl. You remind me of my sister--a worker. I got an old uniform in the back. It should fit you."

She smiled back. "Thank you, Big Mike. I mean, Mr. Big. How should I call you?"

"Big Mike is fine." He looked over at Juan who was beginning to stir for an afternoon feeding. "Listen, after lunch is usually pretty slow. Why don't you finish cleaning up and you can take off? That way you can be refreshed for tomorrow morning."

"I appreciate that, but I don't want to leave you hanging. I can stay around a little longer." Tara was now sweeping the floor. "That way maybe both of us can leave at a decent hour."

He seemed to consider, but looked back at the baby. "No, Ms. Tara. Take Juan, go home—oh, but before you do, look in the tip jar. Take half of whatever's in there."

"But you already gave me an advance," she said, looking over at the jar.

Tara had not noticed the jar before. It was stuffed with dollar bills and coins. Big Mike did not even look at the jar. "Ms. Tara, I know what I gave you. You work for me and I think you are going to work out well. So, I am sharing the tip jar with you. I normally don't share the tip jar until a few months in, but I like your spirit and the way you work. Now if you don't need any more money--"

She laughed. "I need it, yes, sir. Lord knows I need it very badly."

"All right. Well, finish what you're doing, count the money and go home."

Chapter 6

After about a month of renting her room a week at a time, Big Mike introduced Tara to a woman who rented rooms at her duplex. Although Tara had no credit history, the woman rented one of the rooms to her on Big Mike's character reference alone and the fact that she had a steady job.

It was actually a little more than a room. It was a studio with a half stove. The room came furnished with a refrigerator, a bed and a chair. Soon Tara augmented the stroller with a small crib and other necessities for Juan.

She took great pride in cuddling him in the throw blanket she purchased or wiping his mouth with the soft face towels she procured. One evening Tara walked in the room to see a tall, light-skinned fellow screwing in light bulbs in the hallway.

She had learned in her life to size people up quickly. Tara noticed that as soon as she stepped in the door his attention was completely diverted from his task. He stopped what he was doing and was eyeballing her. Instantly he put her in mind of some of the men she had known before Big Mike. The awkward silence was annoying.

"How you doing, girl?" he finally asked.

"Fine," she said walking by him with her hands tightly on the stroller.

Tara hated to go into her apartment with his eyes on her backside. She opened the door and slipped in quickly. After locking the door, she double-checked the lock again.

Carla Brice-Talley   *Tara's Touch*

Chapter 7

The guy was the nephew of Ms. Sarah, the owner of the duplex. He made sure all the residents knew who he was and how he was related. Tara often found him lurking around the place. Supposedly he was cleaning, fixing and working. Tara had made up in her mind that she was not going to call him to fix anything.

It was not long before a few people reported things missing out of their apartments. Ms. Sarah was very protective of her nephew. She would never admit any knowledge of wrongdoing, but she would always accommodate a victimized resident with a discount on the rent.

One Sunday morning there was a knock on her door. Tara was not expecting anyone and did not really like people approaching her space. Although she knew it was not right to inherently distrust, it was hard to hear a knock at the door as just a knock. Slowly she looked through the tiny peep hole in the door. To her dismay, it was Mr. Sleaze himself. He knocked again.

"Who is it?" she asked, allowing her irritation to shine through her voice.

"It's Davis, Ms. Sarah's nephew," he added quickly.

"Okay," she responded raising the sound and tone of the "ay" an octave higher. "It's Sunday and it's early."

"Yeah. Sorry," he paused. "Aunt Sarah asked me to check the pipes. The main pipe is in your unit. I will be in one second and out. You won't even know I was there."

Tara looked over at her son, sleeping peacefully. She took a deep breath. Ms. Sarah had mentioned something about the pipes. Tara doubted she wanted this work done on a Sunday morning, but she did not want him whining to his aunt either. "Give me one sec."

She threw on a pair of jeans and a shirt and opened the door. He came in with that same awful grin he always had on his face. Tara took two full steps back to let him in the apartment.

"Man, you act like something is wrong with me, girl."

She looked him over again. He was about six feet tall with long arms and a long, skinny neck. He was grinning and she noticed his teeth could use some whitening. The thing that had probably helped him most in life was his hair. It was very curly and silky looking. But Tara realized now as she studied that hair, she did not like men with hair curlier than her own. He looked dressed for work. The pants were stained. The shirt was old. Was he cute? Sure, he was. He had a very nice face, but Tara could tell that was probably all he had--his looks.

"My name is not girl," she said and took another step back. "I have no idea where this pipe is you're looking for. Hope you know where it is."

"I know where the pipe is," he said, annoyed. Davis grabbed his tool-kit and walked over to the sink area. "You know--you won't tell me your name, so I call you girl."

"But I would imagine you know my name, so why can't you just use it?"

"Attitude. Why all you black girls got attitudes? Then you wonder why your men are looking at the white and Asian girls."

"Davis, I don't have any men. I am not concerned about any man except for that little one over there asleep. So, you can have all the white and Asian girls you like. I am just saying that you could show me some respect by using my name."

With this she walked over to where Juan slept and took her seat. The angle allowed her to watch Davis from a distance. She did not have many possessions, so she was not concerned about him stealing. She just wanted to keep an eye on his hands.

He laughed aloud, kneeling and turning his back to her. He pulled a few spider webs from a rusty pipe. "Peace, peace. Okay. I get it. Nah, I like my little feisty, attitude-infested black girls--women. Ya'll keep a brother on his toes. I bet you would keep me in line, wouldn't you?"

"I thought you were here to look at pipes," she retorted. Yes, he definitely was a good-looking guy. As he was on his knees, she noticed how muscular his back was. His body looked strong. He turned around again as if he knew no woman could resist how nice he looked.

He smiled in a nasty way. "Pipes? Which pipe you mean?" He noticed she straightened her back when he said it that way. "Girl! Ms. Tara, relax. I don't mean any harm. You the scary type of woman?"

"Look, if you have business here, do it. If not, I am actually going to church this morning and I don't want to be late."

He looked surprised and then shook his head. Davis took a wrench out of the kit. "Church? Why you want to bother yourself with that? I thought you were a smart girl."

"Okay," she responded sarcastically. "I am surprised you would say such a thing. I think your aunt would have some choice words to say about that."

"She would," he said, knocking the wrench against the pipe. Tara noticed he was turning the valve to the left.

"Are you loosening that?" she inquired.

" You are smart," he said. "Yes. I am loosening it because I am going to replace it."

"I did not see you turn off any water. If you loosen the valve with the water on, isn't it going to leak?"

"Good point. Let me switch this off and now let me replace this. But seriously--you believe in going to church and giving that preacher money you don't have?" He looked around at her tiny apartment.

Davis had to admit that it was small, but she kept a good house. He noticed there were some very nice things in the apartment that must have been purchased secondhand. Her son slept in a nice crib with embroidered blankets. Her bed had a nice comforter set on it. There was a little chest in the corner. Her apartment smelled nice.

"I am not saying you doing bad, but you shouldn't be wasting money you could have for that cute little boy."

Tara shook her head. "No. I believe that the Lord has blessed me and my child and I want to acknowledge that. I give to support ministry. The ministry of people has helped me in my life. So, that's me. You should try it."

"Try what?"

"Giving and not taking."

He turned around and looked at her. Tara could tell he was angry because his 'high-yellow' face was all red. "Don't believe everything you hear. These folks lying. Why do I have to take from anybody living here? No offense, but if they could stay someplace else they would."

"Fair enough, but crimes are committed where there is access." After a slight pause, Tara switched back to the subject of church. "Don't be so quick to tell a stranger how to live their life. You don't know me and the things that I have been through that have me going to church. A month ago, I was homeless with my baby. Now I am not. I prayed and the Lord helped me."

"Well, Big Mike and my aunt could get some credit for that, too," he responded matter-of-factly. "Don't make it sound like something you can't see waved a wand over your life and you had a place to stay and food. It was a little more complicated than that." His voice had a mocking tone in it.

"The Lord used them to help me. Trust me. I have seen a lot of people do harm or not help when they could help. So, I know when I am getting help." She looked over at the time. "It's nine. I need to start getting ready."

"So, you a Jesus Nut?" he asked, hoping to make her upset.

Tara smiled. "Certified crazy, thank you for asking. You finished yet or what?" Tara purposely sounded more impatient than she actually was. She had never been the one offering sound advice. She had always been on the other side.

"Yeah, I am finished. Which church you going to?"

"Why?" Her eyebrows were raised. Tara was now standing with her hands on her hips.

"I might come with you," he said in a smooth voice. He walked over to her and was standing very close to her. Tara supposed he thought that he had a sex appeal affect. For her it was a reminder of why she did not like him. He was trying to seduce her.

Davis reached out and put his grubby hand on her shoulder. She shrugged his hand off her, but a man like Davis was not easily deterred. He reached out for her again and Tara moved.

"Did I invite you?" she asked.

"I just figured --" he started to say.

"Well, you figured wrong. Your aunt goes to church every Sunday. If you want to go to church, go with her. I don't date and I don't date at church. And I don't have time for someone to try to use something I love so much to try to lead me into something else."

"You got me wrong. I like you." Tara noticed that his eyes were hazel and that only strengthened her resolve.

"Davis, you don't like me. You don't know me."

"Well, can I get to know you? You a fine young woman. I see you. I see how you care for your son and how you work hard. You don't have men hanging around you. And let me be honest with you. You're beautiful. Everything about you is attractive. I am working for my aunt now, but that's not all I am about. I have plans and someone like you could really--"

"I don't think so," she said, walking him toward the door. "See, I am one of those crazy Jesus Nuts. You wouldn't want to be around someone so dumb and backwards as me. I am sure that is not part of your plan."

"I think you're getting a little offended," he said, softening his tone. He looked around her place again. "I can help you. We can help each other."

"I don't need your kind of help. Have a good day."

By this time he was standing outside the door. Without an ounce of remorse, Tara closed the door in his face. She wondered if her pastor would use this as an example of Christian charity. Probably not, but she knew getting rid of Davis was the right thing to do.

Chapter 8

For a few days, Davis ignored her. Tara did not know if he was embarrassed or mad. For the most part she did not care. However, after day three Tara found herself impressed. She liked the dignity he showed. She considered speaking to him first when she saw him with his arms around a girl who had recently moved into the house.

The white girl seemed nice enough, but she was a little too nice. As Davis passed her with his arms about the girl, he seemed to give her a smug look. His look said, you had your chance. It was not long before she noticed Davis going in and out of the girl's apartment at all times of night. Soon it was common knowledge that he was living with the girl. If Ms. Sarah had an issue with it, she kept it to herself.

Tara was happy she had refused his kind of help. She noticed the young girl was buying more and more groceries while Davis was working less and less around the place. Soon he was doing a "side-hustle." Tara did not know what his hustle was, but it included him sleeping all day while the girl was out working.

She looked over at Juan who was toddling beside her as they walked together down the carpeted corridor. Tara squeezed his hand tightly.

"Son, no one will ever make a fool out of you and me."

Carla Brice-Talley   *Tara's Touch*

Chapter 9

It had been almost two years since Tara broke out of the hospital ward with her son. She was a working mother, had a legitimate job and address and had built a tiny community of friends. However, she was discontent.

Tara would awake at times in the middle of night. She was never one for nightmares. Even when she lived in terrible foster homes, she never allowed those things to haunt her dreams. Tara never thought about the man who fathered Juan. One could say that was the worst day of her life, but she never had nightmares about any of those experiences.

Her fear was not of people or things. Her fear was the thought of realizing that Juan would have been better off if someone else had taken him from her. Tonight she had not slept for a few hours. Tara sat up in the tiny bed and turned on the light. Her large brown eyes fell over her room.

She had tried to make a good home for them. Were there some decent things in the room? Yes. Had Juan known a day without food? No, thank God. She rose up and went over to the little bed she had purchased for him. He slept peacefully. Had he ever known a day without love? No, thank God.

"I know it is not good enough, baby," she whispered.

Big Mike was nice to her. He admired her work ethic and she worked as hard as she could for him. Tara had made a point of arriving early and leaving late. She made sure he never had to ask her to scrub, clean, attend to a customer, pick up something, or tidy something. But if she wanted more for Juan, she needed more than the $250 per week and the tips from the jar.

She leaned over and kissed Juan on the cheek. Tara kneeled down and started to pray. "Lord, I am sorry. I am thankful for all I have, but I just--I know there is more for me. I know there is more for my child. What should I do? Lord, please help me understand what I should do. In Jesus' Name. Amen."

As she prayed, she felt the nervousness and fear subside. Instead of feeling that, she felt a peace and warmth engulf her. It was as if God had put a warm comforter over her shoulders. A nice current began to tingle through her. Tears started to flow down her cheeks, but they were not sad tears. She felt tears of joy.

Tara started to think back on the days she hid herself in the house from a man or the time a woman slapped her face so hard she thought her cheeks would melt off her face. Those things seemed like distance shadows from someone else's life.

"I am thankful. I know you'll show me what to do," she said before resting in her bed. She was then able to fall asleep.

The next day, Tara was working as she normally did. A man and woman were having lunch and opted to stuff themselves at one of the tables at Big Mike's. The lady looked really well put together and seemed overly excited about eating at a "hole in the wall." The man was less excited, but his attitude was shaped by his lady friend.

They both started laughing and admiring the smells around them.

Tara smiled, too. They looked so happy it made her smile.

"Hello. Welcome to Big Mike's. What can I get you?"

"What do you recommend?" the man asked. The lady kicked him under the table. "Look at her. She doesn't eat here. Her waist is too tiny."

"Excuse my wife," he responded shaking his head. "She has hang-ups and thinks that small women do not eat. I keep telling her that you have to eat to keep up your metabolism. Not eating will help put weight on you."

The woman rolled her eyes and looked up at Tara. "Would you please tell him that we women don't have hang-ups? We just know that these men want women like you with hips and tiny waistlines."

Tara laughed. "I wouldn't know. But I will tell you that the steak sandwich with red coleslaw is a guest favorite—mine, too. Also, people love the twice-fried chicken."

The man laughed. "Twice-fried chicken—oh, I got to have that. Give me some fries with it, too."

They looked back at the one-page menu. "What is this butter biscuit and ham?"

"Oh, that is pretty good, too," Tara said, smiling. "But I don't think the portion is big enough. If you get that, add the mashed potatoes."

"Sold me. I will take it." The woman looked back at Tara with a warm smile. She was not a skinny woman, but she was by no means fat. Tara admired her round, pretty face and large eyes.

"Okay," Tara said smiling. "It will be about 10 minutes."

She was gathering up their menus when the man asked her a question she had never considered. "So, you go to school around here?"

"School? Oh, no, I don't," she responded, almost laughing as she spoke.

"That's odd. I thought you were a college kid. You look pretty young. You taking time off school?" He seemed genuinely interested.

"No."

Now the woman seemed intrigued. Big Mike yelled from the kitchen. "What they ordering, Tara?"

"Be right back." Tara walked the three paces to give Big Mike the order. Her intention was to start cleaning off one of the other tables in the place, but the couple called her back over.

"My name is Ted," the man said, extending his hand to her. "What is your name?"

"Tara." She shook his hand after a moment.

"So, Tara, this is Emma," he nodded in the direction of his wife. "You were saying..."

"I was not really saying anything."

"About school," he reminded. "That was the topic of conversation, I believe."

"I work here." Just then Juan squealed in delight. He was sitting over at a tiny table, playing. Tara ran over to check on him.

"That is your son," Emma concluded. Her demeanor seemed to change. She was no longer searching for an answer. She had her answer, but Ted seemed even more interested.

"Yes." Tara could feel her cheeks burning. She was not ashamed of Juan, but these people seemed to be putting too much attention on her. "I better take care of these tables."

"Oh, sorry. We are asking you questions, but we aren't really giving you much to go on. I am a recruiter at the Fillmore College and this is my wife Emma. You seem like a smart girl. You should consider school."

"I don't have time for that. I have to work." In truth Tara had never really thought about it. Did she have time? She had no clue.

"There are different options. We have night classes. There is even child care for students on campus. I don't want to seem too pushy. But if you want more in life, you got to take a few steps and do something you may have never considered possible."

His words shocked her. "What did you say?"

Emma put her hands on his arms. "Ted, don't harass the girl. Sorry, he starts to preach at people all the time. His daddy was a preacher, so I guess he can't help it."

Ted gently shook his wife's hands off his arms. He held up one hand as if to tell her to pause. He then turned his attention back to Tara. "To some it's pushy, but I have a sense about people. This is a nice stepping stone for you, but you need to be in school. I know I am arrogant, preachy and all. However, I am right 99.9 percent of the time. Oh, I said if you want more --"

Tara stood, looking thoughtful. This was her answer. She asked about getting more in life. So, the path for her was school? Tara had never even thought about school.

"I can see you're thinking about it. Let me give you my card. You come by and see me and we can see how we can get you started."

Just then Tara could hear Big Mike screaming for her to pick the food up. Tara gave the couple their order and went back in the kitchen for a moment. Her heart was beating quickly. School had never occurred to her, but all of sudden she could see the possibilities.

Chapter 10

School was difficult, not because of the subject matter she needed to learn, but because of the formalities associated with education. Tara was limited when it came to formal education. She had stopped going to school when she discovered she was pregnant. Her foster parents did not know she was pregnant and they did not know she had stopped going to school. Then one day she left the house as if on her way to school. She never returned. She didn't know if anyone had looked for her.

At that time, she was happy to escape her foster parents, her school and the association with that life. She did not want to be a part of the system and the game of foster care, state intervention, state-run education curriculum and the conventional boundaries the system imposed. She had decided she would be her own system and live outside of the formal system with her son. After all, if she had followed the rules, Juan would be in the hands of some possibly evil foster parents somewhere.

Now she wanted so badly to join the ranks of people her age. Other eighteen-year-olds were graduating high school and/or starting their first year in college. She wanted to join them and she wanted to see her boy one day be the crème of the crop, outranking them all. At this point, Tara could care less about majors or disciplines. She only wanted the opportunity to see if she could operate within the boundaries of the system that had always seemed to oppress her.

Because of that desire, Tara called Ted one afternoon. He was so excited to hear from her. They made an appointment to meet at his office the following day. He was an associate admissions director. Big Mike volunteered to look after Juan while Tara took the bus downtown to see Ted.

Tara was ready to hear about all the obstacles in her way. She was ready for rejection. One part of her thought that maybe it was best if this door closed before she got her hopes up. Then she remembered her prayer and how she met Ted and Emma the following day.

Okay. This has got to be the answer, she thought.

As she walked around the campus, she did not feel out of place. There were so many young people who looked like her. Tara found herself fascinated with their carefree dispositions, clusters of chattering and free spirits. There were diverse groups scattered along the yard as she headed toward the admissions office. Tara saw gothic, hippie, urban and refined types sprinkled among her age group. She wondered how many of them had similar experiences to hers. One of the flyers she noticed blowing across the yard announced a rape awareness session. She shook her head. Perhaps she could teach that one day.

There was not a lot of activity in the admissions office the day Tara arrived. She saw a few people in the lobby. The woman at the front did not even look up at her when she said she had an appointment with Ted. Tara made her way around the corner to his office. He had just hung up the phone with someone when he noticed her standing in the doorway.

"Great. Tara, come in. Excellent timing, my dear." He was so excited to see her.

"Hello."

"You didn't bring little man with you?" He looked around her, hoping to get a glimpse of Juan.

"No, and it feels a little weird not to have him with me." She was still standing near the doorway.

He laughed. "You sound like my mother. I live 500 miles away and she says things like it's so different with me being gone. I haven't lived at home for years," he paused to the let the irony of the statement sink in. Then he gave her a smile as if he had some great secret. "So, can I tell you about something? I am really excited that you called me. Oh, sorry to be rude. Sit down. Want something to drink? Water?"

"Uh, no. I am okay." Tara took a chair in front of his desk and removed her coat.

Tara looked around his office. The lighting was bright because of the large window letting in the sun. All the color tones in the office were tan, beige and brown. He had wedding pictures of his wife in several places and books were neatly lined in a wooden bookcase.

"There's a special program I am piloting," he said with a little smile. "Don't take this wrong, but I need folks like you to prove I am right and make my program a success."

"Right about what?" She asked. Tara did not react to the "people like you" phrase of the statement. She knew she was not like him. She looked at him and noticed that he had on a beige shirt and pants with a nice brown jacket. He pulled up the chair beside her as opposed to staying behind the desk.

"I have always wanted to be an educator. My dad was a preacher and a teacher. Like him, I teach. However, I can't educate enough people a class at a time. My thing is this: there are so many smart folks out there who never get the chances my parents gave me. I wasn't born rich, but my dad and my mom were great to me in every way. If I don't make something of my life with everything they gave me, I am a fool. It's like I have no reason to fail." He cocked his head and smiled at her. "Then there are people like you--people who don't have what I have, but they are doing wonderful things. Tara, you could fail, but you aren't failing."

She laughed. "I just work to survive. It is nothing special or extraordinary. It is what people have been doing since the Fall of Man."

He shrugged and shook his head. "I don't know. You actually strike me as pretty special. Don't minimize what you're doing. I couldn't do it."

Ted noticed she looked uncomfortable with praise. He scooted back from her. "I am sorry, Tara. Let me explain. I need a black woman, aged 18 to 20, who lives on her own and can commit to school. You are exactly what I need to officially start my pilot. So, to me, you're special. I prayed for you and here you are in the flesh. I have about nine other people lined up already and you make number ten. That's enough for me to start using the university funds I have been allotted."

"So, am I just going to start taking classes for free?" she asked, believing he would now give her the twenty pre-requisites she needed but didn't have. "I don't have a high school diploma. I have not been to school in three years. I am not even sure I can locate or get a transcript. I also have to work because I have to pay rent."

"Tara," he said in a rebuking tone, "I would not have asked you here if I didn't think I can work it out. So let's not worry about the high school diploma or transcripts. I am handpicking the first class. Yes. You can start taking classes and the university provides a stipend for living expenses."

"A stipend? You're going to pay me to go school?" Her voice was filled with mirth as well as disbelief.

"If you want to say it that way. It is financial support as you go to school. I know you have a dependent, so your stipend is adjusted to consider that as well."

Tara did not understand why, but she trusted him. "So, what does the university want from me?"

"What I want is that you come in here and knock it out of the park. Complete what you start. Do well and graduate with honors. If you and the other nine do that, I will have a program that I can expand to other universities."

She looked down at her hands. This was too good. She could not have even thought to pray for such an opportunity to come her way.

"What's wrong?" He leaned closer to her.

"I am overwhelmed. I expected to leave here with a list of things to work on so I could go to school one day. I did not expect this all to be so easy."

"Oh, trust me. It's not going to be easy. At the first sign of trouble, they will cut this program. So, don't be fooled. Also, I am fighting every day because there are folks around here who want to use that money for other things. So, I don't want you to be under any illusions. This will be a wild ride, but it's going to be worth every tear in the end. Also, the academic requirements to stay enrolled are the same as those for any other student. If you do not meet the minimum requirements, you're gone. And I have the right to accept or expel any student from the program at any time."

Tara thought about Big Mike. He had been so good to her. Was she just going to quit? She looked around the office again and looked at Ted. Tara thought about Juan.

Of course, she was going to quit if that's what it took to make things better for Juan.

"So, you with me or what?" Ted asked with a very charming smile.

She nodded.

"Yes. Thank you for the opportunity Ted."

Chapter 11

Big Mike could not have been happier for her. Tara could not believe how he responded to her school opportunity. He put her picture up on the wall, highlighting that she was graduating from Big Mike's to go to school. And in typical Big Mike fashion, he set up a separate jar--the Tara School Fund jar. To her surprise, a good number of folks dropped in spare change or larger donations. By the end of two weeks, Big Mike presented her with six hundred dollars from the school fund comprised of donations and her share of her last tip jar.

He grabbed her up on her last day and did something Tara could never remember a grown man doing with her. He hugged her--it was a father's hug. There was nothing debasing about it. Before she knew it, tears flowed down her cheeks. Big Mike was something she never considered having: a man on earth who genuinely looked out for her and cared.

"Why you crying?" he joked. "It's not as if you won't be coming into Big Mike's. I'll only charge you half price. Also, I know I am going to be at your graduation."

She laughed. "I haven't even taken any classes yet. What if I flunk out?"

He gave her a very sharp look. "Girl, you don't know yourself by now? With what you been through in your life? You ain't in jail and on drugs or sleeping around to get your rent paid. If you can come through all you've faced, school will be easy. Just remember: if you didn't belong, you wouldn't be there."

She smiled up at him. If anyone would know, it was Big Mike. He had survived ups and downs himself. He had been in jail for a crime he didn't commit. He was a business owner. Folks stopped in his place to get a good meal. The same type of people who convinced themselves as jurors that he was a violent robber now were the same folks who ate his smothered chicken and burgers.

Tara decided then and there that she was not actually going to school for just her and Juan. This was also for Big Mike. The system had taken away his chance for education, but somehow by miracle her turn had come up again. She was going to boldly take it for him and for herself.

"You make me one promise," Mike asked. You come by here Sundays when you can with my little Juan so I can make sure you're eating right."

"Yes, sir."

Chapter 12

To Ted's surprise and even her own, she scored decently on the placement exams. No remedial classes were needed. So, by miracle--and that's what Tara considered it to be--she obtained admission and started the first semester of her freshman year requirements.

Tara found herself suddenly transformed into a college student. She literally pinched herself as she sat in an ancient literature class listening to the professor talk about various styles of writing. He discussed the books they would cover and how they would study the development of modern thought and education through the writings of those long since passed away.

Tara loved reading. There was something about being able to understand the imagination and thoughts of someone else that captivated her. To help balance her time with Juan, she read aloud to him. Tara never allowed anything to get in the way of her responsibilities with her son. If this meant she had to stay up half the night to do homework, that's how it had to be.

One day, walking across campus, she saw Ted. "Hi, lady," he greeted her with a dashing smile. In his usual fashion, he was dressed in neutral colors. However, Ted was well put together. His hair was groomed perfectly and his facial hair was cut low, sprouting long enough to show bushy, silky curls along his face.

"Hi, Ted!" Tara was happy to see him. The school was small for a university, but the campus was much larger than the high school she had attended. Seeing his familiar face was comforting. "How's it going?" she asked.

"Where you headed?" he replied.

"I was actually going to the library to read a few minutes before class."

"Did you eat?" Ted observed the bag she carried with the large books. She carried the bag on one side, using one of her shapely hips for support, but she had no lunch bag with her. Classes often ran late into the night and he did not want her to try to tough it out without food.

Before Ted asked her about food, Tara had not thought about eating. The fact was she skipped breakfast that morning and didn't plan to have lunch. When she didn't answer him immediately, he took her by the arm and pulled her in the direction of the cafeteria.

"Come on." His tone was commanding, as if he would not take no for an answer.

"No. I am okay. I really just want to get some reading done," she protested. "I need to make sure I am prepared for Dr. Winston's class. He likes to call on people and I don't want anyone to think I am not serious."

"Tara, you are doing great in your classes. I know that. But you're going to burn yourself out if you don't learn how to balance. Come on--30 minutes is not going to hurt. After you eat, you can read and wrestle with Dr. Winston."

Her stomach started to growl. Tara had outlined a budget for herself and it did not include spending money on campus at the café. This morning she had not packed a sandwich. Ted smiled at her.

"You're like my mother--a little on the cheap side, right?"

She walked with him over to the cafeteria. It was comprised of several small eateries. Ted pulled her into the pizzeria. They ordered two slices of pizza and drinks. They found an available table by the window. Ted set their number on the table so the waitress could bring their order.

"Thanks for lunch, Ted," Tara told him, looking down at her fingers. "I will pay you back."

"Please," he said dismissively. "It is a few dollars. So, tell me how's it going?"

After a moment, she couldn't help but drop her reserve and allow her happiness to flow through. "It's the best experience of my life—well, second best after being Juan's mother. I am so grateful to you. I never saw myself here."

"I'm glad. I had a feeling about you the day I saw you. I can't explain why to you, but it's like you were out of place there. I mean, you were at Big Mike's and you needed to be there for the time you were there, but I saw you here."

She laughed. "You're a visionary, because I didn't see anything."

The pizza was soon in front of them. Tara bowed her head to say grace. When she looked up, Ted was looking at her with a slight smile. "That's nice."

"What?"

"You know, praying before you eat. We always did that at my house."

"You don't anymore?"

"I should," he said. "I guess I need to get back to my roots."

She shrugged. "No one ever taught me to do it. I just started doing it. If you skip enough meals, you'll either pray over your food or curse your food. I chose the positive road." Ted was still looking at her. She wanted to break the silence. "How's your wife doing?"

"Good," he said, a little louder than needed. It was as if he was surprised Tara asked. "Yes. She asked me about you last night. I told her you're doing great."

"Please tell her I said hi. You all are really nice people," Tara took a bite of her cheese pizza. As the flavor rolled around her mouth, she realized that she was really hungry.

"Emma is nice," he sighed, although he sounded a little disappointed. "But she doesn't always see the big picture. Sometimes I think she's just focused on maintaining or adding to what we have. She doesn't seem to think about other people. But there is more to life than just worrying about your own house and retirement."

Tara thought about his words. That's not the vibe she got from Emma. "Maybe her role in your life is to make sure you have what you need so you can look outward. Maybe she looks after the details so you don't have to."

"Are you taking philosophy classes this semester?" he asked. That was the first hint of playful sarcasm she had ever detected in his voice. He was always so idealistic. It made her laugh aloud.

"Seriously," she said, looking pointedly at him. "You both can't be out trying to save the world. Don't be so hard on her. A little selfishness can help. I can tell you I am completely selfish when it comes to Juan."

"But are you being selfish or are you being selfless in taking care of him? You don't focus on yourself because you're focused on him."

"No. I am focusing on me right now. I feel bad having him in the nursery sometimes. He used to be with me all the time."

"Yes, but you are in school for him. So, it's still not selfish. You want the best for him."

"I am his mother," she offered. "If I give to him, I still get because he's my son. He's going to be a great man one day. I can honestly tell you that he's going to do something extraordinary."

"All mothers say that about their sons," he laughed.

"Maybe they do, but I am right about mine."

With that, they both laughed. "Peace," he said, holding up his hands. "You win."

"On one condition," Tara said. "You give Emma a break."

Chapter 13

They started to meet for lunch almost every day. Ted and Tara talked about a variety of things. First, they talked about school. Then he asked questions about Juan. Emma could not have children and that seemed to be something he regretted. So he liked hearing about her parental experiences. Tara told Ted more about herself than she had ever told anyone.

She did not know why, but she gave him a glimpse into her life. He seemed genuinely fascinated when she spoke about having no memory of her parents. Her earliest memories were of herself in a room with other children. The woman who was feeding them gave each child a portion of beans. Tara remembered the pot of beans being empty when it was her turn to eat. The woman had to scoop beans from the plates of the other kids so Tara could eat. Tara was certain that the woman in her memory was not her mother.

There was also the time she was told that her grandmother had been located and she might be able to go home with her family. Tara waited with the social worker in her downtown office for hours. As a ten-year old, she was more realistic about her prospects than was the social worker. Half way into the long wait, Tara knew no one was coming. From that moment on, she decided that she would not worry about her birth family. Her best plan for life was to just move forward. So, she made it a point to live in the present and anticipate the future.

Ted even knew that she snuck out of the hospital with her newborn son. He admired her because she took a risk. She bucked every convention to do what she felt was right in her heart. For Tara, it was not right to give up her son. Children without their parents were not protected. That was her personal experience. She was not going to let Juan live his life at the mercy of people who could never really love him as she could. He would not start his life as she started her life.

Then one day Ted asked her a question that was unexpected, but surprisingly welcome to her. "Hey, I have two tickets to the orchestra Saturday afternoon. Would you like to go with me?"

They were at the bistro near campus. Tara had tried the bistro's version of chicken and rice. It was okay, but it did not have the same savory flavor and spicy, lingering taste as Big Mike's recipe had. Disappointed, she pushed it aside and turned her attention to the handsome Ted who was staring at her. Mentally, she promised to swing by Big Mike's with Juan and enjoy a nice meal later on.

"That sounds like fun," she said. "You and Emma have an extra ticket?"

"No. Emma is going to her sister's. I want to go to the orchestra and I don't want to go alone. Would you like to come?"

"I don't know," she said hesitantly. Tara did not mind having lunch with Ted on campus between classes, but spending extended time with him off campus felt a little uncomfortable to her.

"Why? Aren't we friends?" He looked so sincere. Tara noticed that Ted had a look that made other people feel they needed to accommodate his wishes. He had large brown eyes and very long eyelashes. When he used the eyes, it could really make a person pause. She focused her mind back to the conversation and not his eyes or face.

"Well, yes, of course we are friends," she said with a smile. "Saturdays are pretty busy for me. I have Juan, I catch up on work, cleaning, and I have to prepare for Sunday. But sure, we're friends."

"Okay, then you'll go with me, because that's what friends are for," he concluded with a smile.

"Well, I don't have anyone to keep Juan," she insisted, although she was starting to think about the possibility. "I don't think he'd enjoy the orchestra so much as you and I, so he can't go with us."

"My Aunt Mable can keep him," Ted said, as if the conversation was concluded. "You'll love Aunt Mable. She's really nice and loves children. She won't mind keeping him for a few hours while you accompany me."

As he continued to speak about their plans, Tara started to feel the loud environment closing in on them. There was lots of commotion around them in the bistro. People were moving back and forth. Someone was complaining about their portion of rice and chicken. All the movement was distracting to her. It was making it more difficult to just tell Ted she could not go. After all, Tara knew she could not just leave her son in the hands of someone she did not know. She did like Ted and he had been very good to her. She did not know his Aunt Mable.

"Ted, I can't ask your aunt to do that and I don't know her." She tried to be as polite as possible.

"Okay. We'll go over there today and you can meet her. You can see where she lives and then we can go to the orchestra."

"You are very persistent," she laughed.

"Tara, you don't get what you want in this world waiting for people to say yes to everything. If I did that, I wouldn't have anything. Trust me. You'll love Aunt Mable and so will Juan."

After her last class, Tara met Ted at his office. They made the short trip to Aunt Mable's house. Aunt Mable was a kind, plump woman with a pretty, round face and dark, curly hair. The atmosphere in her home was very inviting. It was a nice home, sparkling clean and neatly decorated with heirlooms from someone who had built up valuables over time. Nothing in her home was trendy. There was a classic look about it all. For a brief moment Tara envied Ted. He spoke often of his mother who lived 500 miles away. In addition to her, he also had his Aunt Mable. Then she thought about the off-setting irony. He had no little ones to bring over to this kind woman's home.

Tara could tell that Aunt Mable loved her nephew, Ted. Her only criticism of Aunt Mable was that she talked non-stop. After her extended greetings, repeated inquiries to Ted on his well-being, and explanations that the clean house was not as clean as it should be, Aunt Mable turned her attention to Tara.

Aunt Mable invited her into the living room. Tara followed Ted and soon they were relaxing on a red, velvet couch. "Now, where are you from, honey?" she asked, putting a plate of fresh-baked cookies on the mahogany coffee table in front of her.

The cookies looked spectacular. They were all the same size and they were all perfectly round with big morsels of chocolate chips and pecans. Aunt Mable seemed to look at Tara as if the plate of cookies was some type of test. Ted was on his second cookie before Tara took one.

"Oh, are you one of these tiny little things that don't eat?" Aunt Mable laughed. "Now, that Emma--she'd have three by now."

"Oh, I eat," Tara said. She thought it odd to be compared to Emma. "They are very good."

"Uh-huh," Aunt Mable breathed as if she expected Tara to say something like that, but did not think she was sincere. "You were saying? You're from..."

"I lived in Chicago before I came here." Tara had not expected to answer questions about herself.

"What do you mean, you lived in Chicago? Were you born there? Your mama never told you where you were born? You don't have a birth certificate?"

Tara smiled. Big Mike had the same style of blunt communication. It was something older people seemed to share. She took a slight breath and hoped what she was about to say would satisfy Aunt Mable. "I never knew my real mom or dad. What I know about them I pieced together from documents or things the social workers said. My birth certificate says Chicago."

Aunt Mable seemed to warm a little to her with the revelation that she was a motherless child. "My goodness. You know, when I was younger everyone didn't have a birth certificate." She looked over at Ted. "Your uncle didn't have one. He was born at home and his parents didn't have 50 cents to get him registered. He really didn't have official documents until he joined the army."

Ted nodded. "So I have heard before."

"Tara, I have some meatloaf coming out of the oven. You want to stay for dinner?"

"Oh, I would, but I have to pick up my son. Otherwise, I would definitely stay. It smells great."

Aunt Mable's eyes brightened more. "A son? You look too young to have a son--your waist is too tiny, too." She laughed really hard as if she'd made the best joke ever.

Tara only smiled slightly. It was a little annoying that Aunt Mable kept making references to her size. She was not that tiny of a woman and she really did not like the constant references to her body. However, she knew she would grin and bear it--for her friend, Ted.

Ted looked at his watch. "Sorry, Aunt Mable. We do need to go. We'll have dinner some other time." He stood up and looked over at both of them. "So, we good, right?"

"For what?" they both said at the same time.

"Saturday. You gonna keep Juan--that's her son."

"I sure will. Just bring him over around noon."

The orchestra's performance did not start until three. Tara was about to clarify the time, but Ted jumped right in. "That's a perfect time. Tara, we'll drop him off and I can show you the museum across the street before the concert. You'll really like it. All the pictures are based on African poems and folklore. There is a lot of culture in that place that most people skip over."

She did not respond, but he and Aunt Mable did not seem to notice that she had yet to agree. Just then Tara noticed a picture of Ted in a tuxedo. He was smiling and posing by himself. Aunt Mable saw her looking at the picture.

"Wasn't he a handsome groom? I have more pictures of him on that day. We were all so happy. Ted, your mama looked real pretty that day. Tara, let me show you the picture with him and my sister, his mama. I can show you my pictures of that day, too. I was bad in my green chiffon dress!"

Tara looked through the pictures Aunt Mable showed her. She was looking for the pictures that included Emma. There did not seem to be any and she thought that was very strange.

Carla Brice-Talley *Tara's Touch*

Chapter 14

Saturday came. That morning Tara considered calling Ted and telling him she could not make it after all. There were a few things gnawing at her. First, there was barely any mention of Emma the whole time she was at Aunt Mable's. Also, she could not stop thinking about the lack of pictures of Emma. How could the pictures harvested from the wedding day not include the bride? Then she was not completely convinced that Emma knew about their plans for the afternoon.

She sat up in the bed. "Okay, Lord. I know this doesn't exactly feel 100 percent, but he's a nice guy. Is there anything wrong with me going to the orchestra with my friend?"

As she spoke, Juan came over to her with his favorite book. Tara gathered him up in her arms and they reclined back in the bed, relaxing and enjoying just being together. She so cherished these moments with him. It was nice to have no interruptions and no one else to share him with. He was wedged comfortably in the curve of her body and the warmth of his body made her smile.

She read his favorite story. The little boy in the story had a dilemma. He did not know if he should share his ice cream with his friend. If he shared, he would have less. Ultimately, he decided that sharing is better than not sharing. So, he offered the friend the ice cream only to find that the friend had a chocolate bar. They decided to combine the ice cream and chocolate together. The book ended with the two friends enjoying the sweet ice cream--sharing was sweet.

"Read it again, Mommy," he said pointing to the book. Juan loved to hear her read. Her voice was firm, but had a beautiful rhythm. Because she loved reading to him, she injected excitement in each word. It made him enjoy listening and he was becoming a great reader himself. He did well with sight words and seemed to easily pick up on letter sounds.

"Aren't you hungry?" she asked giving him a kiss on the top of his forward.

Juan had such soft skin. His cheeks were always warm and kissable. She loved the smoothness and even tone of his mocha skin. Tara felt so proud. He was a gorgeous, smart boy.

"Cereal," he said.

"No I think I am going to fix some eggs and toast."

He made a face. "That's a long time."

"No, it won't take long," she said firmly, but sweetly.

Her phone rang. Tara reached over to the get the phone.

"Hello."

"Hi Ted," she said, feeling her stomach turn a little.

"Good morning. Just calling to make sure we're still on. I'll be there around 11:30."

"You know Ted I have been thinking. I know its short notice, but I have so much to do. I think I am going to take a rain check."

"I don't give rain checks," he responded flatly.

"Okay can I be honest with you?"

"Always."

"I am thinking about Emma. Does she know we're going?"

Tara could hear him laughing on the other end of the phone. "Of course. She's right beside me. You want to talk to her?"

Tara felt really embarrassed. "No. I mean tell her hi. I am cooking breakfast right now."

"Okay, so we're on, right?"

"Yes."

"See you then."

When she hung up the phone, Tara looked over at Juan. "Mommy's got to stop being so paranoid."

He pushed the book over to her. "Read it again, mommy."

Carla Brice-Talley   *Tara's Touch*

Chapter 15

When they dropped Juan off at Aunt Mable's, Tara could not help but feel a little jealous. They walked into the house and Juan seemed mesmerized by the grandmotherly personality of Aunt Mable. He loved her fat arms and fat tummy. Aunt Mable's house was full of bright, royal colors--blues and reds and purples. Juan was walking all over the house and Aunt Mable seemed to love it.

"Oh, we're going to have lots of fun," Aunt Mable said assuredly.

Tara was trying to explain some things to Aunt Mable, such as the last time Juan ate. Tara tried to give Aunt Mable an overview of what was in the bag she packed for Juan. Aunt Mable looked up at her with one raised eyebrow.

"Uh, girl, I had three of my own, seven grandkids and five nephews and nieces. Oh, you feed him that pre-packaged stuff?" she asked, glancing into the bag. "No. Aunt Mable's gonna feed that baby some fresh, homemade stuff. You got to come over to Aunt Mable's more often so I can make sure you eat right. You don't want to be skinny like your mama."

Juan was smiling with delight. Tara could feel her cheeks burning. For some reason her hand shook a little when she took her hands off the bag. Ted seemed to notice and took her hand in his. He gave her a look as if to say 'ignore Aunt Mable.'

"Aunt Mable," Ted said, "we're going to get on out of here. We'll be back probably around eight or so."

"Take your time," she seemed to sing. She was bouncing Juan on her lap now and he was laughing.

Tara walked over and gave him a kiss on his cheek, but Juan was having a good time. He didn't even look up at his mother.

"Come on," Ted said. "It's better to leave like this. That way he won't cry."

"Doesn't look like he's missing me right now." Tara looked back with a pout. How could Juan be so happy with Aunt Mable?

Ted laughed. "He will. Just wait until the first time he wants to do something she doesn't want him to do."

"What do you mean?" She stopped in her tracks.

"Nothing drastic. I am just saying it's easier to say no to someone else's kid."

They were outside now walking back to his car. Tara was very quiet. She took great pride in taking care of Juan. Aunt Mable practically said she was not doing a good job as Juan's mother. Ted sensed her displeasure.

"Tara, old people say whatever. You know that, right?"

"I guess so. It's just that no one ever said I wasn't doing a good job."

Ted turned toward her. He had not started the car yet. "Tara, Aunt Mable is a woman who never worked outside the house her entire life. All she did was cook and take care of my uncle and the kids. He died and left her with a nice government pension. Unlike you, Mable doesn't have to go to school, take care of a child, keep her grades up and stay up late. So, don't be so bothered by what she says."

Tara shook her head. "No offense, but I don't see your aunt and I becoming best friends."

He laughed. "I don't know. Sometimes friends come from unexpected places."

She looked at him. "I guess you're right."

Chapter 16

They had a great time. Tara thoroughly enjoyed hanging out with Ted. The concert was lovely. In their time together, Tara realized Ted was a really funny guy. She had never laughed so much in her entire life. They observed a man trying to get into the concert for free. He was explaining that he had purchased tickets in advance, but the will call desk did not have his tickets.

The woman behind the will call desk kept looking through the names on her list. She could not find his name no matter what variation he gave her. Other people were in line waiting and they started to complain. The man seemed unaffected by the fact that there was a growing crowd of irritated concert-goers. He demanded that the injustice be corrected.

Ted was cracking jokes about this conflict the whole time. Finally, he walked over to the man and the woman at the desk. He took out a $50 bill. When he laid it down on the counter, the man turned to look at him. Tara had seen people with that look before and it made her concerned for Ted.

"Here you go. I will cover the ticket. Take it. It's on me."

"I don't need your money. I bought a ticket and this woman or someone lost my name. They need to correct it."

"I know," Ted responded. "But why don't you take this to cover a ticket and then, afterward, you can get your money back for the ticket you bought. We don't want you and all these people behind you to miss the concert."

The man seemed to consider. "Okay," but then he turned to the lady. "We're gonna finish this later. Ya'll lost my name and it's very embarrassing. People probably think I didn't buy a ticket."

The woman at the front desk looked at Ted with gratitude. The man took the $50 and slipped it into his pocket. His steely look melted away and he moved out of the line. It was not clear whether he moved to the line to purchase a ticket.

Ted turned his attention back to Tara and took her by the hand. "Come on. He knows he didn't have a ticket."

She thought her stomach would split open because she was laughing so hard. A few people heard Ted's comment. After a couple more comments from others, it was clear the consensus of the group was that the man had not paid for a ticket in advance. By that time everyone was laughing.

After the concert, they stopped for dinner at an elegant restaurant near the concert hall. It felt different than lunch to her. Tara looked over at another table. There was a couple in the restaurant sitting very close together, gazing adoringly in each other's eyes. The man leaned over and kissed his female companion several times. Tara had never thought much about having a romantic relationship. Juan had always been the man in her life and she was leery of adding someone into their carefully balanced life. But she noticed that the woman looked so happy. It made her wonder. Then it made her wonder about Ted and Emma.

She looked over at Ted, who was looking over the menu. If he noticed the couple near them, he gave no indication. As usual, Ted looked handsome and studious. Tara wondered what he was really thinking. Was he really so focused on the menu? She knew he was always making observations about people, places and settings. But Ted could be very effective in guarding, even hiding, his thoughts when he wanted.

"Ted, can I ask you something?"

"Of course you can," he said, placing the menu aside.

"Where did you and Emma meet?" It had just occurred to her that in all their conversations and his probing about her life, she did not know about his most important relationship.

He didn't say anything at first, then responded shortly. "School."

"Like high school sweethearts?" she asked with a smile.

"No. College."

"You think I might meet someone?" Her voice had an idealistic tone.

He looked at her. "Maybe you already met someone."

"I am serious. You know I never thought about marriage before."

He took a sip of the water he was drinking and shrugged. "Marriage is overrated. You see that couple over there? They look so in love. They can barely keep their eyes off each other and they can't stop touching each other. Just look at her. She prepared herself to be with that man tonight--her looks, the way she carries herself, everything. She came prepared to be wooed."

Tara followed his gaze and considered his critique of the couple. The woman was dressed in a beautiful blue dress that highlighted her coco skin. She had large, soft brown curls that fell about her pretty face. The man was drawn into her. He did not look at another woman in the restaurant.

"They make a nice couple," she said, thinking how nice it must feel to have a man dote like that.

"They are not married," Ted said flatly and sarcastically.

"That's a terrible thing to say! How do you know?" Tara asked, laughing.

"I know because he's holding her and rubbing whatever part of her he can touch. He doesn't see her every day. In fact, they have not had sex yet. He's working on it, though. He might make it tonight."

Tara put the water down she had been sipping. "You ruined that whole vision for me. I thought they were in love and happy."

"They are, but they are not married. Give them a few years and they'll be more realistic. She'll stop preparing to be with him. She'll take him for granted and he'll do the same. If they don't course correct, they'll start to wonder if they made the right choice. They'll start to question if they can live with the permanent decision they made to be married. They will realize that it's not a permanent decision at all."

The waitress walked over at that point to take their order. Tara did not have much of an appetite. She had not seen this side of Ted. He seemed not to believe in anything. She had always seen him as a big thinker who was prepared to move any obstacle out of the way. There were some obstacles he ignored, apparently. Now he seemed like a person stuck in a marriage, resigned to an ultimate finale. She ordered a salad. Ted did not realize he had ruined her appetite. He ordered a steak.

She shook her head after the waitress left. "I am surprised to hear you sound so cynical. This isn't like you--the great educator who changes the world one single, wretched mother at a time!"

He laughed. "I am educating you. Don't lose your edge, Tara. Don't get soft. You know things are often not what they seem."

She sighed a little disappointed. "I guess."

"It's okay. Sometimes happiness can be somewhere else."

"You and Emma are happy, right?" She regretted saying this almost immediately. Tara knew she had no right to probe any further.

"Why do you care? I am having dinner with you right now and that makes me very happy." His voice softened at the end of the statement. He leaned forward toward her when he said it.

"I don't mean it like that," she said. She tried to use a casual tone to make the mood lighter.

"But I do. Look, Tara. I love Emma, but I married Emma because I thought she was pregnant. She was not. We stayed together, but it's not been easy. She can't have children, so I expect that she knew she was not pregnant."

"Oh." Tara was quiet for a moment. She did not know what else to say, so she said the only thing she thought was appropriate at that time. "I am sorry, Ted."

"No, I am not sharing this so you will be sorry. But I am just letting you know. Things aren't always like you think. But, honestly, that is why I like you. You're always the same. You are not fake and I like that about you. I don't want you to get changed by what you see."

They sat for a while in silence. Her salad came. Ted's steak followed shortly. They ate and made small talk. For a moment, Tara was relieved that they had abandoned the prior conversation. They talked about school, the orchestra and laughed again about the man who claimed his ticket had been lost. At this point, they fell into complete silence. The couple who had been the topic of their conversation earlier finished their meal and left the restaurant. Upon their exit, Ted looked at her with adoringly dark eyes.

When the waitress came to ask them about dessert, they both requested the same thing. Tara now realized she had a problem. She liked Ted and he liked her. However, she knew that the fact that Emma had deceived him--or so he said--was no justification for their friendship to develop into anything else.

Her fear was that it already had.

Chapter 17

After dinner, they returned to Aunt Mable's house. Tara moved to get out of the car and Ted put his hand on her arm. Tara looked down and shifted uncomfortably. His touch felt good, but she did not want him to know that. Suddenly she was very conscious of his body heat and how good he smelled. For some odd reason, these feelings were whelming up in her, a sensation she hadn't known before.

"Tara, I am sorry," he said.

"For what?"

"I feel like I said some very negative things at dinner. I would never take advantage of our friendship. You are a really sweet girl--woman. I value our friendship. I don't want you to feel that we can't be friends."

"I thought we were friends. But now I am just a little confused."

"I am not confused at all," he said leaning in closer to her.

"Stop, Ted," she said.

"Okay," he said and pulled back.

Tara was so happy he stopped. She was not sure she really meant 'stop.'

They sat there in silence for a bit longer. Then finally Ted looked over at her again.

"Okay, I am just going to tell you what I am thinking," he began.

"I don't want to hear it, Ted. Don't tell me anything."

"Tara, I like you. You're amazing. The first time I saw you, I felt like a lightning bolt hit me. I can't help it. I have never felt like this about anyone before in my life." He said it very quickly as though it was something he had to get off his chest. His breathing was accelerated.

Tara felt her heart beating a little faster. She had never had a man express sincere desire for her. It was very flattering. But she still remembered Emma's round face and soft smile. Just because she liked Ted, she could not dismiss that. Suddenly her mind fluttered with thoughts of his wife. "What about Emma?"

"She's with her sister. We split up two weeks ago."

"What?" She couldn't understand why she felt sudden anger toward him. "Why didn't you tell me? And if that's true, why was she with you this morning?"

"She was picking up some clothes this morning, Tara. It's over. We have both known that for some time. When I met you, it helped me come to terms with the fact that I did not love her--never did. I do love you."

"No, Ted." She shook her head and started to get out of the car.

"Where are you going?" he asked.

"I am going in to get my son and then I am catching the bus back to my place."

"Why? There is no need for that. I'll take you home."

"No. You can't use me to get back at Emma or buffer your separation from her. The day you all came into Big Mike's you looked happy. Her picture is all over your office. You were happy."

"But she lied and she can't have children," he reasoned. He said it loudly as though his raised voice would help Tara comprehend the betrayal he felt. If she did not have the same feelings for him, at least she could sympathize with him.

"Do you think I want to have your children, Ted?" she asked him. She was standing outside the car now with her hands on her hips. "Yes, I can have children, Ted. Yes, your wife is a little plump and I am not. Ted, you said it yourself in the restaurant. You don't see me every day, so you think I am great. Well, I am not that great. I am like Emma--a regular woman."

"You got it wrong. You're special."

"Right, Ted. I am and you're not going to take that away from me."

She stormed off. He jumped out the car and walked after her. Tara had not been grabbed like that by a man in years. It shocked her at first. He whirled her around and started to shake her.

"Don't act like you didn't know what was going on between us. You can't just play with people's emotions."

"Let' me go!" she half-shouted.

Lights came on in the house and the house next door. Ted pushed her down on the ground. Tara couldn't really see him in the dark. He reached for her legs and Tara started to kick.

"Ted, you stop. You're acting crazy!" she yelled.

He wasn't listening to her. She could feel him pulling her back up and now he had her on her feet. Tara could feel her feet lifted off the ground. He was trying to take her back to the car. She could hear him talking to her. This was not anything close to the Ted she was used to hearing. It had been years since a man had talked to her the way he was talking.

Tara summoned her strength and somehow managed to bite him on the neck. Ted responded with a slap. She found herself lying back on the ground now. She instinctively threw her arms up about her face to protect herself from any further blows. At that instant, Aunt Mable was coming down the front steps. She ran directly over to Ted.

"Theodore! Theodore! Are you all right? What did she do?"

Tara was dragging herself to her knees and holding her cheek. Her face was hurting and she was still in shock. But she could hear Aunt Mable talking to her precious nephew.

"I told you about girls like that. You and Emma need to work it out. You don't need a girl like her dragging you down."

The rest of the evening proceeded in silence. In the days that followed, Tara opted not to press charges against Ted. She wanted the whole thing to be behind her. It was not long before she received a letter in the mail. Her spot in her academic program had been eliminated. Tara decided she was not going to make a big fuss about it. If that was the way Ted wanted it, he could have it his way. She knew plain retaliation when she saw it. She decided to take it in stride.

"Doesn't mean I can't get my degree," she said boldly as she looked in the mirror. Juan was playing behind her. Tara wiped the remaining tears from her eyes and took a deep breath.

"Juan, I promised you that no one would ever make fools out of you and me. I am going to keep that promise. We're still going to do this--even if it's the hard way."

A day later, Tara got her job back at Big Mike's and enrolled at a nearby community college to continue her education.

Carla Brice-Talley	*Tara's Touch*

Chapter 18

A year passed. Tara had settled into her new life of work and school. This was still the college experience at the community college, but it was also different. Many of the students Tara ran across were older, working full-time like her and attending college as students in transition until they could get to a four-year university. Tara carefully and steadily completed her course work and classes. She had decided to focus on accounting because that career path seemed very practical and she could help Big Mike out.

It was not long before she was keeping his books. Big Mike had never formally looked at inventory levels, inventory turns, sales during holidays or summer receipts versus winter receipts. He did not try to think about how many customers entered the store or even the basic concepts of depreciation and capital expenditures.

Thanks to her ongoing education, Tara brought these concepts and an enhanced management system to Mike's operation. He liked cooking, not money matters. Soon, he was cooking while Tara was managing the financial aspects of the store. With the money saved from increased efficiency in his business, he was able to hire someone else. Now, Big Mike was cooking, Tara was managing, and Lindsey was the new waitress.

"Tara, I need to see you," Mike said one evening as they were closing the store. Tara had just hit the enter button to lock the sales of the day into their records.

She looked up from the little corner office she was sitting in and smiled at him. "Yes, sir? Is everything okay?"

"Not exactly. You and I need to work out something."

"What?" She was now really concerned. He looked worried.

Tara stood up and came from around the desk. Big Mike was standing in the small doorway. He was so tall his head reached the top of the doorframe and he had to bow his head a little to look into her eyes.

"Tara, you are doing a lot of work for me. I need to pay you more. It's only the right thing to do."

She laughed and sighed with relief. Tara considered this good training for her. In addition, Big Mike had been so good to her. She wanted to repay him. She still remembered the day she entered the tiny restaurant, lamenting about what had happened with Ted. Without hesitation, Big Mike started to talk about what he could do to help.

"No. You listen to me. There is no way I could find someone to handle all you are doing for me and only pay them a waitress salary and tips from the tip jar. Now I want you to talk to some of your friends at school or a professor. Look into what a fair wage would be and then look at what I can afford. If it will make you feel better, you can even make your job part-time. But, no matter what, I want to pay you more than you are making now. Understand?"

"Big Mike," she said, blurting instinctively, "how about if I become a partner with you?"

"A partner?" He asked almost laughing. "What are you talking about Tara?"

"Well, we were doing some cases in our class."

"Cases?"

"We look at a situation faced by a company and we think about what they should do. Then the case ends with what they did."

"Okay," he replied in a thoughtful tone. "How does this partnership work?"

"Well, some companies that are small and have high growth potential don't pay their employees everything upfront. They give them shares of stock, a small ownership interest. It makes people care more than a paycheck would because the growth of the business becomes part of their future as well."

"Growth? Tara, I am just going to run this little place. Then one day I might shut it down and go back home to Alabama to die. Or I might just die in here over the grill. I haven't decided which one I want yet."

He started to laugh and his brown belly shook a little. Tara crossed her arms now. She knew him long enough to know when he was intrigued.

"First of all, you're too young to talk about dying. So that's not going to happen for years. Big Mike, can't you see the possibilities? Do you know why you don't make more money?"

He shook his head.

"Because you don't have enough space. Your place is packed. People love that taste of Alabama. They can't get that taste any other place around here. I don't want to take money that we could use to put back in the place. However, if we can invest more into the place and you can give me a small ownership interest, that would work."

"You really think so? What are you thinking of?"

"Well, first I want to change the menu—but not the food. I want to put your face on the menu. I want a new sign outside with your face and big letters--Big Mike's. Then I want to start sending menus to the businesses around here and delivering food during lunch time to increase capacity and sales. As it is, everyone can't fit in here. But we can deliver the food to a lot of other people."

"How we gonna do that?"

"Big Mike, you wanted to pay me more. I will take a rain check on that. Don't pay me more right now. Give me some ownership interest and we can pay for a delivery guy and another cook."

He looked at Tara. It was like he was looking at her for the first time. She was not the scared, poor girl with the baby in the second-hand stroller. Tara was not the homeless girl he had met. He was looking at a woman with a gleam in her eyes. Her hips were fuller and she held her body and chin in a way he had not seen before. It was confidence. She was convinced in her plan for success.

"What if this doesn't work, Tara?"

"It will work. Leave it to me. Worst case scenario is we go back to this and you give me a little extra. But I got a feeling, Big Mike. We can't fail."

She was right. The advertising and the delivery model helped to increase sales by fifty percent. Tara wrapped up her associates degree in accounting and declared herself the full-time business manager. Big Mike wanted her to go back to the University for the bachelor's degree, but Tara saw that as something she could do later. She needed to concentrate on building Big Mike's business up to its full potential. She had no time now to sit in classes theorizing about running a company. She was running one already.

Tara also convinced Big Mike to remodel his store. They put down new floors and switched the booths out. Color and styling was updated and brightened. Because of the updates, more tables could be wedged into the establishment.

Next, she contracted for remodeling of the kitchen. Big Mike's was a clean place, but the sanitation grade was never stellar because of the old stoves and rusted refrigerators. Tara had these items replaced with stainless steel and a commercial stove. Big Mike could now turn out food faster. Tara decided they needed another cook, so she had Big Mike write down his recipes. She used this to create a kitchen manual.

Big Mike did not like all the changes. But he had to admit things were running smoothly and he was making more money than he ever thought possible. Tara worked too much, he thought. She was now 23 years old and she only had two activities--Juan and Big Mike's.

Carla Brice-Talley   *Tara's Touch*

Chapter 19

"You need to take a day off," Mike told her one day at the end of the night shift.

The last customer had just left. The staff was cleaning out front and Tara was in the office going through the figures for the day. She did not know that Big Mike had been standing there watching her for almost five minutes before he said anything. The main register had come up short and Tara was very annoyed with this. She had a bad feeling about one of the staff, but she knew how sensitive Big Mike was about such things. Because he was once falsely accused, he was leery about pointing the finger at anyone without solid proof. Before Tara said anything about her suspicions, she would have to be 100 percent sure she was right.

"You need to take a day off," he repeated.

"Me? Oh, no. I need to finish up the night's count. Then I need to prepare the bank deposit. I need to work on the schedule for next week. You and I need to talk, because we need to decide if we want to stay open later with the Super Bowl coming up. I was thinking we could advertise 'Super Bowl Your Meal!' We could give extra-large portions of something, maybe wings."

He shook his head. "Girl, you need to take a breather." He sighed and took a seat. Big Mike had grown to love Tara, but sometimes he felt she was running way ahead of him.

"I don't need to take a rest. You need to take rest," she retorted. "I am fine. I'm feeling really great about how things are going." She turned back to her computer, studying the evening's numbers.

"Yeah, I suppose things are okay."

"Okay?" She looked up at him with raised eyebrows. "Our profits are two times where they used to be. Aren't you proud of that?"

"Yes. Of course--Tara, don't look like that. I am very proud of you and what you've done. But a girl your age--a woman your age should also be having fun. You will never meet anybody. What about that guy that was coming in here all the time?"

"What guy?" she asked, but Tara was only playing dumb. She knew he was referring to a man named Leonard. Leonard dressed well, talked intelligently and had a nice car. He had told Tara he worked for one of the firms in the district. He was also very handsome--the tall and ebony-toned kind of guy with broad shoulders and chiseled cheekbones. Tara had let her guard down with Ted. She was not going to do that again. She had been keeping Leonard at a comfortable distance.

"You know the guy I am talking about. What's his name? Lionel? You liked him, right? He seemed like a nice guy."

She shrugged.

"Okay, Tara, I have never asked you this before, but I am going to put it out there. You like men, don't you?"

She put the papers in front of her down in frustration. "Of course I like men. Just because I am not swooning over every guy who comes in here in a business suit, you think I'm a lesbian?"

He took a good look at her again. She had high cheekbones, full lips, a cute nose and nicely placed eyes. Those eyes hid nothing from Big Mike. Okay, Big Mike thought to himself. Tara was not a lesbian, but she was an emotional wreck. She was someone who had encountered so much disappointment that she had just given up on a social life.

Big Mike liked to jab Tara every now and then with his jokes, so he decided to tease her with his big smile. "Well, okay. I guess you are not--I am not judging you--I mean, we all know what the Bible says. But if that's what you struggling with..."

"I am not struggling with anything," she said sharply.

He laughed. "I am just teasing you. I know you don't play softball all weekend long."

"Okay, bad joke and softball is good exercise," she said, picking up her report again.

"So is basketball and tennis?" he said wryly.

"Ugh!" She cried walking over to the file cabinet. "Big Mike, please. Not funny."

"Okay. Maybe not. No, but seriously, you need to think about your future. Think about Juan, too. You can't give him what a father can."

Tara was sensitive to any criticism of her ability to parent. It always bugged her that someone would offer her advice from time to time. No matter how well fed or well-dressed Juan was, someone always thought she was falling short as a parent. Juan was a star reader in his class and was already advancing quite well in math. Nevertheless, there was always someone who would come along and tell her how she needed a man in her life for Juan. I am his mother, Tara said half-aloud. God gave him to me. She closed the file cabinet rather harshly in frustration.

"Juan's father is completely out of the picture. I don't know if I can picture any man as Juan's father. Maybe God has tasked me to be his father and mother."

"But you're not the father and the mother. You're only the mother--a good one, but that's all you are."

She appreciated that Big Mike said she was a good mother. "You think I'm a good mother?"

He sucked his teeth. "You know I do. But you are terrible at having fun. You told me to think about the possibilities. I am asking you to do the same."

Tara fell silent, but she knew he was right. Juan did ask about his father time to time. He saw other kids with their dads and she noticed a look of confusion in his eyes. She tried to change the subject at first or give him pacifying answers, but her boy was smart. It made her nervous sometimes. She knew other people might think she was not providing all that Juan needed. It would kill her if he ever thought the same.

"I can't go on a daddy hunt, Big Mike. That's not productive. I figure if I work my best here--for you and Juan--that will be enough."

"Okay, so let's talk about you."

"Me? What about?" Tara took her seat again.

"What are you going to do the day Juan runs off to school? The day he starts his own life? Ever thought about that?"

She shook her head. In her view, her life did not start until she carried Juan in womb. Even her dreams were filled with Juan from the beginning. She couldn't imagine life without him.

"Well, he won't live with you forever. You're going to have to be happy at that point without him. You better start having a life now."

She had to smile because of his fatherly concern. Slowly, with a wry smile, she gave him what he wanted to hear. "Okay, Big Mike. The next time a man comes in here and whispers sweet nothings to me, I am going to fall in his arms and run away with him."

He laughed. "You joke, but you never know who might come in here tomorrow."

"Well, trust me. I don't care who comes in here tomorrow. The fact is everybody can talk nice and look nice at first. If you are not careful, you'll be fooled."

"I think you are fooling yourself. You are a woman. You need a man."

"I have a man. My little Juan."

Tara's Touch

Chapter 20

Tara took a rare day off to take Juan to the park. He was riding his bike. She had just removed the training wheels, but he was doing well. He had fallen a few times, which frustrated him. To her pride, though, his frustration didn't turn into fear. Juan was determined to ride that bike and he did. Tara watched him wobble and zig zag. She witnessed the transformation when his zig zagging stopped and he rode the bike with strength and confidence. He was having a great time.

The sun was shining brightly on this crisp fall day. It was really the perfect day to be outside. A slight breeze rippled through Tara's hair. She had brought a book with her to enjoy. Tara prized reading and learning. She made it a point to attempt to train her mind by delving into some interesting topic. But the book was not now by her side. She was having much more fun watching Juan overcome the bike challenge. Seeing him at play filled her with so much glee she was almost oblivious to everything else around her.

"You dropped this." It was a male voice that drew her from watching her determined son.

She looked up to see a tall, ebony-skinned gentleman. He was jogging in the park. In fact, he was still running in place as he pointed to the ground where a twenty-dollar bill lay not far from her feet. Tara noticed quickly that he had a smooth voice and a handsome, well-structured face.

"Oh, thank you." She knelt down to pick up the $20 bill that must have dropped from between the pages of the book. "This is our treat money after the park--"

He nodded toward her and took off running. Tara could not help but look after him. She was so used to a stranger's silly pick-up line or other pathetic attempts to start conversation. This handsome man had stopped only long enough to alert her to the fact that she had dropped money. For a moment, she felt a little silly herself. Why did she start to babble about using the money for treats after the park? He would not care. If she were him, she would not care, either.

"Mommy, look at how fast I can go!" Juan's voice was clear and loud. She was sure everyone in the entire park could hear him. He pedaled quickly away from her. She smiled as he turned and pedaled back toward her again.

"Great job, Juan! You are fast!"

Another child noticed Juan and started to ride beside him. Now that he found a friend, he started to focus his attention on the other child instead of showing off to impress his mother. Tara smiled and leaned back on the park bench. Juan was not looking in her direction now. He and the other boy had put the bikes to the side. Now they were running toward the main playground. It was not long before the two boys were swinging on the monkey bars. Juan hoisted his legs up and wrapped his calves on the bars. He was not hanging upside down. Tara hated when he did things like that. But she knew it would be an unnecessary headache to try to police his play. He had now pulled himself so that he could sit on top of the monkey bars. The other boy joined him and a little girl found her way over to them, too.

Tara looked down at her watch. She would give him another hour of unbridled fun. Then they would grab his favorite treat. The next move would be on to Big Mike's for the evening rush, where Juan would help her with whatever task she asked. He was actually a good little helper. Juan followed directions well and had a strong desire to do well.

She opened the book and started to read. She glanced occasionally in Juan's direction. Tara flipped the pages, admiring the heroine in the book. Was she as courageous as this historical woman? She hoped so. True, she was not leading an army to victory and fighting the Portuguese, but she thought she was doing all right for the time period in which she lived.

"Interesting reading material." Was that the same male voice?

She looked up and smiled. It was the jogger again. Tara immediately put the book down in front of her. "Yes, it's a good book--very well-written and interesting."

"I did a paper on Nzinga in college," he said. He was not jogging any longer. Now he was standing there in front of her, stretching out his calves as he spoke. Tara looked over him. After his jog, he still looked handsome. The sweat patches on his shirt were in all the right places and emphasized his muscular physique.

"Really? What class?" she asked.

"African history. It was a good class. You know it made me feel good to take a class about 'us.' It was refreshing because I never heard about Nzinga in elementary, prep, or high school. Everyone knows about the civil rights movement, but what do we really know about Africa? It's good to see other folks have an interest in African history."

"I read everything and anything," Tara said. She was surprised she was talking so much. Usually she mumbled or gave uninterested grunts. "I try to challenge myself in learning."

"Me, too, "he said. "But I can't take credit for it. Reading is my job. I work for a publishing company."

She laughed. "I see. Well, that's a good excuse to keep yourself reading."

"My name is Tim Benson," he held out his hand.

"Tara Martin," she responded. She took his hand with a smile.

Chapter 21

The first time Big Mike coughed, Tara did not think anything about it. Although his cough lingered and got worse, her first instincts were about the management of the store. He did not need to be in the kitchen with that cold. As the cough seemed to get even worse, she was worried for him. But in all the years she had known Big Mike, he had never gone to the doctor.

"You need to get something for that cough."

"Let me tell you something, Tara. I can go to that doctor and wait for him to tell me I have a cold. I already know I have a cold, so I am not going to the doctor for him to tell me that. I am also not taking that stuff they call medicine. My mama taught me how to deal with a cold."

"Oh, gosh, please don't talk about any of that backwards Alabama root doctor stuff." She was half teasing and half serious.

He rolled his eyes at her. "Root doctor? You been reading too many stories. These home remedies work. I am going to put this onion in this honey with this mint leaf and a shot of brandy and lemon. Warm it up and I will be better than you."

Tara was in the office while Big Mike boiled his remedy, but she could smell the concoction. The honey, lemon and mint produced a nice aroma, but the thought of the brandy and onion turned her stomach. Big Mike was humming a song while he warmed up the mixture. He swore by his mama's remedies. In a few moments, he was sipping it. She knew, because she could hear him slurping.

"You know you should be careful. You have a cough, but you don't seem to have other symptoms. You should see a doctor just to make sure you're OK."

"What?" He started to laugh. "Listen, you can tell Juan what to do and you can haul him to the doctor every time he has a runny-nose. But my mama didn't raise me like that. I will be just fine."

She shook her head. Big Mike was made of steel, she thought. He probably will be fine. Tara did not want to argue. Besides, she had an appointment.

"Okay, Big Mike. I'm out of here for the night."

"What? You are? But it's only nine. Don't you want to stay longer and think about additional work to do? That's how you spend your evenings." He chuckled again.

"Ha!," she said, matching his sarcasm. "No. Not tonight. I have a date."

Big Mike started to cough again. She did not know if it was the ailment or his reaction of surprise. After a moment, he cleared his throat. "Well, you work fast. You decided to give that old boy a chance?"

"No way," she said. "I met a nice man at the park the other day."

"The park? I didn't tell you to pick up strangers in the park."

"No, Big Mike. It's not like that at all. I was out with Juan. He was jogging. We started talking to each other and decided to meet so we can talk some more. He is really nice."

"Kind of late for a talk." He eyed her now.

"Well, I explained to him that I work. He has a deadline at his job, so this time works for both of us. We're just going to grab dinner or maybe coffee at a place by his job."

"Why didn't you come here?"

She laughed. "Because I work here."

"I need to meet him," he concluded. "If you gonna have him around Juan."

"You're never satisfied. Didn't you tell me I had to get out more?"

"I didn't know you were going to get out so quickly," he coughed again. "Enjoy. What's this joker's name, anyway?"

"Tim Benson."

"TB," he joked about Tim's initials. "That's something you get tested for."

Tara's Touch

Chapter 22

Tara had not gone to dinner with a man since the debacle with Ted a couple years ago. However, she still remembered feeling uncomfortable in the restaurant with Ted. As she sat across from Tim, looking and listening to him speak, she took note that she did not feel uncomfortable with him at all.

"Well, there is not much to tell about me," Tim was saying as they sat at dinner.

The restaurant was a pleasure. Tara could not help but study the silverware and cloth napkins. She looked and inspected the décor of the curtains and the uniforms of the staff. Even the menu conveyed an element of class. She couldn't help turning on her business sense for a moment. She felt this restaurant had good staging and marketing. But did the food showcase real taste and class?

Mental notes for later, she thought. Tara turned her eyes back to Tim. He was a genuinely handsome man-- not in the conventional sense. There was a strength in his features and the way he held himself. The attractiveness he displayed was going to always be with him. He could be 90 years old in a wheelchair and girls younger than her would still turn their heads.

He noticed her thoughtful smile. "What is it?"

"Nothing," she replied. "I was just thinking."

"Uh-oh, I am boring you."

"No. It's not that at all!" She laughed. "I have a habit of obsessing over restaurants now. I am always trying to get additional ideas or measure Big Mike's by other places. It is really unhealthy."

"Can't leave your work alone?"

She dropped her head slightly, a little embarrassed. Big Mike was always teasing her about her obsession with work. She hoped that she was not so one-sided so that, in a brief conversation, Tim would reach the same conclusion. "I guess I can't help but see if we can do something we haven't done before. And you know what? I want to do something no one has done before. Maybe that is really for my son to do--not me. I don't know. I just feel like I need to keep looking for that missing piece."

Tim smiled at her pouty, determined look. He could tell Tara was a genuine woman. Her motivations were easy to understand and he liked the pureness of her intent. "Oh, well, I can tell you something. Women like you can't be stopped. You can keep surprising yourself and the people around you. I am a fan already," he said, with a charming smile.

"Hey, I am just a woman with a son trying to give him the best I can." Her cheeks were burning. Tara liked praise. But for some reason, his praise sounded different to her. She had never had a fan before.

"No, it's a little more than that." He took a sip of his sparkling water. "You are driven. I can see that. And that's good. I am somewhat like that, too. But I make myself take a step back every now and then. Working in the corporate world puts more boundaries on you. It does give you greater access to resources. Your company is small, but that's an advantage. You can decide what you want to do. I have to force some balance into my life, though. Too much work is not good."

"I'm sorry to lure you into a conversation about work," she apologized, realizing that perhaps she did dedicate too much of her thoughts to work. Tonight she did not want to focus on that. She wanted to know Tim better and she hoped he could get to know her better as well.

"No apology needed," he said. "Work is part of our lives--a big part."

"But I would like to hear more about you. Come on. You were saying that there's not much to tell. I can't believe that. You seem too interesting to me."

"There really isn't," he said in a matter of fact manner. "My mother died when I was very young. I think she died in prison. My dad disappeared shortly after that, but I was adopted by a great family."

She could not tell if he was keeping back part of the truth. So she decided to ask him outright. "Were they truly great?"

He cocked his head to the side and seemed to think about it. "Yes, in the sense that I ate every night and I went to great schools. They even put me in the will."

"But?" Tara knew there was probably more to the story.

"But I was their project. I never felt like a part of the family. Even when they introduced me, it came with a reminder of my story--my mother, my father. It's like they wanted their friends, church, extended family and business associates to know what good people they were. And I was the proof that they were good people."

"Oh, I am sorry," she said, trying to imagine Tim as someone's trophy. She thought about Juan. What if she had let him go and he became someone's prize possession? She felt an uncomfortable tingle up her spine just thinking about it.

"It's okay. I played the part. I owe them my life. So, I never gave them any trouble. When I turned 18, I left for college. I tried not to be much of a burden and I have been on my own ever since."

"I see." She looked down, feeling pity for him. In some respects, she felt he was a little self-consumed on the issue. If the people gave him that much of their time and attention, he had to be more than a project to them. After all, some people live with their biological parents and don't get those benefits. On the other hand, she felt sad for him. He had things—education and access to resources--but he did not feel loved by these people. According to Tim, he did not really have a family.

"You?" he asked.

"I grew up in foster care. I was never adopted. When I was little I thought I was going to be like Orphan Annie. You know, a rich man will come to rescue me. I knew my parents weren't coming. Then I realized no one was coming. I did not live with nice families. I finally had to run away."

He nodded. Instinctively, he looked at her. "Your son's father?"

"I had to run away," she repeated.

He leaned over and took her hand. "I hope you don't mind me taking your hand like this. Just wanted to squeeze your hand."

"I don't think I mind. I am all right. Honestly, I have had to move on, accept life and be thankful for what I have. I am thankful for Juan. I can show him love. I try to give him what I never had."

"You make me look at myself. I am selfish, aren't I?" He knew the answer already. He was 35 with no dependents, a nice house. He talked to his 'parents' once a month at the most. He often made excuses for Thanksgiving and Christmas to avoid facing them. Here was this woman who had a son and helped an old black man, Big Mike, build a solid brand.

She did not respond. He nodded with an adorable smile. "Maybe I need to adopt a boy or marry a beautiful woman with a little boy."

"Maybe," she said, with a raised eyebrow. "But you know a beautiful woman is not going to just let anybody come and be father to her son. Especially a beautiful woman that was not looking for a father for him."

"She was looking," he said, very confidently. The waiter put his steak in front of him.

"She was not looking," she repeated, just as confidently.

He leaned forward and inspected her salad. "Women are always looking. They just fool themselves into thinking they are not looking."

She shook her head laughing softly. "Women don't look. Women are pursued. Trust me. I know. I have literally had to run away."

"Maybe you should stop running."

"Maybe," she conceded.

Chapter 23

Big Mike's death was a shock. One night after the last customer left, he fell over. Tara was in the office. She heard the noise, but thought nothing of it. Someone was always dropping something. When Lindsey screamed, she immediately rushed to the kitchen. There he was. He lay on his stomach, not moving and face-down.

Tara will never forget how still his body was. The body before her seemed unfamiliar. Big Mike talked up a storm and cracked jokes. He yelled at Lindsey. He yelled at Tara a few times. Tara even heard him yell at one of the customers--a regular, so the man was used to Big Mike's ways. Tara actually thought he liked being yelled at by Big Mike.

Big Mike reminded her of the man she had seen in the hospital emergency room the day she had given birth to Juan. That man did not make it. She was heartbroken to realize that Big Mike did not make it, either. He said he might die in the restaurant. A spatula lay beside him. He must have been about to put it away.

"Call the ambulance," she instructed. But there was chaos around her. Lindsey was crying uncontrollably. The only person who was truly composed was a young man who had started working a week ago. He was already dialing 911.

Lindsey could not pull herself together. The new boy pulled Lindsey away from Big Mike's body and lifted her gently to a chair. Tara leaned over him and turned his head to the side so that his nose was not wedged against the floor. She tried to make sure nothing was in the way of his nose in case he miraculously started to breathe.

It was not long before they heard the sirens and the noise of movement outside. The paramedics were inside the restaurant now. One of them was checking Big Mike's pulse after he gently pulled Tara back from Big Mike's body.

She watched the paramedic lift his wrist to feel for a pulse. Then he placed his hand on the right side of Big Mike's upper neck. The young man's face confirmed what she knew already. There was an attempt to resuscitate Big Mike, but it was unfruitful.

Big Mike was gone, but Tara kept telling everyone that things would be all right. This message was intended especially for Lindsey, who continued to ask why he had not opened his eyes yet. Tara hugged Lindsey and told her to stop fretting and calm down.

Three men were needed to move Big Mike's body. They put him on the gurney, moved him out the store and loaded him into the ambulance. Lindsey looked over at Tara with a lost look.

"They need to turn on the lights and sirens. Why aren't they turning on the lights and sirens? If they don't, people won't know to get out of the way," Lindsey insisted in frustration.

Tara did not answer her. She knew that they did not turn the lights and sirens on for those who were DOA-- dead on arrival.

"Does anyone want to ride with him?" One of the paramedics asked. "Are one of you his daughter? Any family relation?"

"We are all like daughters to him, but I will follow in my car," Tara said.

"Can I come with you?" Lindsey asked Tara.

"Sure, Lindsey."

Chapter 24

After the funeral, Tara invited people to come back to her house. She no longer lived in the studio flat from Ms. Sarah's duplex. She had moved a few years ago from that place to a modest house. It was a three-bedroom house in a decent neighborhood. She received people in the living room and kitchen.

Lindsey was still inconsolable. As he had with Tara, Big Mike had rescued her and been more of a father to her than her actual dad ever was. There were other people who came to pay their respects--mostly regular patrons, employees, members of Tara's church, her pastor, Ms. Sarah and her nephew Davis who had ended up being a good father and taking good care of the children he had by the white girl.

Juan was quiet throughout the funeral and the repass. He knew Big Mike would not be around anymore. It made him very sad. The older man had been a stable fixture in his life. Big Mike had been like a grandfather to him. Juan could see that Lindsey was having a difficult time. He also noticed how his mother had to take care of everything. He would not add to her worries. Big Mike had once told him that he had to be a big boy for his mother. He was determined to do that for his mother today.

Tara had explained the concept of death to Juan when she told him about Big Mike. Her explanation was simple, but it gave him some comfort. He knew that death was not the end for a Christian, because they had discussed it in his Sunday School class. But hearing his mother carefully talk about death and life in relation to Big Mike made the doctrine more real. Big Mike had gone to heaven. His soul, Tara said, had gone to be with the Lord. His body was left so that loved ones could adjust to his absence. When the Lord Jesus returns, Big Mike and every other believer would rise and be united again.

"If he's with Jesus, he's happy." Juan said this with the confidence and purity that could only be spoken by a child.

His simple words had given Tara comfort. She said Juan's words over and over to herself. Whenever she felt sadness overwhelm her, she repeated those words. Big Mike must be happy now.

After people left, Tara found herself alone with Juan and Tim. Tim brought her a plate with chicken and collard greens on it. She waved it away, feeling her stomach turn at even the thought of food.

"I am not hungry," she told him definitively. "I think I'll just go lie down."

"Come on, babe. You should try to eat something." Tim could not remember the last time he saw Tara eat something. She had served, cooked, run around the house, even entertained some folks with humorous stories he knew it pained her to tell. Now Tara sat on the couch looking sullen and drained. Her large, mink eyes were watery, but she held back tears.

"Don't be sad, Mommy," Juan said, giving her a kiss on the cheek and a hug. "It will be okay."

She had to smile in response to him. Tim sat beside her on the couch and put the plate before her on the coffee table. He put an arm about her shoulder and squeezed lightly. Tara felt the comfort of his masculine touch. Juan looked at them both thoughtfully. He liked seeing his mother with Tim because Tim was nice. Juan could tell that Tim made his mother happy. However, Juan had no intention of hanging around with adults any longer.

"Mommy, I am going to play. If you need me, call me."

"Sure, sweetheart." She had to laugh. He was really becoming a big boy.

He trotted off and Tara could soon hear one of his video games playing louder than needed. Normally she would ask him to keep it down, but the noise was comforting somehow. Big Mike had often told her that part of being a child was making noise. As she thought about Juan, she felt sad again. Big Mike was like a grandfather to Juan. She had built no other close relationships outside of the restaurant and now they were alone again.

Tim cleared his throat, pulling Tara from her thoughts. She looked over at him to see him gazing at her. Suddenly she felt bad for ignoring him. "I'm sorry. I am in my own little world today."

"No. I know it's all been on you. Planning a funeral is tough, or so I've heard."

"Yes." She choked back tears. "It's funny. You go from not being connected to anyone to having someone who is like a father to you. Tim, he gave so much to me and Juan. Do you realize when I first met him Juan and I had no place to stay, only the clothes on our back and a stroller? I had a stroller that I bought second-hand."

She laughed quietly just thinking about it. "I walked in and he had just fired a girl—well, she really quit. Anyway, he gave me a job. I really have been working for him since then. He taught me about the practical aspects of running a restaurant. I can't even believe I no longer hear his voice. Do you know he gave me half of the tip jar the first day I worked? He normally would not do that for a few months."

Tim listened quietly. He had met Big Mike and liked the man instantly. He knew Big Mike had given him the once-twice-thrice-over treatment, too. He was a protective older man. With Big Mike gone, someone needed to step in and protect Tara and Juan. He could hear his adoptive dad telling him that women should not be alone with children.

He looked over at her. She looked beautiful even in mourning. Her dark curls fell about her shoulders. Tim loved her side profile because he could study her features and the curve of her chin and neck.

"Tara," he mumbled at first. She was still talking about Big Mike, saying something about how he had certain customers who came to him for advice. Tara laughed at this because, although Big Mike gave practical, common sense advice, he did not possess tact. As she started on another story, Tim blurted out impulsively, "Will you marry me?"

"What?" she asked as if she did not understand him. Then she asked again, more thoughtfully, "What?"

Tim did not know if she was shocked, angry or both. She had turned those large, mink eyes on him and he could not discern what those eyes held. Tara was not saying anything. She was just looking at him as if he was someone else. He felt a little embarrassed now. Maybe he was crazy. He had met Tara a little less than three months ago. But he knew she was the woman for him.

After a few moments, he took her hands in his hands. He looked steadily and directly in her eyes. "Will you marry me?" He had found his confidence now.

"Tim, is this a pity proposal?" she asked, standing up and moving away from him. "What kind of question is this today? Do you think this will make me feel better or something?"

He grabbed her hand before she could move out of his reach. "No. I love you. I know you love me. I don't want to meet another woman or search any longer. I want to be with you and I don't want you to be without me. Marry me."

She was moved by his sincerity and rationale, but she felt conflicted about the timing. "Your timing is odd. I just buried my, my--"

"Your friend and father and business partner—yes, that was Big Mike. I know. Now gain a fiancé and eventually a husband. Tara, don't fight me on this. I have a feeling about us."

"I don't know," she said, feeling a bit guilty. Sensations of happiness were starting to tingle through her. She told herself she did not want to feel happy today. It was not right to feel happy on the day of Big Mike's funeral.

"You don't know if you love me?" he asked in a softer tone. Tim could feel his heart trembling a little. Tara could not tell him she did not love him. He knew she did. He hoped she did not turn away from him.

"No. I know I do, but I just never thought I would be a married woman—well, at least not within three months of meeting someone. This is really fast."

"You will be a married woman and you will be married to me," he said conclusively. "If you say yes to me, then it won't just be you. It will be us together. We can experience all the possibilities of life together."

She sat back down. Tara remembered the many conversations she had with Big Mike about her settling down. Was this a sign? She could feel a nudge to say yes coming from within. "Marriage is a big step," she said aloud, more to herself than to him.

"Yes. It is a big step, but it's a step you and I both need. Tara, I am tired of being alone and feeling like I don't really belong anywhere. I knew I belonged with you the first time we went to dinner. You're a wonderful woman and a great mother, but you don't have a companion to share your life with. You don't have to live out your dream of conquering the world for Juan alone. I want to be with you. I want us to live our lives together."

For the first time, she allowed herself to smile at him. If she was honest with herself, sometimes she was lonely. There were times she had looked at a loving couple with children and wished she had that type of life. She had never known that. She wanted Juan to have every advantage—and a father was a true advantage. On top of that, she did love Tim. Her feelings for him scared her sometimes.

Tara started thinking of what the future could be like. She always saw a future where Juan was very successful, but she could not imagine herself in that future. Now she could see something ahead for herself. She saw Tim and herself laughing together with Juan by their side. She saw herself holding another baby in her arms. There was even a glimpse of growing old together, waiting for their grandchildren to come through the door for Christmas.

Tim was still looking at her with those adorable eyes. "Babe--"

"If this is what you were planning, where is my ring?" she chided. Her question was stern, but warm. Tim was used to Tara's challenges and he was not intimidated.

"I will get your ring tomorrow," he said happily. "Just say yes to us."

"Yes," she said. They shared a loving and passionate kiss. They had kissed before, but this was the first time Tara had allowed complete expression in the kiss. She had spent so much of her life trying to protect her body. It had not been easy for her to yield to his touches. Tim had no intention of spoiling the moment by getting too physical. He appreciated the closeness she gave him and the way she allowed him to squeeze her close to him.

After their kiss, he looked in to her eyes and cupped her face. "I am going to take care of you and Juan."

Chapter 25

Tim and Tara decided to set a date immediately. However, Tara thought there were some key steps that needed to be taken so that their marriage would start on the right track. She insisted that Tim call his adoptive parents and inform them that he was getting married. This brought about their first real argument.

Tim had come over for dinner and Tara introduced the topic sweetly enough. Tim showed passive resistance immediately. He did not say no, but he did not say yes. Suddenly, he was quiet at the dinner table and even stopped looking her in the eye. Tara was not used to seeing him withdraw from her, so she gave him one of her firm statements.

"They cannot find out about our wedding from the same invitation that is being sent to everyone else," she told him.

He seemed unreasonably reluctant. "They're going to make a big deal about this."

"It is a big deal. You are getting married."

"You don't understand. They're going to want us to go there and we'll have to deal with all their assumptions and looks."

"Tim, you are acting like a real baby right now. Did they burn you with cigarettes?"

He held back his response for a moment. He knew Tara would not be able to understand someone treating you well, but as a project. "No."

"Then get over it. Stop complaining. They put clothes on your back and food on the table for you. You can deal with them."

Sure enough, when Tim called his parents, they were excited. In fact, they wanted to meet Tara and Juan right away. Tim had mixed feelings. On the one hand, he wanted to show them what a beautiful, talented woman Tara was. He adored Juan and he wanted to show them that this boy was sweet and well-behaved. He hoped they noticed that he had met a woman who was royalty as far as he was concerned.

He hoped they saw the same.

Knowing his parents, they would try to dwell too much on Tara's past. He begged Tara to underplay the foster care aspect of her life. If they knew about it, that would be the topic of conversation the whole weekend. Then, of course, she would have to hear about how they saved Tim from a life of crime. In their minds, Tim would have surely been a criminal without their intervention.

"You are being silly," she chided. "But if it will make you happy, I will try to come across as an entitled woman with a trust fund. Shall I tell them about the private schools I attended?"

"Ha. You're pretty, but you're not a comedian. You'll see what I mean."

This made her laugh and Tim had to laugh, too. Okay, they were going to make the six-hour drive to his "parents" home in Ohio. He would stop arguing with Tara and let her decide if he was being a big baby.

When they pulled into the gated estate, Tara was both surprised and impressed. Tim had not told her the extent of his parents' wealth. For some reason, she imagined a middle-class home with middle-class inhabitants and furnishing. His adoptive parents lived in a five-thousand-square-foot home made of brick. The driveway was long, winding into a perfect circle in front of the house. The lawn was neatly manicured and bright green.

"Tim," she said, "are you kidding me?"

"I told you they gave me a good life," he said. "It is no big deal. It's just stuff."

"I don't know," she replied. "It all depends on who you ask. I can tell you there were times when I was a little girl that I definitely would have appreciated this stuff."

"Wow, they're rich," Juan said from the back seat. He had put down the action figure he had been focusing on. This estate looked like something described in the pages of one of the books his mother read aloud.

"Yes, they are," Tara said. "But we won't make a big deal about that. We'll thank them for their hospitality and have a good time."

"Okay, Mommy," he said excitedly. "I hope they have a whole room full of toys. You think they have an arcade?"

"It will be fine," Tim said, hopping out the car. Juan had already climbed out of the car. Tim tried to rush to the other side before Tara could open her door, but she stepped out to try to catch up to Juan. Her son was rushing toward the house.

"Juan," she called, "come back here and wait for Tim."

When Juan reached the door, a tall, handsome man opened the door for him before he could reach for the doorbell. The man was Mexican and he looked as if he had been working in the yard. Tim recognized the man and he recognized Tim. They both called to each other at the same.

"Jose!" Tim called out, as though he had just found a long, lost friend.

"Timmy!" Jose called.

They both started moving toward each other. When they reached each other, there was a strong, manly bear hug. Excited chattering ensued for a moment. All Tara could hear was fluent Spanish from them both. She did not recall Tim mentioning his ability to speak Spanish. Although she was impressed, it made her wonder what else she would learn about him on this trip. After a moment, Tim introduced Juan who was standing and looking at them both with fascination. Jose seemed happy to meet Juan and even remarked that he liked the name very much.

"Oh, my Lord!" An older woman was in the doorway now. She was a chubby, older black woman with grey curly hair. "Is that Timmy?"

"Aunt Claire!" Tim called, with genuine happiness.

They were all hugging. Tara stood observing the reunion. Finally, or so it seemed, Tim turned around and called to her. She approached and he pulled her into the circle with a swift, firm arm.

"So, Jose, Aunt Claire, this is my fiancée, Tara. And this handsome boy is her son—well, soon to be our son --Juan."

Aunt Claire beamed with joy and grabbed Tara. "She is beautiful. Come on and give Aunt Claire a nice hug."

Before she could respond, Tara found herself gathered into Aunt Claire's soft, fat arms. The woman mentioned something about Tara needing to eat, but having a nice shape. She then turned her attention to Juan and pulled him into the house.

"I hope ya'll are hungry. I got everything you love, Tim. "

Jose was reserved with her at first. There was no lavish hug. He shook her hand warmly, but kept his distance.

"Where are Ma and Dad?" Tim asked, looking about him. Tara thought the phrase sounded very natural from Tim.

"Oh," Jose responded, "your father had a deal he was closing today, so he'll be back later. You mom went to visit Tina in the hospital."

"I see," he paused. "Tina's in and out of the hospital, huh?"

"No. Not out, in," Jose said.

"Who is Tina?" Tara asked. She had never heard Tim mention her.

"Tina is like a sister to Timmy," Jose jumped in. "Listen, you two shouldn't just stand out here. Take Ms. Tara in the house. I will get your bags."

"Thanks, Jose," Tim said. "Wow, it is really good to see you guys."

Tim shuffled her into the house. The inside of the house was even more impressive than the outside. The décor seemed royal and the design of the house was such that there were open spaces, with no clutter. Tara and Juan were shown past the large living room, family room and receiving room. The staircase was a traditional winding feature. Tara followed Juan as he ran up the steps energetically.

She called to him to slow down, but she could hear Tim telling her to relax. Jose had their bags and he somehow scooted in front of her to show her to her bedroom, which was on the third floor. Tara and Juan were shown to a large room with a queen and twin bed. The room had a large bay window and even had toys and a hand-held game console by the twin bed.

"I hope he likes these things," Jose said. "Mrs. Benson told me to pick up a few things for him."

"That is very nice of her--and you," she quickly added.

He smiled. "Hey, if you got kids coming, you got to get them toys. I hope the beds are comfortable. Let me know if they are not and I will have the mattresses switched out."

"You purchased beds for us?" she asked surprised, but grateful for such kindness.

"Well, the bed in here was old. Timmy hadn't been home in a while, so Mrs. Benson wanted everything to be perfect for you all. I can tell you one thing. You have already scored big points with her and she is hard to please. But you got Timmy to come home. So, she likes you!"

"That is nice. Thank you, Jose."

"Oh, no problem, Ms. Tara. Listen, whatever you need, you ask me. I take care of the house and anyone in the house. But any friend of Timmy's is my friend." His conviction was strong and she could tell he was committed to his service to the family.

She smiled. As he left, Tim dipped in. He was staying on the second floor. Tim gave Jose a mock expression as he left. "Look, man," he joked. "Don't try to put that Latin charm on my woman. I know how you are."

Jose laughed. He turned once again and winked at Tara. When he did that, she noticed how handsome he was. Tim shook his head and closed the door after Jose.

"I been dealing with that since high school--every time I bring a woman around Jose. He tries to charm her."

"Brought lots of fiancées home, huh?" she asked with a smile.

"No. No. You're the first and last," he said, pulling her to him. He gave her a tender kiss. Juan grimaced and made a painful sound.

"Do ya'll have to do that all the time?" he complained.

They both laughed in response. Tim let her go and gave Juan an amused look. Then he slapped her behind lightly.

"I just came to check on you. Aunt Claire wants us to come get something to eat downstairs."

"Okay. I am not hungry right now," Tara said. She looked at that queen bed with that large pink comforter. Suddenly all she wanted to do was get in it and sleep. She could feel the weight of everything that had transpired in the last few weeks. She was also still worried that she had allowed the restaurant to stay closed one more weekend.

"Aunt Claire has been cooking all morning. It would make her sad if you didn't eat."

"I get it," Tara said. "I don't want to offend her. Juan and I will wash our hands and come downstairs."

"Good. I am going to go on down. See you in a few."

"Sure."

As he left, Tara looked around the house again. She had not met Mr. and Mrs. Benson, but there seemed to be a lot of love in this house. She did not understand why Tim had alienated himself from this family.

Chapter 26

Aunt Claire prepared delicious turkey and roasted pepper sandwiches with homemade chips and green salad. Juan ate the same thing, except he had grilled cheese instead of turkey. Aunt Claire told her history.

Tara was looking about the beautiful kitchen. It was on the level below the main entrance to the house. There was a homey feeling in the kitchen. The walls were stone and the floors were a rustic-colored hardwood. Some of the appliances had been updated, but there was still the original wood stove next to the new stainless steel one.

"Timmy was so scared when he first came to us," Aunt Claire was saying. "He thought he was not going to be able to stay. I told him that Mr. and Mrs. Benson aren't like that. They wouldn't have brought him home if he wasn't here for good."

Tim was quiet while she spoke. He was steadily eating the delicious food. Tara could not read his expression. She did not know if he was ignoring the conversation, silently angry, or embarrassed.

"But I think part of it was he was hoping his mama would come get him," Aunt Claire offered.
"You know, no matter who your parent is, you love that parent. Tim would tell me that he was here until his mama came to get him."

Tara looked over at Tim again. He glanced at Aunt Claire and then started eating more chips.

"I can understand," Tara said.

Aunt Claire continued. "I mean, she gave him life. She just made mistakes."

"You knew her?"

"No, but Mr. and Mrs. Benson told me about her history. In and out of jail since Tim was small. You know, on drugs and stuff--running the streets. She didn't even have the getup and go to keep a roof over the boy's head. Her going to jail that last time, though, freed Timmy from her."

Tara listened quietly now. She thought about how the same conversation could have been told about her. She remembered one incident, before she knew she was pregnant with Juan. She recalled that another girl had offered her some powdery substance. Tara remembered feeling completely alone and desperate. No one cared if she lived or died. It was very tempting to think that something could help her escape her problems. She had not thought about it in years, but she had been tempted to take that innocent-looking white powder into her system.

But she remembered hearing a voice. It was a faint whisper telling her not to do it. After she found she was pregnant with Juan, she thought that was the reason. Sitting here listening to Aunt Claire, she realized how important that moment really was. Because she walked away--ran away—from that temptation, she escaped the fate painted so vividly by Aunt Claire.

Tara's eyes shifted to Juan and suddenly she was reminded of how thankful she should be for her son. Tears would have fallen from her eyes, but Juan asked for more chips. His appetite helped lighten the mood. Tara leaned over and put her hand on Tim's shoulder. He felt so tense, but with her touch he relaxed. Aunt Claire was now obsessing over Juan.

"So, Aunt Claire, where did you learn to cook?" Tara asked, taking another bite from the delicious sandwich. "I am always looking for new recipes for the menu at my place."

"What place?" Aunt Claire asked dismissively as she watched Juan eat a cookie.

"Tara owns a restaurant," Tim volunteered happily.

"Really?" Aunt Claire turned her attention to Tara now. "You're young to own a restaurant--I mean, that is such a demanding business. I did some catering years ago. I was so happy when I met the Bensons and they wanted a private cook. Did you inherit it?"

"Well," Tara said, "the owner was like a father to me."

"I see," Aunt Claire said, but it was hard to interpret what she had gathered from their exchange.

"Aunt Claire," Tim interjected, "Tara is being way too modest. She started working there and helped transform the place from a hole in the wall to a restaurant that is a staple of Rockford. It was highlighted as one of the city's best last year in the newspaper."

"Oh, well, you should be very proud of that, Tara," Aunt Claire said, with a gently chastising tone.

"I am very proud. It's just I had the opportunity to take something good and expand it. So I look at it as part of what I was able to give to him before he died. He gave me so much. But I don't want to take too much credit."

"I can understand where you're coming from. You'll have to cook with me over the next few days. I can't tell you recipes, but I can show you what I do."

Tara smiled. "Yes, ma'am."

They all carried on, chattering, eating and laughing. Tara started to feel very comfortable with Aunt Claire. She noticed that Tim started to relax. He actually looked like he was home. Juan was begging for another cookie. It struck Tara that she had never felt like this before. It must be what some people have all the time, but it is so natural and subtle. They probably don't think about it. The big family feeling of security and belonging overwhelmed her and she looked over at Tim. He looked back at her with a wink, but she was sure he had no way of knowing what she was thinking.

Soon they all could hear an authoritative voice upstairs. It was a rich, dark voice and the way it thundered caused everyone to stop what they were doing. Juan even stopped, allowing Aunt Claire to fuss over him and Tim sat up erect. After the male voice, a sweeter, but firm feminine voice soared. Both voices were refined. Although they seemed to speak loudly, they were not arguing.

Aunt Claire smiled. "Okay, everybody get ready. Mr. and Mrs. Benson are here. I can tell they are excited. Tim, you might as well get up there and introduce the family to Tara and Juan."

He stood up and put his second sandwich down. "The fun really begins now," he said, motioning Tara to follow him up the stairs.

When they reached the top step, Tara saw a tall, dark-skinned man. He was older and very handsome, with silky grey hair. Beside him stood a light-brown-skinned woman. They both looked as if they had come from the office or some business event.

Tara wished she had chosen something else to wear. Mr. Benson took one look at her and Juan and nodded. "Tim," he said, "well, it's good to see you, son. Who is this lovely lady here?"

"This is Tara and Juan," he replied.

Mrs. Benson went over to Tim and took him into her arms. She hugged him tightly. "I am so glad to see you," she said.

HIs shoulders relaxed. "I am glad to see you, too, Ma."

"That is my boy," she spoke. She then turned her eyes to Tara. "Well, I have you to thank because you brought my Tim home."

"Hi. I'm Tara and this is my son, Juan," Tara said as Mrs. Benson hugged her.

Mr. Benson was more reserved, but Tara could feel he was genuinely friendly as well. "Well, you were downstairs, so I know Aunt Claire was feeding you."

She laughed. "Yes. We ate very well."

"Well, we are all going out tonight, so I hope you can find more room in your stomach. This is a celebration. Tim is home and he brought family with him."

Chapter 27

That night the family went to the finest restaurant Tara had ever been to in her life. Immediately she was struck by the smells and the aura of the place. When they arrived inside the establishment, the maître d walked from behind his desk and greeted Mr. Benson in the way one would treat a dignitary.

"Mr. Benson, your private room is waiting, sir." He turned and motioned to a lanky boy who quickly came forward with a pleasant smile. "I took the liberty of adding some of the chef's new recipes to your menu."

"Thank you, Markus," he said. Mr. Benson was not a dismissive man, but Tara could tell he had grown used to people treating him with a certain level of respect. He was not seduced by it, however. Mr. Benson knew there was a check that would need to paid at the end of the evening.

Without another word, the Benson clan was led through the restaurant to a private room. A few of the patrons looked up at them. Tara thought it must have been a sight to some of them. Here was a majestic black man in a thousand-dollar suit walking with his beautiful wife on his arm. Mrs. Benson was a woman of timeless elegance. Her hair was not long, but it was thick and full with a shiny black color to it. The parts that were not black were perfectly silver. Her dress was clearly of designer origin and it fit her figure pleasantly. So, although she was older, she had maintained her curves.

Following behind the two older Benson stars was Tim. Tara had to admit that Tim was breathlessly good-looking. For some reason, she was seeing him tonight as though for the first time. Women were swooning over him as he walked by. Even those with dates eyed Tim and had to do a double-take.

Juan must have been quite a show, too. Mrs. Benson had a little tuxedo procured for him. Tara had dressed him in suits before, but he had never dressed so finely. He looked as if he should have been on a magazine cover. As for herself, she did not think her presence made much of a difference. Of course, Tara underestimated the way she shone among the group.

Mrs. Benson had purchased Tara an ensemble similar in nature to her dress. The color of Tara's dress was champagne instead of silver and the dress was shorter, with a younger cut to it so that the bust and hips were accentuated. As they walked, Tim squeezed her hand.

The private room had a spread of food that excited Tara beyond imagination. She did not want to eat any of the food displayed. It all looked so good. There were variants of traditional soul food dishes, but there were also modern dishes with types of seafood she had never tasted before. Tara made a mental note to ask someone for a menu she could take with her. All dishes came in a sample size, so one could try everything at least once.

Tara noticed that there were more than just five place settings. Tim held the chair for her and she sat next to Juan. When Tim seated himself beside her, she glanced at his noble side profile. His eye lashes were dark and long--they seemed to be curling just for her.

She wanted so badly to kiss him at that very moment. Mrs. Benson smiled in her direction.

"It is okay to kiss your fiancée--especially when he is as cute as my Tim," she said with a smile, leaning toward Tara.

Tara felt her cheeks burning. "Am I that obvious?"

"Girl, you love him. That is obvious to me. Besides, Benson men have that effect on women. They are kissable." She nodded toward her husband, who was not looking at either of them.

Mr. Benson had been talking to Tim and they were enjoying whatever topic it was. Mrs. Benson leaned over and gave her husband a kiss on the check. He stopped talking and half-smiled. Juan groaned in quiet disgust. It was bad enough that he had to suffer through random kisses from women. He really hoped he was not going to look at kisses all night or, worse, be kissed all night. Tara leaned over and kissed Juan on the side of his mouth. Juan groaned again and everyone laughed.

"Ma, come on!" Juan sunk a little into his chair.

"One day you'll understand," Tim told him. "But I don't know why you got the kiss intended for me."

"Exactly," Tara said, turning her attention to Tim and giving him a sweet kiss. They stared at each other for a moment.

Juan seemed to give up now and resolve himself to an evening of weird adult affection. He turned his attention from them and started eating a potato cake that a waiter had brought to the table. The salt from the potato seemed to pacify him. Tara also allowed him to have a little soda, so he was happy.

Mrs. Benson looked over at the two of them. "This is all I ever wanted for you, Tim. I always wanted you to be happy. The first day I saw you. I just could not stop thinking about you."

Mr. Benson patted her hand. He seemed to resist going down this road of memory with her. "Yes. Well, Tim has always been happy." He ordered drinks and then turned his attention to the lovebirds. "So, when is this wedding and where is it going to be?"

"We haven't set the exact date yet," Tara responded.

"Well, it's got to be here. I mean, we can turn the whole house into a wedding venue." Mrs. Benson was speaking in a surprisingly insistent tone. Then she had a gleam in her eyes and the idealistic side of her started to show a bit. "It could be a fairy-tale wedding. Tara. Did you ever think you'd meet someone like Tim? I know you didn't. "

"No. No. That is very generous, but it will be a small wedding," Tara said, trying to address the first part of Mrs. Benson's statement. "I wouldn't dream of imposing on you all like that."

"Nonsense," Mrs. Benson said. "We have at least 100 people who need to be there. Then there's your family and I am sure there are people at Tim's publishing company. Marriage is an excellent career move. You must invite a few co-workers. Then, Tara, your friends will be coming. You might even want to invite a few customers from your restaurant. Things like this are important. It is a community, social, business and family event all rolled into one. Tim, didn't I always tell you--"

"Ma," Tim said lightly, but firmly, "it is not a business deal. It's our wedding. Tara and I really want to keep it small. We want it to be an intimate celebration with our closest family."

Mrs. Benson started to talk again. She was outlining her argument in a very structured way. Her tone was very firm as well and her yellow cheeks were taking a little color as she explained to the two of them how wrong they were. Mr. Benson put aside his club soda and looked at her for a moment. He seemed annoyed, but used to her dissertations.

Finally, he shook his head with a sigh of compassion. "You know these two young folks are going to do what they want. So, I don't know why you're wasting time on all this. Notice I was just trying to find out where I needed to be and when, so I could get it on my calendar. No offense, Tim. This is an important moment in your life and it's a decision you'll never regret. But it's your decision, not ours."

Mrs. Benson sucked her teeth delicately and took a sip of her sparkling water. She gave Tara a look of expectation.

Tara was silent, but she had listened to Mrs. Benson. In a way, she could see the woman's logic. Why not leverage the event for multiple purposes? Big Mike's could cater the food and gain exposure to these 100 friends—100 wealthy friends. If they were rich like the Bensons, it could really be a great way to grow the business. However, she needed a new name for the catering service. Instead of Big Mike's, she would use his full name – Michael Simpson...Simple and Savory Catering Company. She instantly loved the new brand name for the catering entity.

Tim noticed that she was quiet and leaned over. "Don't worry about Ma. She'll get over it. As Dad said, we can do what we want."

She nodded. "Right. Oh, I am not worried."

Soon they had gotten into a rhythm of eating and enjoying each other's company. Tara decided that she liked the Bensons. Mrs. Benson was pushy, but Tara did not know any older black woman who wasn't. She laughed to herself. Perhaps she herself was growing pushier by the day and did not know it. Mr. Benson was calm and collected. He did not seem to mind his wife's pushiness. Tara could see he had made up his mind years ago that he would comply with some things and ignore others.

Tara had forgotten about the extra place setting that had remained empty until this point in the night. They were all having such a good time. Even Juan seemed to be enjoying the conversation. She could not believe that she was enjoying a fiancé, future in-laws and her son all at the same time. If only Big Mike could see her in a place like this.

"Well, here we are together again. It's good to see you, Tim. Finally, you've come home and haven't come alone." The new voice came from the private entrance to the room. Tara noticed immediately that Mrs. Benson was very annoyed at the statement as the matron turned toward the tall, mocha-colored man in the doorway. He was well-dressed, handsome and a little drunk.

Tim immediately tensed, but his face showed no further expression. Juan was fascinated. Tara knew this because his eyes were large and he had stopped eating to look at the man. Mr. Benson stood up and pulled the young man to the table. He mumbled something in his ear and the man responded by pulling his arm away.

"I can walk," he hissed.

He sat down awkwardly at the table. For a moment, he looked down at his plate setting. He motioned for one of the wait staff and declared that he wanted something other than the pre-selected foods. After that, he looked up at everyone.

"Well, I was invited here. But you all look surprised that I showed. Why wouldn't your son come to this great celebration where you welcome your other son, my brother, back home? He's been gone so long. I had almost thought he'd never come home again."

"That's enough, Joshua." Mrs. Benson said.

"I don't mean anything negative. I am just saying he's been a ghost and you all don't even question why. Dad just drops a fortune on this little get-together. I ask for $100 and it's a big deal."

At first he was talking aloud to the entire table. Then he decided he would look directly at Tara. "It's been like this since they brought him home. They got stuck with me. God made them take me, but they chose him."

"All right, all right." Mr. Benson seemed to have had enough. His heavy, but steady voice seemed to help

Joshua straighten a little and not appear so drunk. "Good to see you, Joshua. Glad you could make it."

After a little delay, Tim also spoke. "Joshua, you're right. It's been a while, but I'm glad to be home. Good to see you."

Joshua gave a humph for a response. He turned his attention from Tim to Tara. "So, you're the great woman who convinced Tim to come home."

She really did not want to engage with this Joshua, but she felt compelled to defend Tim. "I wouldn't say that. We're getting married and so naturally we came to see the family."

He smiled. "Naturally." Suddenly he turned his attention back to Tim. "You see Tina yet or are you and your lawyer here too preoccupied with each other to do that?"

Tim put down his fork and his tone changed. "Joshua, we'll go see Tina before we leave."

"Don't get upset. I am just asking."

"You're just being difficult," Mrs. Benson chimed in. "I visit Tina more than anyone at this table, including you, so don't try to look so noble. Tim won't have time for all that on this trip. He can visit Tina when he comes back."

Tara decided not to play in the conversation. She had asked about this Tina earlier and Jose told her she was like a sister. There seemed to be a back-story and Tim had never mentioned her. However, he had never mentioned this bitter, drunken brother, either. Tara hated that the perfect Benson family had been ruined by the revelation of Joshua. She really disliked hm. He apparently had every advantage from birth and he became a bitter drunk. No wonder his parents adopted Tim.

Chapter 28

The ride back to the Benson's house was silent. Juan was in the back seat, asleep. Tim seemed deep in thought while Tara pondered the extremes of the night. The first part of the night was out of some enchanted novel or movie. Everything was perfect--the perfect man, perfect family, food, company. Then Joshua walked in and reminded her of the slumming element she had confronted too often in her life. He really lacked class. It reminded her that appearances are so often deceiving.

After ten minutes of silence, she looked over at Tim. Tara admired his handsome side profile, but she wanted to connect more deeply to what was inside him. Tim really was a strong man in every respect, but he was a man with hurt. When she first arrived at the Benson household, it was hard for her to understand where his hurt originated. The Bensons were sincere and there was no pretense about them. However, there was this Joshua she had never been told about and the mystery Tina, whose name was spoken by everyone except Tim.

Finally, she spoke. "Is he their biological son?"

"Yes. Joshua is a strange one. We used to be really close, but he got all mixed up in the high school years. It started when we both ran for sophomore class president. Dad thought there was no harm in us both running if we wanted it. Ma didn't want us directly competing. She wanted us to compete against those outside the family--beat others, as she put it. She didn't think our relationship was strong enough to handle a loss by one of us. I remember thinking how crazy that sounded to me, but Ma was right."

"You won," she correctly inferred.

"Yes, and it's been messed up ever since. It's like we knew that only one of us would win the election, but Joshua must have assumed that the winner would be him. From there it was a battle between us for everything--grades, girls, parents. I got tired of competing with him. He even made cleaning the room a competition. The worst part about it is that I started to dislike him to the point that I enjoyed seeing him frustrated and angry. It wasn't healthy."

"But I thought you said the Bensons always made you feel like a trophy--a do-gooder trophy," she said. She was still confused. It sounded like they gave Tim full support. When Tim called them Ma and Da, it was genuine. He recognized them as his parents.

"They did!" he insisted. "It's as if they were using me to compensate for the fact that Joshua is such a loser. To show other people that they actually could be good parents, they talked about me all the time. That meant that I had to deal with Joshua's backlash. He once turned the entire basketball team against me. I had to get out of here. I just decided I was not going to be their trophy and his punching bag. He reminded me tonight of why I always had an excuse not to come home."

Tim was frowning. As he told the story, his voice grew stronger. His demeanor became more resentful. He looked over at her, but then quickly looked forward again. Tara put her hand on his shoulder.

"But your parents are beautiful people!" She felt so bad for the Bensons. "You shouldn't cut them off because of him."

"I know. It's not fair. So, you even like my mother?" he teased.

"I love your mother. She's a blueprint."

"Oh Lord! Don't try to be like her!" He seemed genuinely scared.

"No. I mean she cares for you all. She's got strong opinions. She's refined. I want to be strong like that for Juan."

"You are strong." He paused, then sweetly, "I need you, too, you know. It's not just Juan who needs you."

She smiled. "I know..." Tara paused. Then she decided she might as well get it out in the open. "Who is Tina...really?"

Tim looked back at her again. He cleared his throat and looked back at the road. She waited because he did not speak immediately. Tara knew him well enough to know he was not deciding what to say. He often paused when he was approaching a subject that he feared would be unpleasant to her. She braced herself. Tara had never really thought about Tim with other women. She had not dated in her life. Prior to meeting Big Mike, her experiences with men were not positive. She decided to completely disregard the unpleasant experience with Ted as a strange lesson. Working and building a friendship with Big Mike helped her see men in a different light.

For her part, she had never inquired about Tim's prior relationships. He had not experienced abuse as she had. To her knowledge, any relationship he would have had would have been consensual. What if he and this Tina were in a relationship and he still carried a torch for her? What if she had to compete with the memory of Tina? It made her nervous. She had always shunned men. She had never desired a man that she could not have.

"Tina is another child, a girl my parents were going to adopt. Joshua and I had crushes on her. She was added to the family later, probably when we were in the sixth grade or so. Ma wanted to do something for a black female, so Tina was hand-picked by Ma."

"What are you saying?" Tara asked, shocked. Tara had been in the situation where she was a girl added into a ready-made family. It could be a precarious place for a young girl with no advocates and no help.

"Oh, nothing like that," he said, immediately understanding her point of reference. "Tina was beautiful, smart, funny and accessible. I mean she was a girl that we could talk to, ask questions of, learn how to relate to. I started to see her as a sister. I could relate to Tina because her parents were like my parents. Her parents had both overdosed on drugs before she came to us. I knew what that felt like, to lose your parents--I mean, to know that your parents cared about some powder more than they cared about you. So, Tina and I bonded."

Tim continued. "Joshua hated that bond between us. He saw it as more than what it was. And, of course, he got jealous. He actually told Ma that he saw me and

Tina in the kitchen area having sex. It was not true, but he told it anyway. Both Tina and I denied it, but it took some convincing. Honestly, I am not sure if they ever truly believed Tina and me."

Tara looked over at him. She knew he was telling the truth. Tim prided himself on his integrity. The sheer possibility that his parents did not believe him would be enough to run him away. She thought about it for a moment, then asked her next question. "So, what's wrong with her?"

"Well, she got sick. She has meningitis. It really debilitated her and she needs constant care. So, she is at a special facility. Ma takes good care of her and that's how it goes."

"Why didn't you mention her before? Don't you want to go see her?"

He shrugged. "I haven't seen Tina in years." Tara could hear the guilt in his voice. "Plus, the last time I saw her--it was hard to see her like that. She is really sick."

"I see," Tara replied. "Well, if you want to go see her tomorrow with your mother, I think you should do that."

"Tara, Joshua only goes to see her because he thinks it makes me look bad. Can you believe he's still competing with me?"

She shrugged and shook her head. As they finished the conversation, Tim pulled the car back in the Benson's winding driveway. Tim lifted Juan out of the back seat and they walked into the house.

Tara was still thinking about the evening when her head hit the fluffy pillow. Now she was thinking about Tina, Joshua and Tim. Joshua's lie and Tim's decision to visit infrequently raced through her head. Could she bridge this family gap? She thought about her own life. There was definitely nothing about her that would make her an authority on bringing families together. Juan had been her family, but she had spent the last seven years shielding him from the elements of the world.

Tim's family had baggage--or maybe it was just Tim. Could he handle being a father to her child?

Chapter 29

On the morning they were scheduled to leave, Tim got up early to visit Tina. Tara did not go with him, but she was happy he decided to go. After he returned from the hospital, they set out for home.

Tara did not ask him much about his visit. He seemed a little shaken, though, for the rest of the afternoon. When she asked him about his visit, he only said that Tina had gotten worst. She was bed-bound now and could do little on her own.

"I'm sorry, honey," she told him gently.

He sighed. "Sometimes..."

He did not finish his sentence. He put the bags in the back seat. Tara watched him. After putting the bags in the car, he placed his hands on top of the car and stretched.

"Sometimes?" she said as more of a question.

"Nothing," Tim said. "Come on. I have to be to work tomorrow and you have a restaurant to run."

"And a wedding to plan," she said, with a reassuring smile.

He looked at her, cheered a little by her words. "Yes, and a wedding to plan."

They kissed. Juan, who had just finished giving Ms. Claire a hug made a gagging noise. That served to lighten the mood. They all set off for home.

Tara was grateful to get back to the restaurant. She had enjoyed the vacation, but she missed the fast pace of the breakfast, lunch and dinner rushes. She missed the customers, the employees and, of course, she missed Big Mike. There was a comfort in the familiar surroundings of work. It was therapeutic to look at receipts and count tills at the end of the night. Tara liked making the deposits, signing the payroll checks and talking to customers.

When they reopened Big Mike's, they opened with a few specials reminiscent of the fairy tale night with the Bensons. People really seemed to like the refinement of the plates and they were grateful to have the reliable, delicious food Big Mike's offered. Tara put a life-sized picture of Big Mike up in the front of the store and patrons seemed to appreciate that. It was the last picture she had taken of him. He was holding his spatula in his right hand with arms crossed. His confident smile beamed brightly.

She remembered that day. He had just finished teasing her about being a lonely old maid by choice. She had shrugged off his comments. "All right," he had said, "you're not going to be able to use me and Juan as your men forever. Better get on that!"

It was as if she could still hear his heavy, rich voice telling her she had better stop pretending she did not care about men and relationships. Okay. She did care-- about one man in particular. Now she was in a place of uneasiness she had never been before. She loved Tim, but in some respects she did not want to concentrate on him. His story about Joshua and Tina bothered her.

Why did Joshua make up such a tale? Why did Tim feel that the Bensons were not 100 percent convinced that Joshua had lied? Then she thought about Joshua and the way he acted. Of course, he lied! He was a spoiled brat. He reminded her of Ted--someone who felt entitled to things and had never really been told he had no right to them. She had never forgotten how Ted had turned on her out of the blue. In that way, she could see what Tim had meant. When they, the entitled people, do not get what they want, they reject you with great venom. And all the more so when they find out that you, with all the terrible things you have been through in your life, somehow exceed them in accomplishment and character.

Tara pushed those thoughts out of her mind as she opened the doors to Big Mike's. It was early morning. There was only an hour before the first customers would be coming in for breakfast. Tara and the staff had been in the restaurant late the night before preparing for this moment. Her heart was racing with excitement and anticipation. For the first time, the gravity of the moment enveloped her. This restaurant business was all hers. She was a business owner in her own right.

There were times when she had even written herself off. Tara remembered being a scared girl, crouching in the corner of a room and praying that the man of the house would not come into her room. She also remembered praying and asking God for more when she was living in the studio apartment with the baby Juan. Now look at her! How could such things be possible?

The place was packed that first day with happy customers. Tara was pleasantly surprised that she and the three-person staff were able to handle the crowd. She had to jump in and wait tables again. It became apparent to her that the loss of Big Mike was like losing three people. She put the Help Wanted sign in the window the following day.

As she focused more on structuring the business without Big Mike, she thought less about planning a wedding with Tim. She still considered him her fiancée, but it was hard to concentrate on that when the business proved to be so demanding.

Three months passed. She promised Tim they would sit down and plan the wedding the following weekend. That weekend came and went.

Chapter 30

Tara was in her office one afternoon during the transition time between breakfast and lunch when she heard a familiar voice. It was a refined feminine voice. At first, Tara could not place it, but when she lifted her eyes from the bank deposit form and saw the designer shoes and tailored dress, she knew who it was.

"Ambitious women," Mrs. Benson said. "I have always liked women who are driven, focused and hungry for success."

"Hi, Mrs. Benson!" Tara stood quickly. Suddenly she was cognizant of the fact that she must look terrible. Her curls were probably flat and she was wearing jeans with flour across them. She was sure her shirt had telltale food stains. During the course of the day, she had changed her chef uniform three times. Although Tara was not a chef, she liked to wear the uniform of the kitchen staff.

"Tara, please don't get up. I thought I would come by. When I talk to Tim he acts like he has no clue what you all are doing. He acts as if he hasn't talked to you. I hope we didn't scare you when you came to visit us. You all promised me a wedding."

Tara laughed in response. "Oh, no. I have been busy. The restaurant--it has really been crazy lately. I just want it to be successful and I have been working hard. He's been working hard, too. I haven't gotten a chance to really do much of anything."

"I think that is not good at all. Tara, can I be candid with you?" she asked, leaning in toward her.

Tara was hesitant to say yes. Mrs. Benson was standing there looking so expensive and refined. All of sudden, Tara felt inadequate, as if she had accomplished nothing over the last seven years of her life. Mrs. Benson seemed to sense her insecurity and smiled.

"Tara, I know what it is like to be busy. I have been busy my entire life. You probably do not know this, but when I met George Benson, he had nothing. My parents had a small business and I had a good life. I loved that man, though, and I wanted him. My father didn't like him. He thought a man like George would only lead to babies and a short, miserable life. He didn't understand that George didn't have any physical possessions, but he had ambition, a strong work ethic, and he loved me. He would do whatever it took to have me."

"Sounds like a wonderful love story." The conversation had put Tara at ease. Now she felt like herself again. She motioned for Mrs. Benson to take a seat.

"Can I get you something?"

"Sure," she replied, removing her leather gloves. "Get me whatever you think is best."

"Hey, Sal!" Tara called. "Can you get us a plate of chicken and rice?"

A strong male voice called back from the kitchen that it would be coming right up. In about 15 minutes he brought a large plate of smothered chicken and rice with collard greens. The food was savory and tasty. Mrs. Benson started to eat, nodding her approval.

"This is really delicious."

"Thank you, " Tara said proudly.

"So here is my thing. You remind me of George and myself, if I may be so bold. You make Tim happy and I want to be of any help I can. Remember when I was talking to you about the wedding? I said the wedding is a social, business, community and family event. Well, marriage is the same. Tim wants to hide in corporate America at some publishing company proof- reading self-help books. He's always tried to run from what he really is."

She looked Tara in the eyes. "I am seeing what you've done here. George and I can help you take this place to the next level. We can give you access to resources."

"Wait, Mrs. Benson. I'm not with Tim for money. I did not know who you all were when I met and fell in love with him."

"Fair enough," she said, taking another bite of chicken, gravy and rice mixed together. "And I admire you for that, but now you know. It is a piece of information you should not ignore. Now I know you are a survivor. You have Juan and you deserve happiness with Tim. Now, in business when you see an opportunity, do you let it lag for three months?"

Tara shook her head in response.

"So why are you letting this wedding lag? You think you're the only woman looking at Tim? Men are funny.

When they feel rejected, they find another woman to help them recover. I would hate to see some lazy woman walk off with him when he should be yours."

"Another woman?"

She held up her hand. "Think about it. Do you talk to him every day now?"

Tara thought about it. He had not called her yet today. It was past noon. If he was not talking to her, who was he talking to?

"So, I have another proposition for you. Since you are so busy, I will hire a wedding planner for you and Tim. The wedding planner will handle everything. You can focus on the business and your man."

" I don't know what to say."

"You're a smart girl. I think you know what to say. Say yes and let's stop putting on hold what promises to be one of the happiest days of my life."

Tara laughed. "I do love Tim, you know."

"I know. You just need a little help. You'll give him ambition and he'll give you love. I think it works well for both of you."

Before Mrs. Benson left, she added one other thing. "Tim doesn't know I came by. How about we keep it that way?"

"Agreed."

Chapter 31

If Tim was suspicious as to how and why his mother got involved in the wedding planning, he did not voice any concern. He seemed amenable to the demands of the wedding planner. He seemed to be okay with the fact that Tara gave general direction on what she wanted, but was too busy to be involved in the details. The small wedding they were going to have soon became a major production. It was a social, business, community and family affair, after all. However, only the guest list was large. The wedding party was still small.

Tara had a maid of honor and Tim had a best man. Neither of them had built enough friendships throughout the years to have an entourage of bridesmaids and groomsmen. They were similar in the fact that the two individuals they chose to play the traditional and important roles of maid of honor and best man were convenient choices, but not really close to either of them in the most intimate sense. They were the best and most practical choices for both of them.

Tara realized she had not really made female friends over the years. She was focused on providing for her son. Her distrust of men carried over to women, as she had seen enough women turn a blind eye to their husbands' activities.

Her maid of honor was the prone to hysteria Lindsey who had never really recovered from Big Mike's death. Tim's best man was a better choice in that he chose Jose. Although he and Jose had not spoken consistently in the years he avoided home, he was a friend. No one even suggested that he try to pretend Joshua was a suitable choice.

So, the wedding party was going to be simple. With no Big Mike, Tara had no one to escort her down the aisle. Tim suggested Mr. Benson could escort her, but Tara did not feel right about it. He was a nice man and he would probably do so without complaint. However, he was really Tim's family. She did not have a father and the closest person to a father had passed.

Overhearing the conversation, Juan chimed in with the simplicity of a child. "I will escort you down the aisle mommy." He was sweet and serious when he spoke.

At first, she laughed but then she grew warm to the idea. Juan was the man in her life. In fact, he was the one who had watched her grow from desperate teen-mother to confident woman. Juan was the one who HAD to approve of Tim before she considered feeling for him. He was her son and he was the only one who could acknowledge that Tim was welcome and now a part of their family.

"Thank you, son. I would be honored if you would walk me down the aisle."

The weekend of the wedding, Tara and Tim arrived back at the Benson's home. When Tara stepped into the luxury space this time, she felt at home. She watched as Juan immediately ran downstairs to seek Aunt Claire in the kitchen. Jose gave her a warm, sisterly hug and she felt completely comfortable hugging him in response. And Mrs. Benson was there to pull her aside and talk to her about some last minute details. She had made executive decisions on flowers, hors d'oeuvres and guest seating. She also emphasized to Tara that she expected a few city council members and the mayor to attend the reception.

Tara knew she should have been overwhelmed, but she was not. This was the life she had chosen the day Mrs. Benson made it clear to her what a union with Tim could mean. This was the world Juan should enter and eventually control.

As far as Tim was concerned, Tara loved and respected him. He was, however, overwhelmed and she had to reassure him more than once in private that the wedding was a one-time event. If it made the Bensons happy to make their wedding a lavish affair, he should be content to give them that enjoyment. The marriage is what really counted. No one would direct their relationship after the wedding. It would be the two of them alone.

Tim reluctantly agreed. He decided to accompany Jose to the store to pick up some items for Aunt Claire. He was grateful there was an errand to run because he was a bit shaken by how settled Tara seemed to be compared to him. He had once thought they had a lot in common and he could take care of her, but she seemed to be more and more dominant in their relationship, while he felt as though he was languishing.

As he watched her ascend the stairs, he shook himself from such thoughts. Tara was beautiful from any angle. Also, she had learned to be adaptable throughout the years. Being adopted by the Bensons had civilized him early to the point that he lost toughness. Tara was tough as nails now. To look at her one would not know. However, he knew if she lost everything tomorrow, she'd survive. He had doubts about himself.

"I forgot to kiss you," she told him, reversing her ascent. She planted a long, wet kiss at the corner of his mouth. This forced a smile from him.

"I'll be back," he told her. Jose was standing behind him waiting. He cleared his throat.

"Come on, bro. You got two more days and then you can spend all the time you want on that."

Tara was upstairs putting her clothes away when she heard a male voice behind her. Immediately she tensed because she knew the voice. The first time she had heard the voice, it was slurred with alcohol. Although the voice was sober now, she identified the arrogant tone and the aggressive wording.

"You know I never got a chance to look at you up close. This is the first time I really got a good look at you with sober eyes. I must say you are fine."

She turned around to see Joshua standing in her doorway. What rock did he crawl from under? He was dressed in a black sweat suit, which showcased his square shoulders quite well. Tara had not really noticed his appearance that first night, but she could see him now. He was a handsome man. However, she was offended by his forwardness. Tara had too many past experiences with men that took liberties with words. Words were not harmless when men decided a woman was only an object. Her guard was up now and she looked behind him.

"Okay, okay," Joshua continued. "Who you looking for? You know your man went to the store with Jose. Aunt Claire is in the kitchen with your son and who knows what Ma is doing? But don't worry yourself. I am not that kind of guy. I know you are his fiancée, but I am just commenting. He did good with you."

He started to step into the room, but Tara shook her head and put her hands up. "I don't think so."

He paused and put his hands up as well, stepping back. "Relax."

"I am relaxed. But I can lose my relaxation and you don't want to see that." She allowed as much attitude as she could muster to flow into each word.

"Ms. Tara," he said in a contrite way, "I disrespected you that first night. And I offended you just now. My apologies."

"And you disrespected Tim. I don't like that."

He seemed to reflect on what she said. "I didn't mean to--"

"Don't lie."

"Okay. I was not really thinking about it in that way. I have always pushed Tim's buttons and he's always pushed mine. It's the way we relate to each other. I guess you can say we show our love that way."

She laughed aloud. "If that's the way you show love I feel for the woman who marries you." With that Tara turned her back on him. She began putting her clothes away again. Her gamble was that he'd be bored with the game if he noticed he couldn't ruffle her.

Joshua was not the kind of guy to be so easily deterred. He used the moment as an opportunity to step into the room. He was standing close enough behind her that she could feel his body heat. Tara decided not to respond. She walked around him and went towards the door.

Joshua grabbed her arm. "I think my mother likes you so much because you're another street kid. She likes people with hard stories. She loved Tim and Tina more than me because they were born in tough circumstances. She even fell in love with my dad because he was poor. I think in the back of her mind she must feel guilty for being black and born wealthy."

"You know it always amazes me that everyone considers themselves a psychologist," Tara said, in a chiding manner. "Well, since you can analyze everyone, may I provide you with my assessment of you?"

He smiled. "Please do. It always impresses me when people like you try to read someone as complex as I am."

"Here goes. Spoiled, privileged boy turns into spoiled, privileged man. He has never had a real challenge in life, so he spends his time envying and picking fights with other people he feels do not count. Does that work?"

This time Joshua laughed aloud. "I am not like that at all. I just tell it like it is. And I see people for who they really are. And Tim has had Ma and Dad fooled for years. But I know what kind of guy he is. He takes advantage. He took advantage of Tina and he'll take advantage of you, too."

He walked over to her and took her by the arm, hoping to look into her dark eyes. Tara's buried toughness surfaced and she yanked her arm out of his grip decisively.

"Get your hand off my arm. Don't ever touch me again. If you do, I will show you what I learned in the streets." She hissed.

"What?" He was taken aback with how aggressively she communicated with him and how suddenly her manner turned from a woman he thought he could intimidate.

"Let me put it this way. Get out of my room and stay out of my face."

He shrugged as he left. "I tried to warn you."

"Consider yourself warned."

Tara's Touch

Chapter 32

Tara decided to ignore Joshua and his deliberate attempt to undermine her trust in Tim. She decided that if Tim had a relationship with Tina, it would have been consensual. There was really no basis for her to question him or be jealous of this relationship. Tim admitted to being attracted to Tina when he was a boy. That was all the history she needed on the subject.

The next day Tara tried to stay focused as she entertained people she did not know. The whole evening was filled with her being introduced to people who would attend her wedding. For the first time, she felt herself empathizing with Tim's feelings. Mrs. Benson paraded Tim, Juan and her around as a rags-to-riches success story. In all her introductions, Mrs. Benson overemphasized her own contribution to Tara's success. The truth is Tara owned Big Mike's before she met Tim. Tim had become an executive at his publishing company before he met Tara. Mrs. Benson was not around for any of those occasions.

Tara even heard someone tell Mrs. Benson she must be so proud. After the twentieth introduction, Tara had to excuse herself from the room. She broke away from the crowd--even Juan--and stepped outside into the beautiful garden.

"She means well," the voice behind her said.

It was Mr. Benson. "I know my wife can be a bit of a handful. She doesn't know how to show her pride and she is not a subtle woman. Also, she has fantasies of a black aristocracy comprised of people of all backgrounds. I know it sounds weird, but just try to grin and bear it. By this time tomorrow evening, you and Tim will be married and you'll be on your way to enjoy your life together. Just get him to come home every now and then. That's my only ask."

Tara smiled, took a deep breath and then spoke. "I am very grateful for all you all are doing."

He shrugged. "This stuff is easy. Money is easy to spend when you have it. Did you know that my wife had money set aside for Tim? He's never spent one dime of it, so this is his money, you could say. We gave it to him already. I think she's only using half of it. You can use the rest for your son."

"I see." Tara paused, then suddenly asked a question that even surprised her. "Do you think Tim and I are right for each other?"

He raised his eyebrows and shrugged. "Who can ever say that? He's handsome. You're beautiful. He loves you. You love him. He's always needed a place to belong. I tried to give him that, but I never could. I think he feels like that with you. You three already look like a family. But I can't answer your question for you and him. Hopefully, you both feel pretty convinced of your love."

"I am. I just wanted you to say so as well. I feel like I have kind of let the sincerity of this occasion be compromised. I mean, I won't even know most of the people there tomorrow."

"The wedding is for my wife, too. Joshua isn't having a wedding anytime soon." For the first time, she saw disappointment in his eyes. He was usually not expressive. Mr. Benson was a strong man and he led his family in a firm way. Tara pitied him. He had everything he wanted except the one thing he couldn't have. It would make his life worthwhile if Joshua could become a better human being.

"He'll get there," she offered. "It's never too late."

"Perhaps," he said with a shrug, then brightened as if he had no worries. "Come on. Take my arm. Let's get back inside. It's my turn to show you off a little bit."

She giggled at his joke. "Yes, sir."

Both Tim and Tara were relieved after the wedding and its festivities. The ceremony turned out to be quick and simple. The wedding reception was an elegant affair. The two of them realized they had the ability and permission to leave after the toast, remarks and dinner. People were dancing and drinking. Juan was already asleep. Aunt Claire insisted that she keep the child for a day or two while Tim and Tara spent time as husband and wife.

For the first time, they were alone as a married couple. The first thing they did was sit side by side in their new home on the first piece of furniture they had purchased together. Tim pulled her to him and wrapped his arms about her. Tara relaxed in his arms. She now knew what it felt like to have an intimate touch from a man that she welcomed. For the first time in her life she wanted to be touched. It was a good feeling. She knew it was more than okay to be there with Tim, her husband.

"I really do love you," he said, snuggling with her.

Tara reclined on the couch. "I really do love you, too. I bought something nice to put on for you. Should I go get it?"

He shook his head. "I always imagined that it would be just you. If you don't mind, we can save the lace and silk for later."

Tara took a deep breath as he removed her clothing. Soon they were both nude together on the couch. She closed her eyes. For a brief moment, she thought about the exhausting events that led to this moment. When she was a young teen fleeing the hospital with her child, she could have never imagined that one day she would be with someone like Tim. She could not see in her future a self-supporting woman with a well-adjusted son and a handsome husband.

Now she lay in the arms of her husband, comforted by his touch. As they lay in each other's arms after love making, Tara kissed him deeply. He smiled at her and then closed his eyes to sleep.

"Tim?" she asked.

His weight was beginning to feel a bit heavy now. She moved from under him. "Tim? Sweetheart?" Now he was snoring. The snoring became louder with each minute. She paused to look at him for a moment as he snored. It surprised her a bit because she did not recall him snoring before. He had fallen asleep at her house a few times in the past, but she always slept in her bedroom while he occupied the couch.

Tara went into the bedroom, found a throw and brought it back in the living room to put over him. She noticed how free he seemed to be as he slept. She wanted to take a shower and cover her body because she had work to do.

She could not sleep. There was so much to think about, especially the several important business meetings she had lined up in the next few weeks.

Mrs. Benson had taken the liberty to introduce her to some suppliers. One gentleman offered the prospect of significant cost reductions. Another person owned a chain of restaurants and was looking for new recipes. They talked about a menu-sharing venture. He could feature some of Big Mike's dishes and pay a royalty. The idea sounded intriguing to her.

Of course, Tim did not know she had these conversations planned. He was busy just passing the time, avoiding Joshua and convincing her to let Juan stay with Aunt Claire on their wedding night. Eventually Tara fell asleep. But in her dreams, she saw a future. Unlike when she was younger, she could clearly see where she was going. Big Mike's was going to be the premier food services company in the United States and she was the chief executive officer.

Carla Brice-Talley *Tara's Touch*

Chapter 33

Time passed and Tara and Tim got in the rhythm of marriage. For the most part they were a happy couple. Tim treated her lovingly and lavished attention on Juan. Tim was successful at his publishing company and had been promoted to senior vice president. The only thing about Tim that frustrated Tara was his contentment at working for the publishing company. She wanted him to quit and join his father in his construction company. Tim preferred the fact that he made his own way in publishing. He had no desire to work in construction, even if he would be an owner of the company.

Besides, he knew Mr. Benson allowed Joshua to hold some titled position in the family business. Tim had no desire to risk seeing Joshua daily. So, Tara had to content herself with the fact that her husband did not mind working for someone else.

For her part, Big Mike's was doing well. The business had expanded to three restaurants now across the city and all three were experiencing increased revenue. In addition, Tara had expanded the profits with menu-sharing arrangements and decreased costs with favorable supplier deals, thanks to the Bensons and a successful catering division that operated more like a food services company. She had three major contracts with companies. Tim's only complaint about Tara was that she worked too much and her appetite for business success was insatiable.

"If you loved sex like you loved Big Mike's, we'd have a baby by now," he said one day while she was sitting in the study reviewing some figures. It was after 9:00 PM. He had just finished reading a book aloud with Juan and was on his way to bed.

Tara only looked back at him with a distracted glance. "I love you, babe," she responded.

"I said you need to love sex," he remarked before disappearing down the hall.

Perhaps that was the biggest underlying discontentment in their marriage. Tim wanted a baby. Tara did not necessarily object to having another child, but it was not a burning desire for her. To say that her mind, soul and body were given to the concept of getting pregnant would not be accurate at all. She knew she was going to have to compromise on the issue of another child sooner or later. She figured that, once she hired a chief operating officer, she would be able to surrender her body to pregnancy again.

So, Tim had to content himself with a wife who was president of the small business coalition, a business owner, an avid supporter of several charities, a mother of her biological child and a prominent member of her church. Did she spend time with him? Sure. She carved out time for him into her day planner. Tara found a note once in her planner and it was Tim's writing.

"Sex with my husband," she read aloud. It was marked for 9 pm that evening. Beside this note, another entry was crossed out. It said call with Troy Simpsons. Troy was the candidate she wanted for chief operating officer. He currently worked for a major food services company. Tara knew it would be tough to afford him, but she had something brewing in her mind that would enable her to afford Troy and others of his caliber.

If Troy could help her build a business, she could take it public and they would both be millionaires. She had not told Tim of this ambition because she knew it would drive him crazy. He liked simplicity, not high stakes.

She took her pen and crossed Tim's entry out. Troy was available at 9 pm that night because he was in China for his company this week. She decided she would call Troy.

"I should be able to work Tim in around eleven," she said, marking her day planner with her pen.

Chapter 34

Joshua knew that he should let his contempt of Tim go. He had sincerely tried to do away with the feeling of hatred he had for Tim. Joshua had tried to drink it away. He even tried to sex and drug it away. Once, during a period of desperation, or so he defined it, he went to a church. After the sermon, he went to the altar and stood before the preacher. The preacher laid his hands on his forehead and prayed for him.

Joshua felt a powerful presence rush over him as the music played and the choir sang. At one point, he thought he would fall backward. Tears flowed from his eyes and he fell to his knees. At that moment, he was a broken man. When he arose, he felt refreshed and he felt new.

But it did not last. Perhaps it was what the preacher had told him. He remembered the preacher looking at him with grave concern. The man's eyes were watery and he put a firm hand on Joshua's shoulder. He told him quite clearly, "God can do it for you, but you got to be willing to let it go. Brother, you got to forgive yourself. If you confess your sins, God will forgive you and you'll be able to move on."

The parishioners around him praised God and erupted in ecstatic singing. He was almost persuaded himself. But then he couldn't get over what the preacher had said. Confess?

What was he supposed to do? Walk into his parents' bedroom and tell them that he was the father of the baby Tina miscarried when she was sixteen? Tell them that he hated Tim and hated Tina because they both preferred each other to him? Tell them that he sometimes wished his parents were dead because he was not enough for them and they wanted to add children to the family? How could he ever breathe those kind of words from his mouth? He could not confess these terrible character flaws.

In fact, he knew his father would slap him to his knees.

So instead of confessing as the preacher had encouraged him to do, he completely rejected this idea as absurd. He would have to hold on to the feelings that burned his soul out. As a result, over the years he had become a man without a soul. Or so he felt.

Now he sat in his office at Benson Builders. Joshua had purposefully closed the door so he could ponder his next move. If someone were to walk by his office, they would think he was going through a contract and reviewing the rent reports. Joshua was good with numbers, so his father used his skills in the finance department.

Joshua turned over the piece of paper and closed his eyes. He flipped the paper back over so that he could read it again. There it was clear as day. Before him was solid proof that his parents had assessed him as not good enough.

At his request and skillful maneuvering, his father's lawyer had given him a summary of his parents' last will and testament. In it he could see that his father had given equal rights to him and Tim. A trust provision had been made for Tina so that she could continue to receive good medical care for the remainder of her life. He could abide that. That was fair. She was sick and could not provide for herself.

Tim was a different case. He was an executive at a major publishing company. His wife had built assets in her own right and now this adopted child, the son of a thug and a drugged-out prostitute, was going to walk off with half of what rightly belonged to Joshua. Not to mention, he could see that his parents had written special provisions into the will. Tim and his children would inherit? The way the section of the will was worded, it implied that, as Tim produced children, his share would increase while Joshua's share would decrease.

Joshua was good with numbers. He had taken a lot of mental abuse from his parents. They were not content with him, but he was not about to be disinherited.

"Well, he hasn't had any children yet," he said to himself. Joshua detached himself from what he was doing.

He made a phone call from the track cell phone he had purchased. Then he stepped on the phone so that he could not call the person to reverse his request. What he had ordered in his phone call had to be done. He would wait for news.

Two Saturdays later, Tim kissed Tara goodbye so that he could take his morning jog. He was particularly happy that Saturday morning. They had spent the morning in each other's arms. He loved his wife--the smell of her body and the curves of her body. He loved the way she spoke and the tone of her voice. He absolutely adored her.

That morning as they lay together, he leaned over and whispered into her ear. "I can't wait to see a little Tara."

"You want a girl?"

"Why are you surprised? Juan is my homeboy. Don't get me wrong. If you give him a little brother, that would be great. But I don't know. I like the idea of seeing you with a little twin of yourself."

She laughed. "I have never thought about a little girl. I have always been so focused on getting Juan--"

"My God, woman! You took care of Juan! He is okay. He is smart, handsome, well-adjusted and he has a good father now."

"Yes, he does," she smiled and gave him a long, endearing kiss. "You are a great father. I love you, Tim."

"You know, I have to get my jog in, but are you trying for a round two?"

"That sounds like fun," she said, pulling him closer to her.

This intimate conversation caused him to leave for his jog an hour and half later than usual. However, he did finally leave that morning. Tim had plans to take Juan to baseball practice that afternoon. His intention was for his father, Juan and himself to have a guy's night out. They were going to eat lunch and then catch a late game featuring one of the local teams.

Tim parked his car at the park. When he got out the car, he looked at the sleek auto before him and shook his head. This was one of the things his mom and Tara insisted he get. If it had been left up to him, he would have still been driving the ten-year-old Mazda. However, he had given in to their nagging. So now he drove a brand-new BMW. The technology in the car was outstanding. He loved the Bluetooth capability, leather seats, and back-up camera so that he did not have to turn his head. The only thing he refused to trust was the self-parking feature. Some things were made for people to do without help.

He locked the car door and started with a few stretching exercises. Tim leapt up and down in the air a few times. Then he set the timer on his watch. He started to run. Immediately he was grateful for the feeling. His leg muscles were expanding and contracting as he ran. The air was filling his lungs and the breeze was hitting his face. Tim loved to challenge himself, so he decided to do five minutes of high knee running.

"Still got it," he said to himself after he paused to catch his breathe. He wanted to bring his heart rate down before transitioning into a nice slow jog. He had told Tara that he would only be out an hour, but it was such a nice day. The temperature seemed just right and he had been cooped up in the office all week. He was going to take the liberty to enjoy a few extra moments of outside time.

He took his pace down and started to run again. Tim was so focused on running and the happiness of that one moment that he did not notice the man coming up behind him. His thoughts were on how great it felt to be a family man in good health.

When he heard the gun go off, it surprised him. Tim had not heard a gun since he was a young boy. It was a common sound in the neighborhood in which he had started his life. However, he was even more surprised to feel the bullet pop through his back and go through his chest. In one moment, the fresh air and feeling of total jubilation he felt turned into a terrible burning sensation and a struggle for air. Another bullet rippled through him and he fell to his knees.

Tim had no intention to die there on the park trail. He wrestled to his feet, or so he thought he did. It seemed he was walking. But in that moment between life and death, it was hard to tell what was really going on. He knew he heard a woman screaming. It was not Tara because she was not there. Someone had rushed to his aid.

"I am okay," he was trying to say. "I don't know what--"

"Don't talk," the person was coaching. "Oh, my God! Help!"

Tim knew he was not walking now. He was not even crawling. Now he was lying down. He was thankful that someone had turned him on his back. He did not want to die face down. From his understanding, that is how his real father had died. His daddy had been gunned down in the middle of the street. Tim lay there in pain, thinking how ironic it was that, even though he lived a completely different life, he was going to die the same way as his biological father. The only difference was that he would be face up and he would be surrounded by people crying.

As it was getting dark, he could see a woman standing over him. She was crying as if she knew him. A man was looking at the wound. Was he a doctor? He thought he heard the man say that it looked like the bullet had gone through the body. Was that good or bad, doctor?

He wanted to ask him that, but he could not talk. His tongue was lodged against the roof of his mouth. Life was slipping away as he lost more and more blood. Paramedics were there. He was on a gurney. They were lifting him or were they? He was in a strange place. He could not see anything, but he could hear people around him. The pain reached a climax in his body and he went into shock.

Suddenly, his pain was gone. He was surrounded by light and he saw angels. Tim put his hand in the hand of one of the angels and followed them into eternity.

Chapter 35

Tara was in her home office looking at a report of new restaurants that had opened in the area. It was interesting for her to see the different restaurant styles. There was food with middle eastern flavors, a Greek diner and a Korean barbecue. She knew Tim loved Korean food, so she made a note that she would visit that one first. Tara always visited the competition. She wanted to assess their service, food and quality herself.

The doorbell rang. She looked at the time. Tim was due home, but he wouldn't ring the doorbell. Her housekeeper did not work the weekends, so she had to leave her studies and go to the door. When she opened the door, she was surprised to see two police officers.

Were they looking for donations? She had not given to a police charity in some time. "May I help you?" she asked, completely unprepared and not expecting bad news.

"Mrs. Benson?"

"Yes." Tara suddenly knew that this was not good news. Her mind began to race. Juan was upstairs waiting for Tim. If Juan was okay, she decided to stop the thought. Everyone had to be okay. Life was too good for anything to be wrong.

"Mrs. Benson, may we come in?"

"Why?" She was starting to panic a little. She looked behind them. Tim's car was not in the driveway.

"Mrs. Benson," the older man said in a consoling tone. He seemed to realize that she was not prepared to receive the news he needed to give her. "I'm sorry to inform you--"

Tara moved back from him, but the other officer caught her hand. He gently walked her into the house. There was a chair in the foyer of the house. They placed her there before continuing to speak.

"Mrs. Benson, I am sorry to inform you that your husband, Tim Benson, was killed today."

The words were like meaningless chatter to her. What they were saying was absurd. She had just seen Tim less than two hours ago. "No. You're mistaken. My husband will be home any minute. He went jogging."

"Yes, ma'am. He was killed at the park."

"What do you mean, killed?" she asked calmly but incredulously. "That is one of the safest parks in the city."

"He was shot."

"That's impossible," she responded, exasperated. "Who would shoot Tim?"

Juan was downstairs now. He had heard the doorbell and knew the ring was odd. They were not expecting anyone and they never entertained people they did not expect. He approached the bottom of the stairs and knew that something was wrong. When Big Mike died, he saw the same look on his mother's face. Adults lowered their voices and whispered when bad things happened. The police officers were trying to keep his mother calm, but she was struggling with waves of emotion.

Juan looked from his mother to the officers. He had never seen this side of her. She was frustrated, argumentative and shaking. One of the officers noticed him and motioned him to come to his mother. Juan put his arms around her and she relaxed.

"We're sorry to bring you this news. We'll need you to come down to the hospital and identify the body. I know this is tough, Mrs. Benson. We can help you call anyone you would like to meet you there."

With that Tara brightened. "Maybe you all made a mistake. Maybe someone stole his wallet and keys. That's possible, right? Who would shoot Tim? There is no reason for that to happen! I bet Tim is out there walking home right now. If they took his cell phone too, he can't call me. That's the problem."

All of a sudden, she jerked her hand away. "He probably needs help right now. You should be out there looking for him! I am going to get my purse and go look for him."

"Ma'am," The older officer spoke. "I have been doing this a long time. You're right. It could be a mistake, but the person who died today had your husband's ID on him. So, we'll need you to come down and help us confirm if it's him or not."

"He just can't be dead," she was saying more to herself than to them.

"Ma," Juan said squeezing her hand. He was older now and he was able to inject a heaviness in his voice that made her yield to the authority he was asserting. "If you go with them, you can clear this up."

His touch seemed to bring her back into reality. Tara looked at the two officers and took a deep breath. "I'm sorry. I know you're doing your job. Let me get my purse."

Chapter 36

After the positive identification of his body, Tara felt as though her whole world had been turned upside down. That morning she had a family unit with a loving husband and a son. By the early afternoon, the family she had enjoyed for the past year was wrecked. Tim was gone. Juan was once again fatherless. She and her son were on their own again.

She couldn't bear to see the grief in the faces of Juan, Mr. Benson, Mrs. Benson, Aunt Claire and Jose. She couldn't stand to look in the mirror because the grief in her own eyes overwhelmed her. Losing Tim made her realize how much she truly loved him. The most powerful feeling coursing through her body at that moment was profound despair. How could life be so good one moment and so disparaging the next?

It had not even occurred to her to pray. In her mind, she kept thinking about all the missed opportunities with Tim. Their life together was just beginning and she knew it would have been a happy life. In fact, she had convinced herself that Tim was a reward for the terrible pain she had to endure as a child, adolescent and teenager. She had even given a testimony at church one day to a women's group. Her premise was that it had all been worth it. Now she was not sure that was true.

Tara was standing in the bathroom after taking a very long shower. Her skin felt a little raw. She had scrubbed herself over and over. At first her scrubbing was therapeutic, but she started to wash with anger. She stood in front of the mirror looking down. Lifting her head was a chore, but she tried to do it. As she looked down into the sink, she watched the tears drop and settle around the drain before the water disappeared.

"My Lord, I don't know if I can take this."

Visions of Tim's cold body flashed into her mind. His beautiful ebony skin was starting to look ashy. The expression on his face would always stay with her. In death, he looked peaceful, not scared or shocked. He could have been asleep if one did not know better.

Tara thought about the times Tim wanted her company and she chose work instead. It seemed they had all the time in the world. She imagined growing old gracefully with him, as the Bensons had. In her mind, she could still see them walking in together at their fiftieth anniversary bash.

How arrogant she had been! Tara forgot that life could be randomly harsh for no reason. You did not have to be an evil person for evil to find you. Tim, the one man she chose to love in her life, was gone. Just as they had found each other that afternoon in the park, she now had lost him in the park.

"I wished I had told you more," she cried. "I wish I had told you more how much I loved you."

Chapter 37

Joshua could not believe the sad news when he heard it. He knew what he had desired. He knew he had made a phone call, but he thought that Tim might defy this fate, too. Tim had overshadowed him in everything since the time they met each other more than twenty years ago. He assumed this event would be another example of Tim coming out on top. However, this time Joshua won the game. In his mind, he acknowledged that the game was unfairly played. Tim was not aware that Joshua would be willing to go to such an extreme.

Joshua had just put the phone down from talking to his mother. Mrs. Benson was utterly distraught. Her voice was shaking and she could barely get the words out. Even though he had not talked to him, he knew his father was in the room with her. He probably was sitting in his large lazy-boy chair, showing hard shell on the outside, not the turmoil within. His parents were in pain because of him.

"I can make it up to them," Joshua thought. At that moment, Joshua went into his kitchen. He poured out all the alcohol in the kitchen. Then he moved into his bedroom and discarded the emergency alcohol he had stored for when he did not want to get out of bed. He searched all his bathrooms and even got rid of cough medicine.

He felt a strange feeling of renewal. Joshua knew he could be the son they needed, now that his parents would no longer be fixated on the son they wanted.

He even picked up the phone to call Tara. She did not answer at first. Persistently, he tried again. Her voice at the other end was shaking, too. For some reason, the sound of his voice resulted in a burst of tears on the other end. After a moment or two, she seemed to gain her composure.

"I am sorry, Tara," he heard himself saying. "Tim and I had our differences, but I could never imagine such a thing. Do you need anything?"

Tara told him she didn't. He felt a blaze of anger. She didn't need anything from him, huh? Tara requested that he check on his parents.

"Your father took it really hard," she told him, before hanging up the phone.

Those words cut into his heart. So, his mother was doing the calling because his father couldn't? Joshua couldn't help but conjure up an imaginary scenario. If it had been him instead of Tim who had been killed, his mother would have been more upset. His father would be making the phone calls.

With that in mind, he felt something turning in his stomach. A feeling of nausea engulfed him. It was a violent feeling, as if he was coming out of a drunken slumber. Now his dinner lay on his chest, pants and floor. This will pass, he told himself, wiping his face on a towel. It will pass.

Chapter 38

The funeral was delayed because the autopsy needed to be done. Tim's body had not yet been released to the family. With the help of Mrs. Benson, Tara was able to make funeral arrangements. This time, however, Mrs. Benson did not talk about the advantages of making it a social, community and family event. The whole affair would be private, for family only.

Tara opted for a closed casket. She did not think she could bear viewing his body again. And she did not want anyone staring at him and inspecting his appearance. She did not want any discussion of how peaceful he looked. Those conversations had almost driven her crazy when Big Mike died. People chose the oddest conversations to try to console the survivors of the person who had passed away.

Tara had spoken to her pastor several times. She had tried to keep a close eye on Juan. Juan had grown close to Tim in a short amount of time. He seemed to be holding up okay, but she could not be sure. Jose offered to take Juan fishing and Tara allowed it. Juan seemed thankful for the distraction and it gave her time to reflect.

Tara was alone on the day she received the revelation that Tim's shooting may have been more than just a tragic act of violence.

Tara was sitting in her home office, just staring into space, when Detective Charles Monroe knocked at her door. At that moment, she could see Tim. The day he died replayed repeatedly in her mind, but the events of that day were different each time. Instead of letting him leave for the park, she kept him home for a round three of love making. In her mind, they were happy together. Tara fantasized that Tim, Juan, and she had snuck away on an impromptu vacation to a Caribbean island. Of course, this was what she wished had happened. He would be alive if the events of the day were different. At least that is what she told herself.

Her housekeeper, Mrs. Day, brought Detective Monroe into the room. The detective was alone. He was a tall man with dark eyes. His skin tone was like the color of graham crackers and he was dressed in a nice suit. He did not say anything initially, but waited for Mrs. Day to speak. He studied Tara's posture and demeanor as she sat in the chair.

As he observed her, he made a mental note to place her very low on a list of possible suspects. This was clearly a woman who mourned the loss of her husband. However, he was not prepared to eliminate her altogether. He was a young police officer in his thirties, but he had seen enough to know that murder cases took surprising turns.

In the seconds before Mrs. Day spoke, he gathered his impressions of Tara. She was a very attractive woman. She was well organized. She was obsessed by her work. Even now as she stared out of the window, looking at nothing, there was an open ledger in her lap.

"Mrs. Benson," Mrs. Day said gently, "this is Detective Monroe."

At first Tara did not respond. Mrs. Day had to repeat herself before Tara was pulled from her thoughts. In her reverie, she was laughing with Tim. Mrs. Day's distinct voice yanked her from these pleasant thoughts to the reality of life without Tim.

"What can I help you with?" She turned in her chair. Tara looked over the detective. Her immediate assessment was negative. To her, he looked young and incompetent. More than two days had passed since Tim's death and she had not heard a single lead in her husband's case. Perhaps it was because of this fellow standing awkwardly before her.

"Hello, Mrs. Benson. I am Detective Charles Monroe of the Springfield County police department. I want to ask you a few questions."

"Question away," she sighed, sounding more sarcastic than she intended.

He seemed to be used to a cold reception. "May I have a seat?" he asked, motioning to one of the leather chairs in the office.

"Sure," she said, reluctantly putting the ledger away.

Mrs. Day excused herself after offering the detective a glass of water. He declined and turned his attention back to Tara. She had not taken her eyes off him.

He took a seat in front of Tara and leaned in to speak to her. "Mrs. Benson, we wanted you to hear this from us first. Obviously, you know your husband was murdered. But we do not believe that it was a random act of violence in the park."

"What do you mean? It was a random act of violence in the park. That's why he's not here with me. What are you even talking about?"

"Your husband was not robbed. All his belongings were on him, including his wedding band and a very expensive watch. There was no struggle. He was shot in the back at close range. There were other joggers and people in the park who went unmolested. And quite frankly it is unlikely that someone just spotted your husband jogging and decided to shoot him. We believe your husband may have been targeted by someone he knew."

He stopped speaking to give her the opportunity to digest his words. Tara felt as if she would faint. She placed her hand on his shoulder for support. Detective Monroe had worked several murder cases and had experienced this reaction before. He called to Mrs. Day.

"Can you bring her some ice water, please?"

After a cold drink of water, Tara looked up at him. "There is so much coming at me all at once. Please forgive me. Now, you're telling me that someone we know could be responsible for this? Tim and I know the same people. I mean, I may not know everyone he works with, but all of our friends and family are people we have in common now. So you are telling me that I may know the murderer?"

"It is certainly possible. Would any of these friends or family have a reason to hurt your husband?"

She couldn't believe her ears. "You don't know Tim. He was a great guy, loved by everyone he knows. He was an example everywhere he went. He worked with the youth at church. He was one of the top up-and-coming executives at his company. He wasn't the type of person who makes enemies."

"Mrs. Benson, I understand. We often struggle with putting ourselves in the mind of someone who would target such a good man. But I need your help, no matter how obscure or minor you think a detail might be. This question is no reflection on your husband. Someone took his life and we want to hold that person accountable." He paused. "Were the two of you having any marital problems?"

She shook her head. "No. I mean, he thought I worked too much and he was a little frustrated that we had not had a baby together. I wanted him to work in his father's company, but he liked what he was doing. We loved each other. I guess we had normal couples' issues," she laughed. "We were still merging our personal entities. The only thing I can think of is...but, no, that would be insane."

"Mrs. Benson, at this point anything might help us get to the bottom of this. What's insane?"

"Well, Tim was loved by everybody. But his brother, Joshua--they really didn't get along."

He nodded and took out a notepad. Although Detective Monroe was young, he preferred writing his notes to recording them. Besides, this was not an official interview. He just needed to get some insights from Tara.

"Tell me more about that."

Chapter 39

Mrs. Benson decided to visit Tina as she did every Saturday. Through the years, Tina's condition had worsened. She was no longer physically able to go to the bathroom, wash, or eat without help. Her mind was not as disabled as her body, but there were times that she seemed to speak of things years ago as if they happened today. As a result of Tina's mixing of time and audiences, Mrs. Benson was already aware of the things Joshua needed to confess.

It was ironic that Mrs. Benson knew that Joshua had a sexual relationship with Tina years ago. She just chose to not let Joshua or Mr. Benson know. She had even opted to let Tim think that she even entertained the thought of an inappropriate relationship between and Tim and Tina. Now she sat in the nice recliner beside Tina's bed in Tina's private room. The female nursing assistant had given Tina a bath. After that, they both helped get Tina dressed.

Mrs. Benson knew she should keep herself active rather than to sink into despair over Tim's death. She kept herself moving. If she stayed in one place too long, she felt she would sink into misery forever. She awoke early that morning, went to the hair dresser, purchased a new outfit and bought Tina an outfit, too. Mrs. Benson was adorned in her new silk blue, shimmering blouse and white dress slacks that stopped right above the ankles. She had purchased new shoes, too—with two-inch designer heels.

Now she settled into her chair, reaching over to give Tina a chocolate muffin.

"Tina," Mrs. Benson said. "I brought you a muffin. You want some?"

Tina shook her head. "I just ate."

"I don't think you just ate," Mrs. Benson corrected. "You just finished with your shower, honey. Okay. You want to sit up? Yes, don't lay her down," she told the attendant. "Yes, that's good. Let her sit up so she can be comfortable while we talk."

Tina ignored the fact that she had just taken a bath and had not eaten. She repeated herself again before the attendant left the room. "I just ate."

After they were alone, Mrs. Benson smiled at Tina. "You look very pretty today, Tina."

Tina smiled. "Thank you. This is the dress you bought me." Mrs. Benson smiled at what she said. She bought all of Tina's clothes, but the girl insisted on thanking her for every outfit.

"Next time I am going to get the pink one, but I like the way that yellow looks on you."

"I like yellow, too," Tina said sweetly.

"You want to watch television?" Mrs. Benson asked. She already had the remote in-hand and switched the screen on.

The television defaulted to a local news station. The lead story was the aftermath of a shooting in the downtown area. Mrs. Benson started to switch channels. She had her fill of violence for a lifetime. And she wanted no reminders of Tim's death. But Tina pointed to the television.

"Sad. That is so sad," she said, more emotional than usual.

"I know," Mrs. Benson said. She could feel tears wailing up in her eyes, but she pushed them back. She did not want Tina to know about Tim yet. Mrs. Benson did not know how she would tell Tina that Tim was gone. Although Tim had not visited Tina often, she knew he and Tina remained close.

"Sad about Tim," Tina said. "So sad."

Mrs. Benson rose up in the chair. "What did you say?"

"Sad about Tim. So sad. I miss Timmy."

Mrs. Benson studied the woman's face. She seemed to be quite aware of what she was saying. "Tina, what are you saying?"

"Tim got shot. Joshua told me."

"Oh, my God!" Mrs. Benson felt so angry. "That boy never makes the right decisions. He never thinks of anyone but himself. He just flies off the handle all the time. At least he could have told me that he told you before I came here today."

Tina looked scared at Mrs. Benson's reaction. She did not like to see Mrs. Benson angry. Mrs. Benson saw the look of fear across Tina's face and calmed herself. Leaning back into the chair in a more relaxed posture, she apologized.

"I'm sorry, Tina. I am not angry at you. I just wanted to tell you my way. I have to get you a dress so you can go to the service."

"He's sorry, too. Joshua is sorry," Tina offered.

"Not as sorry as he's going to be," Mrs. Benson hissed. "He doesn't use sense."

"He's sorry about Tim. He didn't mean it. He didn't mean to hurt Tim."

"Tina," Mrs. Benson said very slowly. "What are you telling me?"

Tina hesitated. Then she decided it was okay to repeat. "Joshua is sorry about Tim. He didn't mean it."

Mrs. Benson decided at that moment. She looked at Tina and then she rose up and put her arms around her shoulders. "Sweetheart, I know Joshua is sorry. He told me, too. But let's not tell that to anyone else. They won't understand the way you and I do. They'll start asking questions and we don't want Joshua to have to say anything else about it."

"Okay, Ma."

Mrs. Benson made sense of it in this way in her mind. Joshua did not use good judgement and talked too much. Tina was not 100 percent coherent anyway, so you had to take the things she said with a grain of salt. Tim was dead and there was nothing she could do about it. If there was a possibility of losing the one son she had left, she'd have to do what she could to avoid another loss.

Chapter 40

Tara found herself pacified and somewhat encouraged by the funeral services. Pastor Jenson spoke from II Corinthians 5:8: *We are confident, I say, and willing rather to be absent from the body and to be present with the Lord.*

She imagined how happy Tim must be to be in the presence of the Lord. Heaven was a place where there was no more sorrow, pain, sickness, and death. All former things were passed away. Tim did not have to worry about anything anymore. Even though she missed him, she knew he was in a place where he did not have to miss her. The preacher read Revelation 21:4: *And God shall wipe away all tears from their eyes and there shall be no more death, neither sorrow, nor crying neither shall there be any more pain: for the former things are passed away.*

Still, it hurt to be separated from him. She had to endure the knowledge that Detective Monroe had come to the funeral. He had come to observe her and anyone else of interest there. Tara sat in the front pew. Juan was beside her. The Bensons were also with her. Although she resented it, Joshua was also there. On his arm was a blonde woman Tara had never seen before. In that moment, Tara really hated him. Who brings a date to a funeral?

Tina was in her wheelchair between the Bensons.

The soloist stood and started to sing. *Precious Lord* was one of Tim's favorite songs. The woman who sang had a power to her voice and a precision in every note. Her tone pulled on the heartstrings stirring a strong sense of the power of God creating comfort and peace.

When the song ended, one voice rang out in the church, distinct and clear: "So sad, Timmy. Joshua is sorry," Tina said. "Joshua didn't mean to hurt you."

At first Tara thought she must have heard incorrectly. Tina repeated it again. Over and over again she said the same thing. It soon had the attention of everyone, including Detective Monroe. Tara's survival instincts from years ago kicked in. She immediately started to watch everyone in the room.

It was not lost on her that Mrs. Benson did not appear as surprised as everyone else. For sure she was trying to get Tina to quiet down, but she had heard these words before. Perhaps she heard them this past Saturday. Mr. Benson was horrified and he looked from Tina and buried his head in his hands.

Joshua?

Joshua sat there, looking as hard and cold as nails. He was entirely unmoved. Finally, one of the nurse's assistants came in and rolled Tina out of the sanctuary. A church usher had also gone to see if she could be of assistance. Juan turned to his mother.

"Ma, that was weird. I don't understand."

"Me, either, baby."

Chapter 41

It was not long before Detective Monroe connected the dots. But he knew that his case was circumstantial against Joshua. He did not have the murder weapon and he did not have the killer. Joshua had a viable alibi. Coincidently, the woman with him at the funeral claimed he was with her the day of murder. Eye witnesses' descriptions of the shooter were definitely not the tall, handsome Joshua Benson.

However, Detective Monroe had been doing his job a long time. He knew there would be a break in the case somewhere. Killers always messed up. In addition, he did not think that someone like Joshua Benson would handle such a dirty task himself. He doubted Joshua would have had the guts to pull the trigger while his target could see him or catch him.

The expected break in the case came two months later when a disgruntled hitman tipped off the police. Apparently, he had never received the full payment. Joshua had banked on the fact that there was no consumer protection agency for hitmen. What he did not count on is that people who are career criminals know police officers well.

Detective Monroe knew hear-say testimony was inadmissible in court. But it still might be useful in getting a confession from Joshua. The detective decided he would start where logic dictated.

"If I were a killer," he postulated aloud in his office, "and I was not used to killing, I might want to get the crime off my chest. I might confess to my mentally deranged sister because I wouldn't think she would say anything. And who would believe her? I wonder would I have the nerve to tell my mama, too?"

With that he picked up the phone and called Mrs. Benson for an appointment.

Tara noticed that the phone calls from Mrs. Benson had stopped. Tim was buried and so was their relationship. However, Tara was not done being a Benson. As if her prayers—or, more realistically, Tim's prayers--had been answered, she was pregnant. In fact, she was almost eight weeks along at the funeral.

She decided not to tell anyone yet, especially the Bensons. Tara wanted this awful business with Joshua to be over. If he was held accountable for Tim's murder, she was willing to tell the Bensons they had a grandchild. But if Joshua walked around a free man, she would let him be their only son, their only hope, and probably their eventual downfall.

Detective Monroe decided to talk to Mrs. Benson in person. He met her at her office downtown. People scheduled private interviews in the strangest locations, he thought. Joshua was also in the same office building, along with Mr. Benson. Perhaps he could question all of them together. He thought he would make it a point to drop in on Joshua today. Tara had been frustrated with the detective because he had not brought Joshua in for questioning. She did not know that Monroe was waiting for Joshua to get comfortable enough to slip up.

Mrs. Benson welcomed the detective into her office with a warmth that would have been disarming if he was not experienced at his job. She looked stunning. He wondered if she always dressed and looked like this in the office. She wore a shimmering dress that showcased her golden skin perfectly. Her hair was full and she had it colored light brown. Although she was an older woman, she still had sex appeal and he suspected she used it when she thought it was advantageous to her.

"Detective Monroe, please come in. Any news on Tim's case?" she asked, with the utmost concern.

She shuffled him into her office. It was a large office with a prominent desk and a section with a large couch and chair. There was a mini bar in the office as well, stocked with soda, soda water, juices and lemon aids. He took it all in with one glance, noting that it was in sharp contrast to the food area in his precinct.

"Actually, I was hoping you can help me with some questions so that I can move this along."

"Me? What about?" she asked innocently, motioning him to sit on the comfortable chair in her office. Without asking, she set a drink before him. "It's club soda," she said, annoyed when he looked hesitant. "I know you're on duty."

"Thank you." He made a show of pulling out his notepad. It served to break the mood she was trying to set. He was not there for a social call.

"Mrs. Benson, I wanted to ask you specifically about the funeral. Tina's outburst was unexpected and troubling, to be frank."

She took a seat opposite him on the chocolate sofa. Mrs. Benson took a sip of water before responding.

"Oh, yes. My daughter Tina's words must have been troubling. She was very close to Tim and she just did not know how to handle it. I tried to explain it to her before we got there, but I just was not clear enough."

"I understand that you have power of attorney for Tina. I would like to question her, of course, in your presence and with your permission."

"I don't see how that would be a good idea or helpful at all." Her words were firm and her tone was rigid.

"Why not?" It was his turn to play innocent.

"Tina is not able to care of herself and she merges memories from the past into the present. Her sickness has really taken its toll on her mind, body and soul. She'd only babble and lead you down blind alleys."

"Hmmm," he paused for effect. "She did not seem incoherent at the funeral. She was not babbling, either. She said that Joshua did not mean to hurt Tim. It sounded like she knew what she was saying. What do you think she meant by that?"

"I did not say she was incoherent. But she's on various medications and it's difficult sometimes for her to understand the implications of what she says."

"But why do you think she would say Joshua was sorry?"

She shrugged. "I told you, she merges memories from the past and the future. Who knows what she was referring to? Joshua and Tim have not been close in recent years. It could be as simple as that."

"What if it's not as simple as that?"

"It can't be much more complicated than that," she retorted.

He took note of the show of emotion.

"Tara said that Tim and Joshua did not get along well." He purposefully did not add anything to the statement and he waited for her reaction. For Detective Monroe, it did not matter if she spoke. He would gather information from her body language and facial expressions.

He could see her face flush red. "Tara....well, yes. Tim and Joshua had not been close in years. As I said. When Tim and Tara married, Tara and Joshua didn't exactly mesh well together and there you have it. I am sure he's sorry they did not remedy the situation before this happened. By the way, do you have any real leads or is this how you're spending your time?"

He nodded. "We do and I am following every lead. I think we're very close to bringing the right persons to justice."

"Persons?" she asked, with raised eyebrows.

"Oh, yes. I am sure more than one person was involved."

Mrs. Benson spoke abruptly. "You know, detective, I must say this. Tara is hurt. She never liked Joshua, so I don't think she's necessarily thinking straight, either. I wouldn't consider anything she says or her accusations as a lead. When she comes to her senses, she'll be better able to handle this."

"Okay, that may well be. Well, I am sure with the support of her family, you all will get through this together. But Mrs. Benson, I have to tell you. I need to eliminate Joshua as a suspect and the only way to do that is to get to the bottom of all of this. So, can you give me your honest perspective on Joshua and Tim?"

He noticed she stopped looking him in the eye when he mentioned family support. Had she cut Tara off from the family already?

"They were brothers," she said, as if trying to convince herself. "They didn't choose each other. Their father and I chose to put them together. They didn't click. They did not get along. And it's been that way since high school, maybe earlier. I think Joshua resented Tim for being so likable. I think Tim saw Joshua as unappreciative for being born to people like my husband and me, whereas Tim spent the first few years of his life being passed from relative to relative. I doubt that makes Joshua a murderer!"

"No. That wouldn't make him a murderer. But I have seen jealousy do terrible things. And if an inheritance is involved, you'd be surprised what people would do for money."

"That is a cold view of the world. I raised my children to value people more than money. Besides, Tim, Joshua and Tina were provided for in our wills. There would be no reason for them to try to get rid of one another."

"If a person wanted the whole inheritance, it might make them want to get rid of a competitor – especially one you thought deserved no share at all."

"I think that is a terribly cynical way of thinking. No child of mine would do such a thing!" She was shaking now.

"Unfortunately, it is a realistic one. Parents aren't always able to pass along their character traits to their children. Then, again, I have seen the opposite. I have seen a mother have her own child killed for insurance money. I certainly wouldn't put it past a brother."

She shook her head in disagreement. "Well, I feel sorry for you. I am sorry you have to deal with that type of thing every day. But that's not the case here. I am sure the killer is out there. It will likely turn out to be some random thief or drug addict."

"Are you sure about that? Nothing Tim had was taken. There was no struggle. The only thing that was taken was his life. That's not something a crackhead would do."

There was silence for a moment. He wanted to appeal to the mother instinct that must be in her. But he did not know if that mother instinct really extended to Tim. At the end of the day, Joshua was the son born of her body. If Tim was one big experiment to her, the experiment was over. She would protect her son Joshua now.

"You know, detective, I don't feel comfortable continuing this conversation without a lawyer." She stood and walked over to her office door. He rose behind her and moved toward the door. Before he walked out, he turned and looked at her directly.

"I think I have what I need. Mrs. Benson, I didn't mean to upset you. But please consider cooperating fully with us on this case." Before leaving, he emphasized a principle in which he genuinely believed. It was something he had learned after years of watching parents have to deal with the fact that their children were not who they thought they were. For some parents, that realization was a heart-breaking revelation, leading them to respond with rage and revenge. But that was the minority. Most parents thought they had to make up for whatever they felt they did not give their children in the first place. "You know, so many parents think it's their job to shield their children. But sometimes a child has chosen his path and there is nothing more you can do for him."

"Please leave," she said, without looking at him.

"Yes, ma'am. Talk to you later, for sure."

When he left, she closed her door and set the lock. Then she went over to her desk, sank down into the chair and sobbed uncontrollably.

Chapter 42

Mrs. Benson shook herself and decided to check on her daughter-in-law. She knew she could not look Tara in the face just yet. But she thought if she could call her, it might help. Tara needed to feel connected to the family. Perhaps a call would convince Tara not to attack the family. Mr. Benson had no knowledge of what his wife wanted to do. He asked about Tara, but he was not a man to contact her in a social way. He allowed his wife to arrange social and family connections.

Mrs. Benson drank several glasses of cold water to take the phlegm out of her throat. She did not want to sound as if she had been crying or was not in control. Tara had often listened to her counsel. Mrs. Benson was ready to gamble that she still had enough stature in the younger woman's eyes to give her advice.

The phone rang several times before Tara picked up. "Hello."

"Hello, Tara dear. How are you?"

Tara did not respond immediately. When she didn't speak, Mrs. Benson repeated herself. "Tara, dear. It's me, Sheryl Benson."

"I know who this is." She said these words flatly and deliberately.

"How are you?" Mrs. Benson said, ignoring the anger she thought she heard in Tara's voice.

"Oh, I am fine. I am just dandy for a woman who lost her husband."

"Tara," Mrs. Benson said calmly, "I lost my son."

"I don't know. Was he really your son? He was really my husband and he's gone."

"Yes, Tim was my son. He is my son. I fed him, clothed him and I loved him."

"You didn't love Tim," Tara said impulsively. "You were fascinated by him. You thought he made you look good, but you didn't love him."

"I beg your pardon!" Mrs. Benson was outraged at the accusation. "How dare you say that I did not love him? I still love him. You didn't love him! You're the one who spent so much time on your soul food shack that he felt neglected. I told him to hang in there. I told him you didn't know how to have family, so he had to teach you how to have one. So, don't tell me about love."

Tara was devastated by the thought that Tim would talk to Mrs. Benson about any problem he had with their marriage. She knew he did not like the enormous time she spent on the business. But Tim also knew that running a business was a challenge. At the end of the day, he respected what she had to do for success and why she did it.

"You are a liar," Tara responded evenly. "I don't believe you."

Mrs. Benson was stunned at the degree of confidence and venom in Tara's words. She decided to retreat. The purpose of her call was not to fight with the younger woman. She softened her voice.

"Tara, I am sorry. I know you loved Tim. Believe me, I loved him, too. We all loved Tim. My husband, Jose, Aunt Claire--we all loved him."

"I know," Tara said, apologetically. "But what about Joshua?"

"Tara, Joshua is Joshua. You know that. He talks too much. He drinks too much. He's insensitive and stupid."

"But is he a killer?"

"Of course not!"

"I don't know about that."

"Tara, you can't say awful things about him."

"Why not? Tim is gone! Tina said Joshua was sorry for what he did. Sick, medicated Tina just popped out with that at the funeral in front of everyone. It's too strange to be ignored."

"Those are just words, Tara. Tina is sick and medicated all the time. You can't use words to start telling Detective Monroe that Joshua is a murderer."

"So, that's why you called me? You didn't call to check up on the widow of the son you say you loved. You didn't call to check up on the son he adopted. You just called to protect Joshua."

Mrs. Benson waited. She could hear Tara sniffle on the other end. She wanted to say something, but she knew it was best to be silent.

"Mrs. Benson, I looked over at your son at the funeral. I looked at him. I saw it. He hurt my Tim and I think you know something about it. I don't know how much about you know. But I am sure you know it in your heart. I can't deal with this. You say you love Tim, but you're willing to act like it's okay that he got shot down in the park like a dog. So, if that's your love, I can't deal with you anymore. Please don't call me. Juan and I don't need you."

"Tara--"

"The law will do its job and if the law doesn't, God will."

With that, Tara hung up the phone. Mrs. Benson sat for a while staring at the phone. Women like Tara did not understand. She was hurting right now, but one day she would understand. Mrs. Benson hoped Juan never disappointed Tara as Joshua had disappointed her.

Chapter 43

Tara threw herself back into her work. It was therapeutic to have some level of normalcy again. Visiting and spending time at fast-paced restaurants, listening to the issues the staff were experiencing and planning the next move for her own business helped keep her mind off the loss of her husband.

The other bright spot was that her pregnancy was showing. Everyone talked about how cute she was as a pregnant woman. For her part, Tara didn't see what was so attractive about her. The first time she was pregnant, she was a 16-year-old girl. Her body seemed to barely change. Now she was a woman approaching her thirties and this pregnancy was noticeably different.

Her stomach was bigger. Her skin certainly stretched more. She had bags under her eyes and she had terrible head congestion. It did not matter how many times she blew her nose—the congestion just wouldn't clear. Also, her hair would not take on its usual vibrant curls. She had no choice but to wear it stiff and straight.

Her mobility, sense of smell, taste and her ability to digest food were all affected by her pregnancy. She felt lousy. But everyone else told her she was glowing.

"Maybe glowing with fish oil," she mumbled, taking her prenatal vitamins and DHA pills. It made her feel even sicker to take the pills. Forcing a large pill down with water sometimes resulted in an awful gag reflex, resulting in vomiting.

Tara knew she would have to suspend visiting the restaurants until she got through the first trimester. The sound of gagging in the back of the restaurant was not exactly the ambiance she wanted for her customers. Also, she noticed that the staff was a bit troubled by her condition. For those who had never been around a pregnant woman, the experience was unnerving.

She thought it best to send Juan away to a summer camp. He had tried to be strong for her, but Tim's death hit him hard. He went from having a pal and a father figure to a large void in his life. When he was younger, he would ask about his father. He had stopped asking. He seemed withdrawn and depressed. Should she have kept her son by her side instead of sending him to camp, she wondered? Tara was not confident she projected the strength he needed. She hoped the constant activity of camp and new friends would help him. For this reason, Juan was not home the afternoon Joshua paid her an unexpected and unwelcome visit.

The doorbell rang and Mrs. Day dutifully answered. She showed Joshua into the house and led him to the room where Tara sat with her feet elevated. These were doctor's orders to alleviate the swelling around her ankles and calves. Her eyes were closed and she was deep in thought. It took her a few moments to realize that she was no longer alone in the room.

Unlike Detective Monroe's first visit, Joshua tried to assert control in the atmosphere immediately. "Well, I knew you'd be surprised to see me. I didn't know I'd be surprised to see you."

Tara opened her eyes and looked up at him. When she comprehended who it was, she rose to her feet with surprising agility for a pregnant woman. "What are you doing in my house?"

"Tara, I came to see about you and Juan. I asked Ma about you and she really did not have much to say. I thought I would come by. She didn't mention you were pregnant."

Without acknowledging his attempt to play nice, Tara called to her housekeeper. "Mrs. Day!"

The woman made her way back into the living room. She was noticeably startled--Tara rarely raised her voice. "Yes?" She could see that Tara was upset. Mrs. Day glared over at Joshua, the obvious offender.

"Mr. Benson was just leaving," Tara said, putting her hands on her stomach and nodding her head back toward the door. "Get out of my house, Joshua."

"Tara, please," he begged. "I know you think horrible things of me and I deserve most of it. But, please, I am not--I would never hurt Tim."

"I don't believe you," she hissed.

"Ms. Tara, come on!" he implored now. His large eyes looked sincere. "Okay, I am mean, I drink too much and I don't know how to show my feelings. But I am not someone who could take another man's life."

Tara shook her head. "Another man? He was your brother! I know you never considered him your brother, but you lived in the same house, shared the same parents, went to the same schools. You even had a sister in common! He was your brother--and my husband. He was the father of this baby and he's gone now, Joshua. He's gone. Do you realize what you've done?"

"I know," he said, closing his eyes as if he had not really considered all this before. After a moment, he looked at her again. "I know. You don't understand, Tara. It's not that simple."

"Yes, it is. It is just that simple. Joshua, I grew up in horrible conditions. My son, Juan, isn't from some love-child relationship. I was raped. But he's my son. You may not like everything you get in life. Sometimes you feel let down and mistreated, but you don't lose your basic faith in God, your decency and your humanity."

"So, what do you think Tara? I didn't kill Tim. I was with--" he started rehearsing his alibi, using the same lie he had told to Detective Monroe.

"I know, your date from the funeral. I saw her. I don't believe her, either."

He looked down in shame. Was he avoiding eye contact only to concoct his next lie?

"Come on," Mrs. Day was saying. "Let's go. I think you upset Ms. Tara and I don't like that much."

"No. I am not going," Joshua declared. "Tara, you're going to hear me out." He jerked his arm away from Mrs. Day. "I don't need an escort."

"Joshua, I don't want to hear anything you have to say unless it's a confession about how you were involved."

"But I was not--"

"Joshua, I don't believe you. No matter what you say or what you do, I do not and will not believe you."

"Fine," he said angrily. "I was just trying to step in and mend the gap. I was trying to make amends for my relationship with Tim. I thought I could make it up to you and Juan."

"If you come near Juan, I will make you sorry for it. I don't ever want to see you come here again. Just so you know, I told your mother the same. Don't come here and don't even speak my name. Consider us just like you treated Tim--people not worth your time."

"I think Ma and Dad will be interested in a grandchild," he said in an antagonistic tone.

"Well, Joshua, I have no intention of bringing up my child around a murderer or a family that would protect him. We're not family now."

"Well, I don't agree with that. I was a lousy brother to Tim. I was not a good brother-in-law. But I want to be a better uncle. I am sure my parents could sue for visitation or something. They have very good lawyers and a lot of influence with people who do count."

"Mrs. Day, show Mr. Benson out."

"Okay, okay. I am leaving," he said. "But it's your loss. It's that unborn child's loss, too, because my parents made provision for Tim and any of his children in their will."

"Well, Joshua, I am just a working woman. I don't want any money that would require me to overlook the murder of my husband. Unlike you, I have had little and I have had more. But I have always had my integrity."

He seemed to consider her words. Integrity? He did not have much respect for the word. People used it when they wanted to assert their superiority over him. For now, he conceded defeat. "Okay. Have it your way."

When he left, she called Detective Monroe to tell him about the exchange.

Chapter 44

The break needed in the case came a few days later. The actual shooter was arrested on another charge. He did not want to face time in jail, so he gave the police the information they needed on the Tim Benson case. The man named the people who contacted him. The detective was soon able to link Joshua and a drinking buddy of his who had the underworld contacts. Before the investigation was concluded, more than five people had been arrested in connection with the murder, including Joshua.

Tara attended the arraignment. The whole event was surreal. Instead of being a part of the Benson entourage that entered in dazzling procession, she walked in alone. She sat behind the prosecutor. On the opposite end, behind Joshua, sat Mrs. and Mr. Benson. Tara did not resent Mr. Benson. She knew he was there out of sincere love for Joshua. As for Mrs. Benson, Tara felt resentment and disdain. Mrs. Benson was there only to defend Joshua. Needless to say, the lawyer representing him was one of the best in the country.

The prosecution asked that bail be denied because of the heinous nature of the crime and Joshua's ability to travel. His defense attorney argued that Joshua had no prior criminal record, was no threat to the community, and would be released into the custody of his parents. The prosecution countered that for most other individuals charged with murder, bail had been denied without exception. There was no reason for the court to make a distinction between a hired shooter and the ultimate mastermind of the murder. The defense countered that Joshua was innocent until proven guilty.

In the end, the judge was persuaded by the defense. Tara watched in dismay, but she had prepared herself for this result. On paper, Joshua might appear to be a low risk for release on bail into the community, especially under the supervision of his parents. The Bensons were well respected and well known in social circles that Tara was only beginning to enter. Joshua looked over in her direction and smiled.

Mrs. Benson looked over at her, too, and immediately noticed the baby bump. Mr. Benson did not seem to focus in any direction. He appeared to be thirty pounds lighter and his skin had dropped its ebony glow. He looked sick to Tara and she pitied him.

"God help him," she whispered aloud.

As if Joshua was following a script Tara had written, he disappeared. He did not appear at the grand jury hearing and he was declared a fugitive. Tara knew Mrs. Benson had helped him avoid the consequences of his actions. This must have been the last straw for Mr. Benson. Tara read about his death three months later.

Tara thought about the older black man she had seen in the emergency room years before. Mr. Benson had been a strong, healthy, happy man. At least that was how she had thought about him before Tim's death. Tears flowed down her cheeks. She put the business journal she had been reading aside. Tara felt sincere pity for Mr. Benson. He had been a nice man and he had not deserved a son as disappointing as Joshua. She guessed the cause of death must have been a broken heart.

Chapter 45

Time flew--or so it seemed. Weeks turned into months and months into years. Before she knew it, Tara was dealing with a teenage son. Juan was sitting in front of her with the sour look only a teenager can give his parent. He was not looking at her, but neither was he looking away from her. She was talking about his report card. He was counting the minutes and wishing her to be silent. She had no intention of stopping her lecture anytime soon. She felt the divide between them.

Over the years, Tara had done very well financially. She had sold her ownership in Big Mike's to a public company in exchange for cash and common stock. Since then she had diversified her business portfolio by providing seed money for some successful start-ups and investing in property. She also remained as a consultant on the Big Mike brand, which proved flexible and lucrative.

Some would question her decision to sell Big Mike's, but the business was growing by leaps and bounds in the immediate years after Tim's death. She needed to devout 100 percent of her time to it. She just could not do that with two children. When Tara was growing up, having a parent who cared about what was on her Christmas list to Santa meant more than actually getting anything on the list. She didn't want Juan and little Kacey to have money and toys, but no father and no mother present. Mrs. Day had been more than accommodating and helpful, but it was Tara's job to raise and love her children. She took a break from work to focus on them.

"A lot of good that has done!" she was saying looking pointedly at Juan. "You have access to excellent education--and I know you understand the material."

He did not respond. Juan had learned to let his mother vent. It helped her to talk aloud. Soon she would realize that his report card was just a moment in time. In fact, it only measured a time period in the past. There was no indication of how he would perform in the future.

They were in the kitchen. Juan was sitting in the eat-in dining area with a bowl of cereal in front of him. It was turning soggy, since he dared not eat while Tara vented. His peaceful, sugar-filled breakfast had been interrupted when his mother discovered his report card tacked by a magnet to the refrigerator. Tara held the report card in her hand, disappointment and annoyance oozing from her. Juan hated that he had hurt her, but he knew his report card was not the end of the world.

As if knowing he was minimizing the gravity of the situation, she continued. "Juan, you can't take such a relaxed approach to your grades. Now explain to me how someone with your intelligence has a D in Chemistry."

An explanation? Juan almost laughed. What explanation would satisfy his mother? He could tell her that he thought Chemistry would have no use to him in his chosen profession. He could argue that the D grade did not reflect his performance on tests. It was a summary of his class participation and attendance. His teacher, Mr. Marks, factored those elements into the grade. For students who struggled with the material, this methodology resulted in a benefit. For someone like Juan who already knew the material but had other things to attend to during class time, these factors were a detriment.

"Ma, I am sorry. I will do better," Juan said. His voice was now deep and rich-toned instead of the high-pitched, boyish voice he used to have.

"No. It is not that easy. You will do better. Juan, I mean it. I'll take those car keys. Maybe that will help with your studies. You can take the bus."

His car? He needed his car to get around. Juan actually was not too worried. His mother trusted him with his little sister more than anyone in the world. So his car was actually a benefit and necessity for his mother as well as Juan. After all, his mother had many business- and philanthropy-related activities. That did not include her church activities. She couldn't take away his car without ruining her own schedule, Juan reasoned.

Kacey had joined them in the kitchen now. When she heard her mother's raised voice and her brother's response, she hurriedly put on her shoes and came downstairs. She loved her mother and adored her older brother. Since Juan had entered his teenage years, Kacey seemed to be the glue now that held the family together and ensured they always had common ground.

"Mommy?" Her tiny voice was a welcome change to Juan's.

"Kacey, good morning. I am talking to Juan right now," Tara said, turning to look at her. She motioned her to the table. "Come here, sweetie."

"Sounds like you're yelling, Mommy. You said not to yell." Kacey was not being smart-mouthed. She spoke as a child would speak. She took everything her mother said in a literal way. If Tara said no yelling, that meant no one should yell, including Tara.

Juan shook his head and looked down at his little sister as she made her way over to the table for breakfast. Her words made him smile. Kacey seemed to be so pure of heart. He wondered if he had ever been that way.

Tara had started talking again, but Juan's mind wandered back to earlier years. When he first realized his mother was pregnant, he did not know what to expect. However, when Kacey was born, it was clear she was the rescue he and his mother needed. He could still recall the baby's first moments in his mother's arms. With Kacey's first yawn, his heart melted. There was something sweet about her that always made him and his mother smile. And to say she was cute was an understatement.

She had a beautifully formed face and petite body covered by dark, coco skin. Her thick, soft hair was braided, the ends hanging down her back with pink beads. This morning she was wearing a red dress that fell right above the knees.

"Kacey, you and Juan have nothing to yell about. By the way, I was not yelling," Tara said in her corrective tone.

"Mommy, can I get French toast?" Kacey asked, looking at the pancakes on the plate beside Juan.

"Kacey, your breakfast is on the table and you see what it is. It is not French toast."

"Okay. I wanted French toast, but I guess I can eat this," the little voice said in dramatic resignation.

Now Tara was smiling a little bit as Kacey climbed into the chair, said the blessing over her food and started to eat pancakes unenthusiastically. Of course, Kacey knew that the difference between French toast and pancakes was not significant. However, the act she was putting on served to lighten the mood. She loved the attention of both her mother and brother.

After a moment, Tara turned her attention back to Juan. "I am going to talk to your teacher. I'll see what he has to say about your work, since you can't give me a good explanation."

Juan nodded with a hint of sarcasm, but nothing so obvious as to arouse his mother's anger. "Thanks, Kacey." He winked at her. Kacey looked over at him with pride and smiled.

"All right, you two," Tara said. "I have a meeting this morning. If you all could finish up, you'll get to school on time and I'll be on time."

Juan saluted as if he was in the military. For Kacey's part, she did not see the need for Tara to continue fussing at Juan. Although she did not understand the entire context of the conversation, she knew it was not going anywhere. Her brother was stubborn and strong-willed. He was not going to do anything differently because of a single lecture from his mother.

Tara was stubborn and strong-willed, too. Kacey was the sweet, easy-going one among the three of them. She had heard many times that her father had her same personality traits. Kacey wished she had known him.

Chapter 46

Juan parked his car downtown at the Department of Child and Family Services. He had taken the warning that the report card provided. Instead of running errands during school hours, he decided not to risk skipping classes. Today was an early dismissal and it was still early afternoon. There was plenty of time to get the paperwork he needed, scoop up Kacey from after-school care, and make it home for dinner, as prepared by Mrs. Day.

She made all the meals for the family and cleaned three times a week. He knew she was also Tara's spy. Sometimes, when Tara had late meetings, Mrs. Day would dutifully report to her if someone came over, the exact time Juan got home, his mood, if he started his homework immediately or waited. He had grown to love the older woman, but he often found her pseudo-grandmother position annoying.

He walked into the building and enthusiastically ran up the steps to the main office. The people around him were from a mixed bag of socio-economic, ethnic and racial backgrounds. Some of them looked as though they must have been there for information, as he was. Others looked like they really needed help.

There was a mother with a big round belly. She had three kids hanging about her legs. Two of the kids looked white and one looked as if the father was black. He idly wondered if the same black man was the father of the baby she carried now. Perhaps she went Asian this time.

He took a number and took a seat at the back. While he waited, he tried to focus on the magazine he had brought with him. When it was his turn, he walked up to the window. The bushy-headed white woman behind the window already seemed to be out of patience with him. For a minute, he thought about how difficult her day must be every day. Perhaps he could find an advantage in using the fact that she wanted to clear her line and get to the end of day. He would have to turn on the charm.

"Hi. My name is Juan Benson," he said, placing his identification on the counter. "I am doing a school project on the foster care system. I wanted to know how one would find the former foster parents of a particular child."

"School project, huh? Do I look like I have the time for this, kid?" She raised her eyebrows at him. Her hand was on his ID, but she didn't look at it. She pushed it back toward him and was about to call to the next person waiting behind him.

"Well, I know you have a lot of people to help," Juan said quickly. "I was talking to Director Wally and he suggested I come here to get help with my project."

James Wally was the director of the Department of Child and Family Services. Juan knew him through Tara, who had worked with Wally on a variety of civic and charity initiatives. What Juan told the woman was not exactly a lie. He had talked with Secretary Wally about the important work of the Department. In fact, Secretary Wally had told him once that good information could be found just by visiting the downtown offices.

"You know Director Wally?" she asked, skeptically.

"Sure do," he said with a smile.

"And what is it that you need again?"

"I won't take much of your time, I promise. For my project, I would like to interview children who are now adults who have gone through foster care and the people who took care of them. I have a former foster child already, but I just wanted to get the names of her foster parents."

"All that information is confidential, young man."

"I thought the foster parent could opt out of confidentiality. Also, I thought there was a way for me to have a letter sent to her foster parents and they could respond if they wanted to."

"You've been watching too many movies," she said flatly. "The biological parents have more rights than the foster parents."

"Ah, so I would imagine the same rules don't apply for foster parents. If I give you the name of one person, can't you look it up to see if you have a record of the foster parent? Just give me the last one on record."

"Kid, depending on how long ago, there may be nothing there," she reasoned. The woman was intrigued by Juan. She felt there was more to his story than just a school paper. He was the most interesting person she had spoken with all day.

Now that she had engaged in some conversation with him, she did not consider him a menace. He was an intelligent, handsome, determined young man.

Someone had done a good job of helping him with his confidence and the ability to articulate his ideas. Regardless of whether he really knew the director or not, she decided to help him with the information he needed.

"True, nothing may be there. I guess I was hoping it might work. The time frame was about sixteen years ago." Juan was still looking at her. Inside he was beginning to feel anxious, but he was still showing her the confident teen who had impressed her.

"Sixteen, huh? I might have something. Okay. Give me the name and date of birth. I will try. If the foster parent did not indicate they wished to remain anonymous, I will give you whatever I have."

"Tara Martin. June 5, 1983," he could hardly contain his excitement.

"Tara Martin," she said while she typed it in. The woman gave a humph. "Interesting."

"What do you mean?"

"Lots of entries for foster parents for Tara Martin. That's unusual. We generally try to place a child in long-term care as opposed to moving them from house to house. She did not stay in the system long enough to age out. It's like the entry abruptly ends."

"Really," he said, hiding his excitement. Tara really did not talk much about her life before him. The life he knew was just with the two of them until Tim came along.

The line behind him was filling up with more people. All of a sudden, the woman stopped playing the game with him. "I need to get back to work. Why can't the foster child, or adult, just give you this information?"

"All right," he said. "It's just Ms. Tara doesn't remember exactly where the folks were located. I told her I would run this down for her. She works all the time and I know she can't come down here. I don't know how I am going to finish this project. It counts for 50 percent of my grade. Maybe I can just interview her."

"You're good," she said. She hit the print screen button, stepped away from the window and came back with a sheet of paper.

At first, he thought she was joking when she thrust it at him. "I didn't see any indication of privacy. Now get out of my line."

"Thanks," he said. He was so grateful.

"Yeah, yeah. Tell Director Wally I said 'Hey.'"

Juan's hands were shaking as he sat back in his car looking at the paper he had been given. His mother had lived with seven different families before she gave birth to him. All seven families had addresses in Chicago. His eyes were drawn to the last entry: Dina and Darnell Baker, at an address on High Street.

He didn't know how he was going to pull it off, but he planned to take a trip to Chicago to visit them personally. He knew who his mother was and he loved her very much. He admired her strength and was extremely appreciative of all her sacrifices for him. Although he did not remember everything, he had vague memories of the rented studio room and having to sit in the corner at Big Mike's while his mother worked. He knew that there were times that they ate beans out of the can because that's all they had. Now he could have what he wanted, when he wanted it.

Yet he was not satisfied. Tara had never really told him about his father. He wanted to know this man. He hoped that the foster family on High Street could give him the answers his mother wouldn't.

Chapter 47

Mrs. Benson nervously waited at the hotel. She looked at her watch. Her granddaughter was supposed to be there already. Although Tara never failed to hand over the child as they had agreed, it always made her nervous when she was late. She always feared that Tara would change her mind or that Kacey would suddenly not want to come see her.

As she waited, she walked over to the mirror in the bathroom. It seemed only yesterday that she was an older, but still attractive woman who turned the heads of young men. There was a time when she dressed to show the world that not even time could take away from her looks and charm. Now, she said to herself, she looked like an old woman. Her hair was still elegantly curled, but it was all grey. Her skin wasn't wrinkled, but she felt it lacked the freshness and glow of youthful skin. Her makeup and the clothes did little to hide her signs of age. Perhaps I am just old and lonely now, she sighed to herself.

Was that the sum of it? In frustration, she walked out of the bathroom. If she could help it, there would be no more mirrors today. She looked about her in disgust. The hotel was nice, of course, but it lacked the personalized touch of home. It was someone's else notion of what "home" should look like for a business person seeking temporary accommodations. Well, ultimately this was business. It was the business of seeing her granddaughter, the only grandchild she had.

Mrs. Benson hated the look and feel of a hotel room, but this option was the only one Tara would agree to. It would have brought Mrs. Benson great joy to show Kacey the glorious home her father had grown up in. She would have loved to show the child how much she had loved Tim and the privileged life that had been given to him. However, Kacey's mother--that woman, Tara--flat out refused to ever come to the Benson estate again. Mrs. Benson feared to push Tara on this point. She knew Tara suspected that she, Mrs. Benson, had somehow supported and protected Joshua through the years as he evaded justice.

Joshua had never been brought to trial nor had he seen the inside of a courtroom since his arraignment seven years ago. Under a cloud of suspicion from Tara, Mrs. Benson was resigned to travel a few hours every two months or so to meet Kacey in a hotel suite.

Mrs. Benson had never seen the inside of Tara's home and she knew she never would. There was a time when she entertained thoughts of sending a private detective to spy on Tara's life. She had dreamed of proving her unfit to be a mother and ripping Kacey from her. She even maliciously thought how ironic it would be if Juan ended up in foster care, after all. However, after having the private detective follow Tara for a month, she realized it was a bitter and fruitless exercise. The woman was motivated by only two things, her children and work—and she prioritized her children maniacally.

Mrs. Benson had dropped the ill-conceived spy endeavor and decided to seek a compromise with her enemy. The hotel arrangement was the compromise--

waiting, on Tara's time schedule, to see her granddaughter, Kacey.

Mrs. Benson was in the sitting room of the suite with three large, gift-wrapped packages at her feet. Kacey always walked away with new clothes or toys after her visit with Mrs. Benson. Mrs. Benson had two primary motives for these gifts. First, she felt guilty. Kacey would never know her father or grandfather. Mrs. Benson felt responsible for both losses.

She believed the terrible truth about Joshua had called George Benson's cancer out of remission. He was dead within six months.

Tim had not known about his father's bout with cancer and Joshua was too selfish to care about it. In the past, her husband had wanted to be more strict with Joshua—"tough love," he called it--but she had always stood in her husband's way. By the time she realized Joshua was a selfish, ruined man, it was too late. However, even she would have never pegged her son as a murderer.

Tears welled in her eyes every time she thought about her remaining son.

The second motive was she wanted Kacey to associate her grandmother with gifts, fun and happiness. Mrs. Benson never disciplined Kacey. She never corrected her or yelled at the child. Perhaps it was the same parenting mistake she made with Joshua, but she knew Kacey had Tara for structure and discipline in her young life. Mrs. Benson figured if Tara ever decided not to let her see Kacey, Kacey would be her advocate and want to see her. Was she buying her granddaughter's affection? She hoped so.

As she pondered these thoughts, there was a knock at the door. Mrs. Benson felt her heart beat skip in elation. Thank God, she thought with relief. On the other side of the door, she could hear Kacey's little voice. When she opened the door, the child burst through, running straight over to the three gifts wrapped especially for her.

"Kacey, I am so glad you are here. Now I can order some lunch." She said this gently to the child, but there was a little bitterness in her voice. Tara was late. Now that Kacey was there with her, Mrs. Benson realized how hungry she was.

Tara always came with Kacey, but never spoke much. If Tara caught the bitterness in her voice, she gave no indication. As usual, Tara carried her laptop with her. She looked over to where Kacey was ripping off wrapping paper, nodded stiffly toward Mrs. Benson, and went into another part of the suite to work. This gave Mrs. Benson time to talk to Kacey, watch her play with her toys, and eat lunch with her before saying good-bye.

"Grandma," Kacey said, bringing the new doll up to her, "can you fix the doll's bow?"

"Of course," she said, reaching over to straighten the bow on the doll's dress. "This doll is pretty. She looks like you."

"Grandma! I don't look like a doll. The doll is plastic," she giggled.

"Oh, I don't mean that way. The doll's dress is pretty. Not as pretty as yours, of course, but pretty."

"Oh," Kacey responded, satisfied with the answer.

"What do you want to eat, Kacey?"

The girl shrugged. "I don't know. You eat, Grandma."

"Well, I will just get you something, too. How about French fries?"

"Okay," Kacey said, dismissively. She went back into the other room and began pulling open one of the other boxes.

Mrs. Benson felt sad as she watched Kacey play. The other downside to Joshua's crime was that she had no heir old enough to run the Benson family business if she suddenly passed away. Tim was gone and Joshua was a fugitive from the law. Kacey was her heir. Outside of the trust set aside for Tina, Kacey would inherit everything. The irony was that Tara would need to administer Kacey's inheritance for Kacey. On the one hand, Mrs. Benson knew that Tara would not mismanage the inheritance. However, it irked her that she would have to leave the fruit of her husband's life work to someone with whom she had such an acrimonious relationship.

"Mommy, look at this!" Kacey ran right past Mrs. Benson to show Tara the new charm bracelet.

Mrs. Benson's eyes followed Kacey. She saw how Tara looked up, inspected the bracelet and complimented Kacey. Tara never said thank you to Mrs. Benson for any of the gifts. Kacey ran back to open the last gift. Mrs. Benson decided not to order anything to eat. She felt like a pathetic, lonely soul. The only people who really needed her were Tina and Joshua.

Tina lay in a nursing home unaware she was in the world. Joshua spent his life floating from one place to the other, taking odd jobs and gathering in frequent sums of money his mother provided for him. She knew it was wrong to enable his evasion of the law, but he was her only living son. If he needed her help, she would give it to him. Detective Monroe reached out to her every now and then to see if she had heard from him. Of course her son had contacted her, but she was not going to tell the police that. It was not her job to bring Joshua to justice for his horrid crime. If the police were too incompetent to find him, that was their fault.

In this way she made herself feel better about helping one son who had murdered her other son.

"Grandma, I am hungry," Kacey chirped. "I want some French fries, chocolate candy, and juice."

The tiny voice pulled Mrs. Benson away from her thoughts and made her laugh. "Now, Kacey. You know Grandma is not going to let you eat all that sugar. I am going to get myself a salad. How about if you and I share a salad and fries? If you eat the salad, I will make sure you get some chocolate candy."

Kacey was very satisfied with this compromise. Without another word, Mrs. Benson picked up the phone and called room service. Kacey was rolling around with her doll on the bed. Occasionally she would inspect her new, beautiful charm bracelet. She was singing and smiling. Mrs. Benson sat there watching her. She felt proud and sad at the same time. After all, Kacey had run past her many times and never once gave her a hug. Oh, well. She would take whatever love she could get.

Chapter 48

Juan drove up to the row house on High Street. He avoided parking in the small driveway, but instead found a spot on the street in front of the house. He got out of his car and looked about the neighborhood. It was a reasonably well-kept neighborhood, probably populated by middle to low-middle income people, he thought. It reminded him of the first house his mother had purchased for them. The homes on High Street were modest, with a distinct working class feel to them. Most of the residents were at work this time of the day, Juan speculated. Only an occasional car made its way along the grey street.

It appeared to be a decent place to start a family. Children could probably peacefully play outside without their parents obsessively looking out the window. The yards were tiny, but there was room enough for children to play. Of course, he did not expect to see any children. They were at school. He should be at school at this time, but he was not. Juan had decided that this education was much more important than listening about someone else's history. He needed to know about his own.

He had to smile. His life was so different now. His mother had really done well financially. In addition to her financial success, she was a respected woman in business, church and home. He had almost forgotten that the majority of people lived in modest homes like these. Most people did not have a housekeeper or have to be annoyed with the details of how to plan an estate or what to do with an inheritance.

For some reason his heart was pounding within him. Juan could sense that he was on the verge of something that would change his perspective. He cared about his future. He loved his mother dearly, but he found little satisfaction in being a rich kid.

He was so hungry for more knowledge about his history. Tara had not shared the past much with him. She seemed to always be running from it and pushing him toward some great destiny. He appreciated it and he wanted to meet her expectations, but he felt it would be incomplete without full knowledge of those who had come before him. If he could get some insight, perhaps he could get energized to be what she dreamed he'd be.

After taking a deep breath, he jumped out the car. There was an old Volkswagen in the driveway. Juan had not tried to call ahead. He did not want anyone to prepare for him. He was afraid that he'd get a no or someone would ask him to come at some other time. This was his opportunity. His mother and Kacey were together, busy with Mrs. Benson. They would not reach home until well into the evening. By that time, he'd be back home. Maybe he could even avoid seeing Mrs. Day. He took the liberty to move forward with his personal project--the project aimed at finding out more about himself.

Before he knew it, he was standing in front of the door. Juan tucked his notebook under his arm, prepared to flash his charming smile and knocked. He was about to knock again when the door opened.

There was a short elderly woman looking up at him. She had spots of grey in her hair and very wide hips. She gave him the inquiring, impatient look that older people give younger people at times. Juan had to adjust his gaze downward because she was so short. He wanted to look her in the eye with the confidence he had been taught to exude.

"Brant?" she asked sharply.

"Excuse me?" he asked, confused.

"Brant, why didn't you tell me you were stopping by? Come on in, boy," she said, motioning him to come inside the house.

He laughed a little and did not move. "No, ma'am. My name is Juan Benson. I was wondering if I could ask you some questions. I am looking for the Bakers. Do you know them?"

She reached into her pocket and pulled out the glasses. It took her a moment to put them on and the minute seemed like an eternity to Juan. He decided to mask his impatience with a smile.

She shook her head. "You look so much like my grandson. I thought you were him. I am Marilyn Baker. Who are you looking for?"

"Well," he cleared his throat, "I was actually looking for Mr. Darnell and Mrs. Dina Baker. I wanted to ask them about caring for foster children some years ago."

"Come on in," she invited again.

As he walked into the house, he immediately smelled moth balls. As if she knew it, she went to the windows and opened them. "I am sorry. I know it gets stuffy in here. Sometimes I forget to air it out. I need to throw away some of this stuff, but it gets hard to do that. You don't have that problem yet."

"It's not a problem," he said, standing near the doorway. She walked deeper into the living room and he decided it was safe to follow her.

He found himself liking her. There was a natural kindness about her. His eyes dropped over the house and he realized that it was well maintained. The carpet was clean and the furniture was polished. She had a few newspapers lying around, but other than that, it was a neat house. There were pictures on the fireplace mantel. Juan was tempted to go right over and look at them, but he took a seat on the couch instead.

"You are young," she observed. "Now, what are you doing inquiring about Darnell and Dina and foster care?" She took a chair opposite him.

"I am doing research on foster care. I thought they could share some information with me about their experience, since they had foster kids."

"Oh no. They did not have foster kids. They took in one foster girl and, well, that did not really work out for them. She was an older child and Dina and Darnell were somewhat young themselves. I don't think there was enough distance in age between them and her."

"But do you think I could talk with them about their experience?" he pressed.

"You can talk to Darnell. Dina and he split up not long after the girl ran off. Last I heard, Dina was living out in California somewhere. I don't think Darnell has seen the foster girl since the day she left here."

He seemed surprised. "She ran off--the girl ran off?"

"Yes," she said. "She had been in and out of different homes. I think she had too many problems to be with those two. I don't know why Dina tried to take in a teen. But then, that was Dina--she was always trying to look at something other than what was right in front of her. She and Darnell had not been long married and instead of trying to have a baby with her husband, she brought a foster girl into the home."

"Oh," he said, disappointed.

"What's wrong? Oh, my manners! Can I get you something to drink?" she asked, then took another look at his face. "Don't let me paint you too bad of a picture. Darnell can tell you better. I think he enjoyed having the girl around."

"Oh, no. I am fine. But...well, you think Mr. Darnell would be willing to talk to me?"

She shrugged. "Probably, although he doesn't really like to talk about that girl or that time. I think his intentions were good, but he feels like he didn't get anything good out of it."

He was confused. "Why?" He couldn't think of anything his mother would do or could do that would leave someone else worst off.

"I don't know," she said, sensing his discomfort. Mrs. Baker seemed to sink back into some distant memories. "I remember her as being a nice girl--you know, nice enough. She was quiet, though. She was pretty and quiet. Honestly, I think Dina was a little jealous of the child. You know, she even accused

Darnell of messing with that girl? I don't know what made her think of that. It was a really crazy time around here."

Mrs. Baker shook her head at the thought. As if she saw a scene in her head, she closed her eyes for a moment. She could still see Dina's distraught face and the tears in her daughter-in-law's eyes. Mrs. Baker could hear the screaming and her son's reaction. He did not scream back. Darnell did not levy one protest. He only dropped his head before his wife. She had always interpreted his response as embarrassment over her accusation and nothing more. Juan's voice drew her back to the moment.

"Really? Why would she say that?"

"Crazy," she laughed, pushing the memories away. "Then, when the girl ran off, that just left this open question on the whole matter. Their marriage was pretty much over by then."

"She ran away? Do you know what happened to her? Where she went?" He knew his mother was quite young when she had him. If she was a runaway, did they even try to look for her? It made him feel sad that her disappearance could be treated so casually.

"I think Darnell tried to find her, but she didn't turn up. He reported it, as I remember, but nothing materialized. So, we just left it alone for his peace of mind. I am assuming she's okay and that the rest of her life took its course. We never heard about anything happening to her. Speak of the devil," she said, as the front door opened.

A tall, coco-colored man walked in the door. He was around 50, Juan guessed. Juan stood up because he could see that the man noticed him immediately. He was probably wondering what he was doing there with his mother. Before he could speak, Mrs. Baker broke the silence.

"This is Juan. Doesn't he look like Brant? He is researching foster care. I told him you wouldn't have much to add, but he came here to talk to you. I told him Dina is long gone."

"I see," Darnell said, looking away from his mother and putting his eyes back on Juan. The young man did put him in the mind of his son. Physically, they shared the same height and complexion. Both were handsome young men. However, this young man had a more polished look than his son. He wondered what he was really doing here, talking to his mother. "Your name again?"

"Juan Benson," he replied. "I just wanted to see if you could share your experiences with me. I am doing a paper on foster care and I wanted to do some interviews of people who had direct experience. I am talking to former foster parents and former foster kids. It would really help me if you talk to me."

"Where are you from? What are you doing this for-- school? Where would my input go? You got to give me more information, young brother."

"Of course," Juan said, pulling out a paper that outlined the parameters of the assignment. He had put his school's logo on it to make it look official. This was the first time he felt it necessary to use the document.

Darnell took the paper out of Juan's hand and glanced at it without any real study.

Darnell looked over at his mother after handing Juan back the paper. "Ma, could you get us something to drink?"

"Sure," she said, excusing herself. "I'll make you some tea. You like tea, Juan?"

He shrugged and nodded. "Yes, ma'am."

When she left the room, Darnell motioned for him to sit down. "Why don't you tell me why you're really here? You look mighty young to be doing field research for some think-tank. And I doubt a school would ask a youngster to find former foster parents and interview them. What's really up?"

"I am doing research," Juan tried to persist with his plan. But he could see that the older Darnell was unmoved by this line of thought.

Darnell raised his eyebrows. "If you're not going to be honest with me, you can leave right now."

"No, please. Okay," Juan sighed. "I know this is going to sound weird. But I am trying to find some information about my mother. I believe she was in your care as a foster kid. She got pregnant when she was very young--with me. I never knew my birth father. She won't tell me who he is or anything about him. I thought if I found her guardians, you might be able to give me information about him or at least some hint about who he might be. Anything you could tell me would be helpful."

Darnell did not speak immediately. He studied Juan, then leaned back into the chair. "I only had one foster child in my care. What is your mother's name?"

"Tara Benson – well, she was Martin then. Tara Martin. She had me when she was around 16 years old."

"She got married?" he asked.

"Oh, yes. Years after having me...well, my step-father--he passed." Juan added, to round out what happened to Tim.

"He adopted you."

"Yes. He was a really good man."

"So, why are you here asking about some man you never met when you had a good father who gave you his name?"

Juan had not expected the question. "I don't know. I guess I have to know about my birth father if I can. I mean, my step-father was good to me, but he got killed. I only had him for a year or so."

"I see," he studied Juan some more. "And your mother is good to you? Is that your car out there? I don't see too many kids your age around here with a car like that. But you're not from around here."

"Yes. My mother took really good care of me," he said, a bit embarrassed. People always wanted to zero in on the obvious things that mattered the least. "And no I am not from around here. I live in Rockford."

"Rockford? You all living off insurance money from the dead man--I am sorry--your father?"

Juan shook his head vehemently. "No. My mom did well before she met him. She's worked so hard for me and she doesn't know I am here. She'd freak out, probably. I just wish I could find something, some information. I need to know about my past. I mean no disrespect to my mother or my father, the man who adopted me. I love them both, but for myself, I have to know."

"Okay," he said after a moment. "So, you want to know who your daddy is."

"Yes. I do."

"Okay. Who do you think he is?"

"What?" Juan was thrown off by the question. He had never even considered what his birth father would be like or who he was.

"Well, you are asking about him. What if you find him and he's dead? What if he's in jail or a drug addict, drug dealer, murderer? Have you thought about that? Maybe your mother didn't tell you because she knows something about him that you don't know. What if she's not hiding him from you, but hiding you from him?"

Juan shrugged. "I hadn't thought that far ahead. He can't be too bad if my mother was with him."

"What if she wasn't with him, but he was with her?" he asked, with raised eyebrows.

Juan did not like the thought. "What do you mean? I just want to get some information."

"Okay, but what if I can't tell you anything?"

"I don't know," Juan said frustrated. "I figured I would get here and find out what I could. Can you help me or not?"

"Look. I am not trying to discourage you. I think you're a fine young man. You're smart and you know how to go after things. Your mother was that way, as I remember. I just don't want you to have some television show in your head. You might find your birth father and hate him."

"To be honest, Mr. Baker, I've already dealt with my anger. I am not mad. I just want to know. So, what can you tell me about what you know?"

Darnell leaned back. He lit a cigarette and took a long puff. "Your mother didn't have boyfriends or anything. So, I don't know of a young man who would have been your father from a romantic relationship."

Juan was disappointed to hear that, but he knew that the man was going to say more. In fact, Juan was certain that Darnell knew more about the situation. His dark eyes focused intently on the older man. He watched him start to drop his gaze under his intense stare. Darnell took a deep puff of his cigarette and began his narrative.

"Your mother was young and pretty. She had no family, no friends. I am not sure if she ever knew her mother or father. When she came to us, she had been in several homes. Each time she was moved for her own safety."

"Okay, but she found safety here, right?" Juan asked, protectively. Tara never talked about such things, but he had listened to her prayers and conversations with others. He remembered once hearing her talk about another girl fighting her over food when she was around ten years old.

Darnell looked ashamed. "No. I mean, yes--at first. Shortly after she came to live with us, my brother also came back home. He had just gotten out of jail and I gave him a place to stay. I shouldn't have. I broke the rules and everything to give him a place to stay, but he had no place else to go. I couldn't turn him away. So, he lived here with us."

"So, what are you saying?" Juan asked, feeling his heart speed up and his cheeks begin to burn.

"Juan, my brother was not a nice man. He was cruel and rough. He didn't know how to survive in society outside of prison. He certainly didn't know how to be around a young girl like your mother and respect her. So, I believe he hurt your mother several times. I think that's why she ran away."

"You think or you know?"

"I never spoke to her about it, but he came to live with us and she was gone within the month. I noticed that she started to act differently. She didn't want to spend time with the family any more. She stayed to herself or tried to hang around my wife. When my wife made it clear that Tara was being too clingy, she started coming home later and later."

Juan was silent for a moment. As the gravity of what was being told him sank into his ears, he almost regretted seeking out the truth. He shook himself from that train of thought. He was committed to understanding his origins, no matter what the cost.

"And I am the result of that hurt," he responded. "This brother of yours--a criminal. You let a convicted criminal move into your home and gave him access to a defenseless 15-year-old?"

Darnell put his hand up. "Hold on, Juan. That is my brother. You have to understand. I didn't think bringing him into the home was dangerous."

"But she was in your care. You said that you broke the rules. The rules were in place for a reason. I am just saying you did not use the best judgment." Juan was quite upset and thought it strange that he was lecturing this older man. However, he was bold enough to do it. His mother was not there. Someone had to speak up for her, even if it was years after the events.

"You're right. If I had known what would happen, I would have been more careful. I guess I thought between my wife, my mother and myself, it would be okay. Also, you have to understand, I never thought it was a risk. He wasn't in jail because of women. He was in jail for being dumb." Darnell put out his cigarette and shook his head.

"Well, I guess we can't anticipate everything." Juan knew his tone was a little sarcastic. But he knew that no one had perfect foresight. "I can't believe I'm hearing this about how I came into the world."

"I don't know if your mother has raised you in church. I learned that God makes no mistakes. You were born because He wanted you to be born. Man doesn't control that. So, it really doesn't really matter how you came to be."

"But my father raped my mother," Juan said, angrily. "She had no choice. She did not want to get pregnant with me."

"You would have been born with or without that crime. That's how I see it. Or you can see it as something good that still came into your mother's life-- you. Juan, your mother had no one in the world at all who cared for her. She was all by herself as a child. If she had stayed with us, my wife would have sent her away on her eighteenth birthday. Tara would have started her adult life as she started her childhood life-- alone. Because of you, she did not. And from what I can see, you gave her purpose. So, while my brother had become an example of the worst of humanity, you are just the opposite of that. For your mother, you are the best."

Juan thought about these words. Then he looked over at the older man. "May I see a picture of him?"

Darnell raised his eyebrows, surprised. "I have a few pictures. We pulled some together for the funeral. Mama insisted."

Darnell went over to an end table and pulled out a few pieces of paper. Within the papers were three photos. He sat down beside Juan on the couch and handed him the photos one by one.

"This is him when he was a teenager. That's before he went into lockup. Charles Baker was his name, by the way."

"What did he do?"

Darnell shrugged. "He was young, but he always wanted to be tough. You see his baby face? He started hanging around some guys who didn't care too much about rules. It started with skipping school, bad grades and, before you know it, fighting and stealing, then jail."

Juan steadied his hand from shaking as he held the picture. He stared at the image of his birth father. A handsome teen smiled back at him. He had even, brown skin and dark, sparkling eyes. The cheekbones were well structured and his smile was bright. This certainly did not look like the face of someone who was about to destroy his own life and that of others. Juan did observe the young man's baby face. Juan tried but could not find any resemblance between the teen in the picture and himself.

"How old was he here?"

"I think he was 16 or so. Yes, he must have been, because he's got on that red varsity jersey."

"Oh, he played sports?"

"Yeah, he was very good in football. Just stupid in life. This picture was taken after he got out of jail the first time." He handed Juan the second picture.

Juan looked at the image. The man who stared back was still young and handsome, but there was a hard, cynical look about him. He looked mean in the eyes. Juan shuttered to think that the wrath that must have been in this man was unleashed on his young mother.

"I know," Darnell said, as if he knew Juan's thoughts. He handed him the last picture. "This one was taken right before his last arrest."

"Last? What did he do?"

"I don't want to tell you. You really want to know this?"

"I guess I have to know."

"He took some money to kill a guy. You know my brother was a lot of things. I knew he was mean. I mean, sometimes I didn't feel comfortable with him because he could act crazy about ordinary things. But I never thought he could have killed someone for money."

The statement sent chills up Juan's spine. He thought about Tim and the utter grief that had engulfed his family immediately after his death. If he was honest with himself, he would acknowledge that his mother never recovered from the blow of losing Tim.

His thoughts shifted to Tara. Darnell was right. She had been alone a great deal of her life. When she finally found a family, it was torn apart by violence. He thought about himself. Even he had come to her as a result of violence.

Darnell was still talking. "He killed a family man. A young man jogging in the park. After that, I cut him off. My mother went to see him, but I just couldn't. It's as if the Charles I played with when we were younger was no longer there. So what was the point of visiting this guy who would probably kill me for money, too?"

"A man jogging in the park? How long ago was this?" Juan asked, feeling that the description of the murder sounded all too familiar.

"Oh, I guess six or seven years ago now. The man who paid him skipped town. It was all in the papers.

But, you know, my brother didn't get away with his part in the crime. I'm glad he didn't. Really I am. He died in prison about four years ago. Cancer." Darnell sounded bitter and resentful as he said this.

Juan abruptly turned the pictures over and pushed them back into Darnell's hand. Juan did not need to know anything else about Charles Baker. He stood up and gathered his notepad.

"Thank you so much, but I think I will go now. My mother will probably go crazy if I don't show up soon. I don't want to worry her."

Darnell realized that Juan was very shaken by the conversation. He stood up and caught his arm as he was walking past him. Juan dropped his head because he did not want to look at Darnell. Suddenly, Juan felt tears well up in his eyes. He could not remember the last time he had cried. It certainly had been years.

His emotions were so mixed as he stood there with Darnell. He was sad about his mother's plight in life as a child and young adult. He was sad that his father was a murderer. He was sad that he had come all this way for such disappointing news. He was sad that the murder his birth father had participated in sounded shockingly similar to Tim's murder. Was that coincidence? Did his biological father take Tim from him and his mother?

"I know this is heavy. I should have warned you," Darnell said, feeling terrible. He could see the young man's bowed head and drooping shoulders. Darnell didn't know why he hadn't just told Juan he didn't know anything about his birth father. Now this young man had to live with the ghost of Charles Baker.

"Listen, let me call your mother. I don't think you should drive home like this."

"No, I am fine. I don't want her to know I came here. I don't think it's fair to her and I don't know how she would react."

"I see," Darnell paused. "Juan, I don't know how you're going to take this. My brother was terrible, but my family's not so bad. Perhaps you got to me so we could make a connection."

Juan raised his head.

"I don't know now," Juan told him honestly. "I don't know if I can say I have a right to find a second family here. I don't feel like family. My father didn't love my mother. She didn't love him. I mean, I hear what you're saying about God's purpose. I don't feel like a mistake, but I don't think I can say I am family."

"Look, I am not a religious man, but I tell you what. You knew nothing about us when you knocked on our door. Now we've gotten a chance to know you. You seem like a nice young man. Why don't we all sleep on it? Let's pray about it and see what happens. You and your mother made a family. Perhaps you and I can be one, too."

Juan nodded. When Darnell mentioned prayer, Juan felt a load lift from his shoulders. The tears were still there, but his emotions did not confuse him any longer. His mother had once told him that life could be hard, but God made His people tough. He did not always appreciate her lectures, but he realized how much she loved him. She loved him enough to see him, not his father, when she looked at him. She only saw her beloved son, not memories of brutality and violation. Juan knew where he belonged. He didn't feel anything was missing any longer.

Juan shook Darnell's hand. It was a firm handshake from one man to another.

"Thank you for seeing me. Thank you for your honesty. Please thank your mother for being so nice. I am going to talk to my mother and I'll be in touch...maybe."

"Fair enough, Juan."

Chapter 49

Juan was thankful that he was able to slip into the house without much explanation. His mother was in her office, writing something. When he walked in, she looked up at him with her familiar look of love. Kacey was playing with some of her new dolls on the floor next to Tara.

"Hey, Juan," Kacey said. "Look at what my Grandma got me. Aren't they pretty?"

She held up two dolls with beautiful yellow dresses. He smiled. "Yes, Kacey, but not as pretty as you."

This sentiment seemed to please Kacey and his mother very much. Tara was about to say something, but before she could speak, he walked over and gave her a big kiss on the cheek.

Tara jumped in surprise at first, but her heart melted. It had been so long since Juan had done that. That was something her little boy use to do. She looked over at him and smiled. "Juan, what was that for?"

"For being the greatest mother in the world," he told her.

She laughed and shook her head. "I am sure there are a lot of people in the running for that title. What's going on? What did I do to deserve that?"

"Nothing, Ma--and everything. I want you to know that I am going to talk to Mr. Marks tomorrow. I will do whatever extra credit work he gives me and I will make up that grade. You won't see anything else like that coming from me in the future."

"Okay," she said, sympathetically. "I appreciate that, son. I know you think I am hard on you, but you have so much potential. Besides, you have to take the empire to the next level one day. I want you to have everything you need to do so."

She laughed. In part, she was joking. Tara did not really consider her success at the empire level, but she was building a solid future for Juan and Kacey. If he didn't know how to manage what she had built, he would lose it.

He nodded. "Understood, Ma. Kacey, did you practice reading yet?"

"No," the girl said, begrudgingly. She tossed her dolls aside. Juan's words spelled doom to her. Playtime was over.

"Well, come on, then. I need to catch up on some reading. You can come with me."

The prospect of reading with Juan put a smile on her face. She happily took his hand. Tara watched both of them as they left the study. She always knew she was blessed, but she was beginning to feel waves of unfamiliar satisfaction.

Chapter 50

When Joshua heard the news of his mother's death, he was devastated. He sat in the tropical breeze outside the hotel where he was staying. The hotel was set right off the ocean and he was enjoying a cool breeze from the water as he lay back on the orange wicker furniture. He had been working abroad for years. He had managed to save a modest portion of his paychecks as well as the funds that had been funneled to him by his mother.

Thanks to his mother's regular routine of sending him funds as well as covert disbursements from Tina's trust, Joshua was living in reasonable comfort. People around him knew him as Benson Laws. They assumed he was from a small country in Africa.

He liked the irony of his assumed name, Benson Laws. Who would expect him to use part of his real name? "Laws" was his way of scorning the legal system, Detective Monroe and Ms. Tara. He had decided that Tim was in the way of his happiness and his deserved inheritance. It was his decision to remove the obstacle. Thus, he had become the "law" over Tim and his destiny.

In retrospect, though, he wished he had handled it differently. Death was so final.

His father's death had come as a complete shock to him. Now Joshua was isolated and alone in the world. Joshua took a sip of his vodka-laced grape juice. It was ironic that he was now like one of the children his parents had been obsessed with helping. He was a motherless and fatherless offspring, like Tina and Tim.

"Benson, we are all meeting at Sarah's house after work. You make sure you come." The lilting female voice, heavy with an Australian accent, pulled him from his thoughts.

He smiled, sipped the juice and smiled. "Okay. I'll try."

He did not know if his accent he had taken on was authentic or not. He wanted to make sure he did not sound American. The Australian lady smiling at him seemed overjoyed. He had learned over the years that his dark complexion was a definite benefit with women. Joshua never lacked for female attention or companionship. And when he laid on his accent, it made them all, foreign- or American-born, melt before him.

He winked at the pretty brunette and tugged on his thick, curly beard. Joshua allowed his eyes to roam lustfully over her. The woman responded as he expected she would. She giggled and walked off, making sure to look behind her as she moved her hips lovingly. He liked the shape of her buttocks. Joshua shook his head and focused his thoughts back to the more important matters at hand.

In reality, Joshua did not know if he would go to the party or not. His mother was dead. Although he had not always liked his mother, he did love her and he would miss her. It felt decent to grieve for her, especially because he could not attend the funeral in the United States. He could at least skip a party.

He knew he had to plan what made the most sense now that she had passed away. Who would look out for him and try to funnel money to him? Jose was still around, but Jose was no money manager. Jose was a property manager, the trusted tradesman who had never liked the selfish Joshua. Jose had always loved Tim. Jose was even the best man at Tim's wedding! So, Jose would not help him now, even though he must have known that Mrs. Benson was sending Joshua money over the years.

His mother was too shrewd to let other people in on her secret. Mrs. Benson would never risk exposure in such a case. Joshua also surmised that his mother had not planned to die in her sixties, so there was no back-up plan for sending funds to him. He would have to figure out how to survive on his own.

His thoughts drifted to the fact that both his parents were now dead. He figured that the estate money, the house, the investments, the summer house and the Benson name should really fall to him. He shook away the thought. Obviously, he was in no position to assert a claim for the Benson estate. The only person to inherit would be Tim's offspring, Kacey.

In his mother's letters to him, Mrs. Benson talked often about Kacey. He could tell that she had genuinely loved the child. In his mother's eyes, Kacey was smart, beautiful, and funny. Mrs. Benson liked to say the girl looked like her, although Joshua knew she biologically could not. After all, Tim was not a blood relative. Kacey was not blood. Of course, his mother never really thought of these folks as outsiders. She had always seemed to prefer the outsiders to him.

That was a moot point now.

She also wrote about Tara in her letters. Mrs. Benson admired Tara, but it was clear that the younger woman held Joshua's mother responsible for his evasion of justice. There was no repairing of that breach before her death. To make it worst, Tara was Kacey's mother and therefore her guardian. She would be the one to look after everything on Kacey's behalf until she reached the age of majority. She would be the one to stumble on the payments from the trust to the offshore account. She would be the one to prove that his mother knew where he was all these years. Everything could come crashing down on him. Perhaps the law would finally catch up with him, after all.

"That woman hates me so much," he said aloud. He had to check himself because he sounded like his American self. Thankfully, no one around seemed to be paying attention to him.

Joshua did not know the best course of action. For sure, he had lost his appetite for death. With the passing of his father and his mother as well as Tim's death, he did not want more to do with death. One of the odd jobs he had to take while on the run was work in a crematorium. He actually took the dead bodies of men and women and fed those bodies to the fire. Perhaps it was God's way of making him do penance. He had to smell their flesh, look at their faces, pick up their heavy bodies and gather their ashes into urns for their families. The process was not pretty.

The urns were deceptive. Porcelain and elegant-looking urns held ashes of people who a week earlier were laughing and living. One man even reminded him of Tim. He was alone with the strong-looking corpse. That was the one time Joshua thought he had gone insane. In that time with the corpse, he cried, cursed, blasphemed and almost repented--almost. He just couldn't get the wickedness of his act out of his head and heart. However, Joshua couldn't bring himself to turn himself in. He knew the only path to true repentance was to face prison time or a possible death sentence.

That path was too steep for him. Perhaps God would be merciful to him in the end. His mind started to drift back to his dreams of inheritance. Joshua stood up and shook his head as if to clear it.

"Hey, you need something more?"

He turned to acknowledge the bartender. The man was ready to give him more vodka. Joshua smiled at him and took his seat again. "Nah, mon. I'm good."

He swallowed the rest of the vodka in his glass. He then stood and eyed a woman in a thong walking past him. As he watched her tan buttocks dance before him, he thought again about the money. Women loved him even though they thought he was poor. They would absolutely adore him if they knew he was rich. It had been some time now since Tim's death. The actual shooter was dead. If there was no one to ID him and the rest of the case was circumstantial, could he return home? Could he actually be acquitted of the crime and inherit his portion of the Benson estate after all?

He imagined contesting the will and getting it all. Kacey was not blood, he reminded himself.

He also imagined the look on Tara's face when she watched him walk out of the courtroom a free man. It made him laugh aloud. Maybe his mother's death was a sign. Perhaps he should go back to the United States and face the hangman. Joshua had a strong feeling that he could end up beating the rap.

Chapter 51

About a month or two later, Tara received a phone call from Detective Monroe. She was surprised to get the phone call because she rarely heard from him now. Shortly after Joshua left the United States, they stayed in frequent contact. They even tried to collaborate in getting Mrs. Benson to give her son up. However, Tim's case soon lost the luster it once had. The world moved on and, to a certain extent, so did Detective Monroe's activities. With the arrest and conviction of the actual trigger man, there was at least some satisfaction for law enforcement. He had done his job.

Tara felt Detective Monroe's appetite to bring Joshua to justice had subsided over the years. He had contented himself with allowing Joshua to remain a fugitive at large. In fairness to Detective Monroe, it was not all his fault. Mrs. Benson was as hard as nails. She could look you in your eye and lie without flinching. In addition, the woman did not scare easily, so threats or even hints of threats did not work with her. She called everyone's bluff and won the bet. There was never any proof that she aided Joshua. Despite a Joshua sighting every now and then, there were no leads.

Department resources were directed toward other, more current cases where the guilty party could be apprehended in short order. Days turned into weeks and weeks into months without progress on the case against Joshua. Tara had learned to live with the delay, but she was by no means happy with the way Tim's case had been handled.

For Tara, there was no closure to that part of her life. She could not move on. Tara did not date and she was not interested in another relationship. It would be a betrayal to Tim, she felt, to meet someone, marry, have this other man's child and act as if life was good and pleasant. Her obligation to Tim was to raise Juan and Kacey. Raising the two children would fulfill Tim's heart's desire.

Tara's behavior had perplexed several men over the years. Handsome, smart men of all backgrounds and races had tried to make a connection with the beautiful, astute widow. None had even come close to being successful. Tara remembered seeing pictures of Detective Monroe's family on his desk. She complimented him on his lovely wife and handsome set of triplet boys. They all looked like him, with the same complexion, serious eyes and wide smile. However, part of her resented his ability to enjoy his family while she could no longer enjoy her married life with Tim.

Another part of her knew it was wrong to resent Detective Monroe. But she could not help but hold him partially accountable. He was responsible for the case-- and the true murderer got away. Detective Monroe was not completely ignorant of her resentment. He did not take it personally, though. He believed he had done all he could.

The reality was that people were killed every day. New cases needed to be worked. Other families needed him to give them hope of closure. To his credit, he never failed to touch base with Tara every so often-- especially whenever there were Joshua sightings from somewhere in the world.

Tara recognized his voice immediately on the other end of the phone. "Detective Monroe," she said when she raised the phone to her ear, "I am surprised to hear from you. Where was he seen this time?"

"Hi, Mrs. Benson. Are you sitting down?"

"Yes," she responded. Tara was actually reclining. She had just come home and had kicked off her high-heels.

"Mrs. Benson, we have him."

"Have him?" She could hear the words, but she did not want to be roped in for yet another disappointment. Tara waited. Was he telling her what she had waited seven years to hear?

"Joshua Benson. He has come back into the United States. He surrendered his passport and we are in the process of extraditing him."

"When? How?" She was no longer reclining. Now Tara was on her feet, pacing back and forth in excitement.

"Well, the story is really crazy. I wish I could tell you it was all due to good police work. He just entered the United States and turned himself in at the nearest police station in Queens, New York. He told them he was a wanted man. They looked him up in the FBI database and called us about an hour ago."

"He turned himself in," she repeated, somewhat numbly. Tara felt disappointed. She had always imagined he would be brought in kicking and screaming, while his mother watched with her best poker face.

"Yes," he said. "He'll finally see the inside of a courtroom again. I wanted you to hear it from me before it might hit the news."

"I appreciate the call," she said.

After they hung up, Tara shook her head. She knew Joshua Benson well enough to know that he did not have a change of heart. He had been on the run for years. His mother had now passed away. And he chooses this moment to surface? She surmised that he was so greedy for money that he would risk a death sentence to get his hands on an inheritance.

Chapter 52

On the day Joshua saw the inside of a courtroom again, Tara was sure to be there. She took a seat beside Detective Monroe, who seated immediately behind the prosecutor's desk. There were several procedural steps to follow before trial. But Tara was hopeful that Joshua would receive a "speedy" trial, as promised in the constitution. She wanted him in jail—or worse.

He came into the courtroom with the same air of arrogance he always had. At first, he did not look her way. However, after he adjusted himself to his surroundings, he turned as if to look for her. Their eyes met for a brief second. Tara sized him up immediately. As she suspected, there was no change in him. He looked older, but not a bit wiser or more contrite.

He had aged well, Tara noticed. Joshua was always handsome, but he now had the deep-rooted handsome looks of his father. He stood tall in a well-tailored suit. He was clean shaven, too. What a deceptive image he put forth, Tara thought to herself. Joshua looked like a business man, not a murderer.

"All rise," the bailiff announced.

Everyone dutifully stood. The judge entered the courtroom and took his seat behind the bench. He eased his glasses onto his middle-aged face and took a brief, appraising look at Joshua. Soon his eyes turned toward the district attorney. He called her name and she stood.

"Ms. Bernadette, you are aware that the defense counsel has entered a motion to dismiss this case based off insufficient grounds to indict Mr. Benson." The judge said this without any emotion or inflection in his voice.

"Yes, your honor. The state finds this motion utterly incomprehensible. The defendant, Mr. Joshua Benson, was arraigned seven years ago for the murder of Tim Benson. He was granted bail against the state's recommendation and has evaded justice for the past seven years. The case, therefore, never proceeded. The state asks to have a grand jury hearing, as proscribed by law. In addition to the grand jury, your honor should hear the evidence and then make a judgment on whether there is sufficient evidence to present charges to a jury of Mr. Benson's peers."

The defense lawyer was a pudgy man with long sideburns. He wore a brown, baggy suit. When he spoke up on his client's behalf, Tara was surprised to hear his heavy Southern accent.

"Your honor, the case against my client is circumstantial at best. Your review of the evidence that the state has right now will surely conclude there is no case here."

"Your honor," the prosecution interrupted, with outrage. "Tim Benson was gunned down while he was jogging in the park seven years ago—a murder arranged and paid for by Joshua Benson."

"And the murderer of Tim Benson died in prison," the defense interjected. "The only link between my client and that murderer is the murderer's words. He is now dead. There is no physical evidence or eye witness who can connect my client to that crime. But if the state wishes to waste time and resources on this, we'll allow him to be exonerated procedurally."

The prosecutor shot back, "I am surprised the defense would characterize the murder trial as a waste of time and resources. Tim Benson was a father and a husband. The people have a case and fancy motions should not allow his murder to go unaddressed."

"Your Honor!" the defense attorney complained.

Tara watched in quiet frustration. She knew Joshua had to have had this legal gamesmanship in mind when he voluntarily returned to the United States.

The judge banged his gavel. "To you both: we are not going to change the procedures of this state to accommodate either side. Mr. Carson," he said, directing his attention toward the defense. "Your client fled seven years ago and will face a grand jury now. Ms. Bernadette, the state's argument for trial will be heard there."

"Thank you, your Honor," Ms. Bernadette replied. Tara liked her instantly. She was spunky and intelligent. Although she was a young lawyer, she had an air of trained competence and intelligence. Ms. Bernadette also exuded passion. It was nice to see someone believe in their work and not just practice it.

The defense and prosecution were both silenced now under the judge's direction.

"In the case of the people vs. Joshua Benson for the murder of Tim Benson, a natural person, how do you plead?"

"Not guilty," Mr. Carson replied loudly for his client.

Bail was denied this time. Joshua turned and looked in Tara's direction again. Detective Monroe turned to Tara. He placed his hand on her hand. He could feel the vibration from the anger she was feeling.

"Is he right?" she asked the detective. "Is it possible he could walk out a free man and not pay for what he did?"

"Nothing is certain, but there is still a solid case against him."

"Are you sure?" She asked.

Detective Monroe did not answer her immediately because, in fact, he was not sure. The strongest link had been the word of Charles Baker, the person who shot Tim. Charles Baker had confessed on video and, in that confession, he had implicated Joshua. But common sense suggested that a man like Charles Baker and a man like Joshua had no reason to interact with each other. They seemed to be from different worlds. The defense would argue that Charles Baker's claim of Joshua's role in the crime was just the ravings of a desperate murderer.

The authorities had never found a money trail between the two men. Nor had a motive for Joshua's involvement ever been proven beyond a reasonable doubt. Detective Monroe had been sidetracked with other cases during the seven years that Joshua had been on the run. As the case had grown colder, the elements for conviction had grown somewhat stale and shaky. Now, as he looked into the large, dark brown eyes of Mrs. Tara Benson, he knew he may have let her down after all.

Chapter 53

Tara was in her living room, mulling over the events of the past week. Juan was upstairs and Kacey was in her room, asleep. It was a little after 8:30 pm. Tara had a quiet moment to reflect.

She was not going to hop on the emotional rollercoaster Joshua had planned for her, she decided. Joshua Benson and his mother loved money--that was the one thing they had in common. They used it to cope with everything in life, including friendships, influence, events, business ventures and legal woes. Tara thought about this truth as she sat on the couch, trying not to sink into sorrow.

Stepping over to the fireplace, Tara took the picture of Tim and herself on their wedding day into her hands. In the picture, they were both so happy. He looked back at her with those piercing ebony eyes and that compelling smile. For her part, she was truly happy on that day. She had been oblivious to how quickly happiness could disappear.

Tara thought Tim had marked the end of her sorrows. She flopped back on the couch and tears welled in her eyes. There was an overwhelming sense of regret. She mourned most of all what could have been. If she had known their time would be so short together, she would have cherished it more.

Tara did not drink her sorrows away or look for other escapes in sex or drugs. Her escape lay in her children. Tara made sure she focused on every minor detail of their lives. As Juan grew older, he needed her less. As she turned her focus to Kacey, she parented her in a different way. Kacey was a pretty black girl with a successful mother and a wealthy grandmother. Tara felt Kacey would naturally find a path to continued happiness in her life. For Juan, it could be different. He was her son--her black son. He had known what it was like to be without. Tara had to forge a path for Juan that would give him room to be successful. If he was successful, he would be happy.

Her other escape was her business life. When she divested her ownership interest in Big Mike's, she chose to work on a variety or civic projects and business ventures. Tara was always starting to work on something or finishing something. She did not allow herself periods of idle time. Down-time, she worried, might awaken a realization that she was not content with her life.

She looked at the wedding picture again, then turned her attention back to Joshua. Seven years had been enough time to wait for closure. Her life was on hold all that time and she was weary of it. He was not going to get away, she vowed. In fact, Tara knew she would not be able to take another disappointment at Joshua's hands. After seven years, he was not going to walk in with his snake-like manner and slither his way out of a murder conviction.

"Tim, I am sorry," she said this placing one of her manicured figures over his smiling face. "I have let this go on too long. This time, I am going to be smart about it. I know the system doesn't always work for people like me. I will step in to make it work."

This was her new project—and a business venture as well. With the death of Mrs. Benson, Tara was the trustee of Kacey's holdings. Everything--the assets, the house, the construction company--had passed to Kacey. Tara had anticipated that Mrs. Benson would put some odd clause in her will, attempting to cut Tara out of the administration of its terms. She had not. By recognizing Tara as Kacey's mother and guardian, it was almost as if the older woman wanted to continue her feud with Tara from the grave.

It was time Tara reviewed the extent of her daughter's inheritance and the activities of the Benson estate.

She picked up the phone and called a short, dumpy, but experienced auditor she had worked with in her years of doing business. This woman was a bulldog. She made the tiniest audit finding into a major headline. Tara usually found this behavior annoying. But Tara respected this annoying auditor for not letting things go until she was satisfied with the answer.

Smiling, Tara dialed the auditor's number. Suddenly, she felt energized. When the woman's raspy voice answered, Tara greeted her with an enthusiasm she did not expect to muster. "Hello, Cheryl Winsome."

"Yes, this is Cheryl Winsome. This is surprising. Is this my friend?" The woman said, with a bit of sarcasm. Cheryl and Tara were not exactly enemies, but they were not friends. "This is a surprise. What can I help you with?"

Tara paused before speaking and then placed her request steadily. "I need a very thorough and quick piece of work on the Benson estate. My daughter just inherited some significant holdings upon the death of her grandmother. I would like you to look into money balances, money movements and transactions over the past ten years."

"Sorry to hear about the loss in your family."

"Thank you. What do you say?"

"Well, you know what I would say. That sounds fun. But we have a number of cases we're working." She broke from her personal tone to a professional voice. "Quick work? How quick?"

"I need this matter finished in a month--the sooner the better. I can pay more if you're done sooner."

"That type of forensic work takes time and costs a pretty penny. I have to put extra folks on it to get done in that timeframe."

"Money is no object," Tara said flatly. "I am not concerned about the cost."

"Okay, great. I will send a team over Monday morning to get started right away."

"Cheryl," Tara said in a softer, more intimate voice. "I was hoping you would be personally involved in this case. I need your type of relentless expertise."

"Oh? Hmm, so you need someone to get it done by any means necessary. You must think there are skeletons in the closet if you want me to be involved." She laughed in that nerdy way that Tara generally did not like.

"I just need an independent point of view, but I need it quickly."

"Okay. I will rearrange staffing on other projects and I will see you Monday."

Chapter 54

Juan, like his mother, knew finding a money trial was the key to bringing justice in the murder of Tim Benson. He decided to connect back with his new-found uncle and family. If Charles Baker received payment, did he spend it all, hide it all, confide in his brother or mother? How could a poor man like Charles Baker hide his coming into thousands of dollars. There was no way he could. The temptation would be too great.

"So, what did you buy and who did you treat?" Juan thought as he drove the two-hour highway stretch.

Juan remembered how nice the inside of the Baker home was in contrast to the modest neighborhood. There were some nice pieces in the home and he wondered if those pieces were procured by Charles Baker's ill-gotten gain. Even the worst son would want to buy his mother a nice gift.

Once again, his mother did not know he had gone to the old Chicago neighborhood. Juan did not have time to feel guilty because he knew she would more than approve of his propose. This time he called ahead. Mrs. Baker waited for him by the door. When he pulled into the driveway, she flung open the front door widely. He stepped out of the car and she motioned to him wildly to come into the house.

The warm, bear hug surprised him, but felt more natural than he expected. He thought she represented a real grandmother so much more than Mrs. Benson. Mrs. Benson had been too glamorous. She was always dressed lavishly and always attempted to mask her age with form fitting dresses, dyed hair and make-up. Mrs. Baker was the opposite. She seemed to enjoy her age. The silver curls were tight and framed her face beautifully. Around her body was a dress with a pattern that could have graced a quilt as well. Around her ankles she wore support socks.

"Come on in! I am so happy you wanted to come back and see us. This is more than any prayer I could have prayed."

He relaxed his body to accept her gracious hug. Juan followed her into the house. He could smell chicken and fresh baked bread. It put him a bit in the mind of Mrs. Claire's kitchen except Mrs. Baker's cooking was less refined. Mrs. Claire had passed away just a few years ago and he realized at that moment that he missed her. Suddenly, his stomach was growling. Home cooked food sounded and smelled good.

Juan washed his hands and joined her at the table. She blessed the food and then piled a massive amount of chicken, mashed potatoes, candied yams, green beans and three dinner rolls on his plate.

"Let me know if you need more. There is plenty of food."

"Yes ma'am," he said, feeling doubtful that he would be able to finish this first portion.

As he started to eat, Juan was enjoying the taste so much, he forgot about the notion of full. He was just enjoying eating and Mrs. Baker seemed to enjoy watching him eat. Her smile relaxed him, but Juan knew he was there on a mission.

"May I ask you something?"

"Sure, anything."

"It might seem like a strange question."

"You want to know about your father. He was a good boy. He went wrong though. That first time he went to jail ruined him. He came back to me a different boy. I didn't get a chance to finish raising him – the system raised my boy."

"I'm sorry," he said. The pain in her voice really struck him. Her wound was fresh. Juan realized a mother's wounded heart was not easily healed.

"Not your fault. I just wish things had been different. I don't know why they couldn't be different. Like if my husband had lived would everything have been different? I don't know. Did I just do a terrible job? I worked so much when they were younger and I couldn't afford good day care. I had to leave them with whoever would take them and keep them for me. Did they influence my baby the wrong way? I ask myself these questions all the time."

She dropped her head, wiped a tear away, then looked back at him with a half-smile.

"I guess I will never know. Then I see you and I think maybe I did something right after all. You go to church? What church you go to?"

"Yes, ma'am – Victory Rockford."

"Nice. I don't think I have ever been down there, but maybe I will come one weekend and spend some time with you all. I bet you know this song. We'll understand it better by and by."

Without another word, she started to sing:

"By and by Lord when the morning comes. All the saints Lord gather together at home. We will tell the story Lord how we overcome and we'll understand it better by and by."

After she stopped singing, she gave him a real smile. "I'm not worried. Charles was no saint--I know that. And he died in prison. I don't know what he said to the Lord before that day. I have hope that he got it right. God can do anything."

"Yes, ma'am." Then Juan decided to just blurt it out. "You think he was telling the truth about being paid to kill the man?"

"Of course he was telling the truth!" she snapped. "He did not know that man. He had no problems with that man. I think it's terrible that they let the real killer, the guy who planned the whole thing, get away. But isn't that the way of money--black and white matters, but money matters more. Poor Charles Baker dies in prison. This rich man escapes and lives out his days in freedom someplace. I can't believe nobody knows where he is! I remember his mother, too. I saw pictures of her. She knows where he is--you can tell by her smug looks and what she doesn't say. And the police sat right there for years as if there is nothing they can do. I think it's shameful!"

The bitterness in her voice surprised him. It made him look at her differently. She did not seem to hold her son responsible for the choices he made. The sweet, singing, demure grandmother he saw just moments ago was gone. Mrs. Baker was upset now. Juan wondered if she was angry with him for asking the question. He decided to try to give her some comfort.

"He--the rich man--turned himself in a few weeks ago."

"Really?" she asked. "I stopped looking at the news after Charles was arrested. They report the same thing over and over. They make your children sound like wicked people with no soul. I just stopped listening. He turned himself in?"

"Yes, ma'am," he said again.

"So, he turned himself in? Good. It won't be like Charles' death is the end of the case."

"Maybe. There is one problem—or, a potential problem," Juan added quickly, when he saw the look on her face.

"What problem?"

"Some people feel that there might not be enough evidence to convict him. If it turns out it is Charles' word against his and Charles--I mean, my dad--is dead, there is no one to finger the person who hired Charles now. That guy might just walk away. If that happens, Charles'--I mean Dad's--death would be the end of it."

Mrs. Baker stared back at him for a moment with complete shock. "That is terrible! How can they allow that?" She was outraged. The woman's demeanor was now more acrimonious, almost like that of a woman scorned. "Black men don't get justice--no matter what side of the law they are on."

"It made me upset, too," Juan said. "I don't know why, but I don't want it to look like Charles--Dad--was a random murderer. Then I thought, if we only had some proof. If there was proof of the payment Charles received from the guy, we would have some physical evidence pointing to the guy who originated the crime. But it was all so long ago. How could we even trace or find anything?"

"He never paid it all to him," she said, coldly.

The way she said it put a chill down Juan's back, as if her knowledge of the money and the crime was deeper than he realized. He decided not to let the loose ends sidetrack him.

"Well, if we could show that Charles was paid something by the guy. I mean, just like you said of Tim, there is no legitimate relationship between Joshua Benson and Charles Baker. The defense would then have to explain the money. If we could prove he gave the money to Charles, that would be a much stronger case."

"You're sneaky," she said suddenly. "Charles was like that. He was not always direct with the things he did or wanted. Okay, so if I could help you with this proof, how would you use it?"

"I guess I would call the lead detective. I don't know exactly what to do with any new evidence, but I think I would turn it over to the authorities."

"Okay. Finish your food."

When she said that, Juan's stomach tightened. However, he had resolved that he would not leave there without something to help with the case against Joshua. Because of that he did his expected part and stuffed another piece of food in his mouth.

Mrs. Baker excused herself from the table. When she returned, she came back with a little bankbook. She sat down beside him and opened it. There were two entries in the book, a deposit for $9,999 and a withdrawal of $2,000.

"Who made the withdrawal?" He asked.

"That is none of your business. Charles didn't have a bank account, but I did. I let him deposit the money into my account. I did not ask him where he got it from at first, but after I knew, I kept the money in my account. My son died for this money, so it's his money."

Juan had to hold in his anger. Charles Baker did not die for the money! Her son killed for the money.

"Is there a way to show where it came from?"

"I don't know. You're slick and I am sure you must have a plan."

He nodded and put the fork down. He would stay a few more minutes and then he needed to take this information to his mother. Juan wanted to disappear before Darnell came home. He was not interested in a family reunion.

Chapter 55

Juan waited a few days before broaching the subject with his mother. On one hand, he was fearful of talking to her about his covert operation that resulted in uncovering information she obviously had no intention of sharing with him. On the other hand, he had always wanted to be his mother's hero. This was his opportunity to show her that he did share her courageous and enterprising ways after all.

He decided to wait until Kacey was snuggled in her bed and asleep. Juan held the bankbook tightly in his hand as he walked up behind Tara in the kitchen. She was sipping hot tea with her back to him. This was one of the nightly rituals Tara enjoyed. She would wait until Kacey was asleep, go into the kitchen and sip mint tea. Sometimes it would take her an hour to get through one cup of hot tea. It was the way she relaxed after her full days.

She must have been in deep thought. When she turned from the cabinet, she jumped, surprised to see him standing there. "You're up late, Juan."

"I wanted to talk to you."

She raised her eyebrows. "Is that so?"

"Yes."

She walked past him to go into her office. Juan sighed and followed her. Tara was wearing a big, pink, cotton robe that hugged her like a blanket. She reclined on the couch in her office and tilted her head back. It was obvious to him that she expected bad news.

"What is it, Juan?" She was trying not to appear as though she had a preconceived notion of the conversation. But she was failing miserably. Parents were interesting creatures, he thought, as he leaned forward and revealed the bankbook to her.

He placed the bankbook down before her. She looked down from his face to the object on the table. Perhaps she expected to see a bad report card or a note from one of his teachers. Tara had actually received a note about school absences, but with all the focus on Tim's case again, she did not confront Juan. Tara knew her son was too smart to allow his grades to plummet completely. Her only wish was that he would follow the rules more carefully so that the doors that were destined to open for him would fling wide open.

"What is that?" she asked, curious.

"It's a bankbook."

"I see that. Why do you have it?" There was a hint of sharpness to her tone.

"Ma, don't get upset."

"Okay. Now I am getting upset. Why are you telling me not to get upset?" Her voice was sharper now and instead of reclining, she was sitting upright.

Juan took a deep breath. "It's the bankbook with the bank account number that holds the money Charles Baker was paid to kill Tim."

For a moment, she did not speak. Then Tara tilted her head and focused on him fully again. "Juan, what in the world are you talking about?"

"Ma, I talked to Charles' mother. I figured that maybe Charles had given her money. Turns out she has the money—well, most of it--he was paid by Joshua. I was thinking we could research this account. If we can show where the funds came from, Joshua will have a hard time explaining why he gave it to him."

"Juan--" His mother had a scowl on her face.

"Aren't you happy?" he pressed. Juan could not imagine any news better than what he was sharing with her right now. If he had to sell her on his ideas, he would, but he had no intention of this accomplishment being overshadowed with a pointless scolding.

"Well, yes, but you have to take a step back for me. How would you know about this bankbook? Where did you find Charles' mother? I can't believe she just walked up to you and gave you this bankbook. How did you get it?"

"I met her at her home in Chicago and, yes, she gave it to me. I had a long talk with her. She wanted me to have it, Ma, as long as needed for the case."

Tara was on her feet now. "When did you go to Chicago? Juan, do you know how dangerous Chicago can be? You don't know these people. How could you do something like this without telling me?"

"Ma, don't yell. I put together a personal project at school. I was in search of your history--my history, too---so I went to talk to your foster parents. I found

Darnell Baker and I stumbled on news about Charles Baker. After I talked to Darnell, I did a little more research and realized Charles was convicted as the shooter. I wasn't going to go back, but with Joshua turning himself in, I had to go back." He paused. Then blurted it out. "So, I know everything. Darnell told me everything. I had to go back and get what I could to help--I had to help you."

"Go back? You have been there more than once?"

"Yes, ma'am. The first time, I went to talk to them, the Bakers. I thought maybe they could tell me who my father was or at least give me some hints. I went back after Joshua turned himself in. I know everything, Ma, and I am sorry if it upsets you."

"Everything like what?" She was much calmer now. Her eyes stared at him as if seeing him for the first time. Juan had done all this? It baffled her in some ways because she had no idea he cared so much about the past. Tara was impressed by his obvious resourcefulness. But when she thought about how dangerous the Bakers could be, it scared her. As she stared at him, she was thankful to see her son standing before her in one piece.

Tara felt guilty. Juan was a young man in turmoil, with raw emotions she had overlooked for so many years. She wanted him to be content with only the knowledge she gave to him. However, she realized that Juan could not move forward without a thorough knowledge of the past. Tara had been running from the past since she was 16 years old. In fact, she had made it her life's business to shield Juan from the life she had lived for her first 16 years. As far as she was concerned, there was no benefit, only pain, in those years. Why would she pass that suffering on to her beloved son?

"I know what happened to you," he continued. "I know what Charles Baker did to you." He was a little angry as he spoke. "So, we'll seal this chapter and you can move on."

"Charles?" she inquired. Tara looked at him again. Her son had a deep look of shame on his face. She could also see that he had been deceived and she was responsible for that. How could she let Darnell Baker flavor his version of events to her child?

"Juan, sweetie," she started. But now he had the look of determination she was used to seeing. Tara had always considered it stubbornness. Now she knew that it was partly stubbornness, but also passion, leadership and a sensitivity to justice that made him sometimes go his own way.

"Ma, it's okay. I know what happened. I know what Charles did to you. And I am sorry for it."

"Charles," she repeated. "Is that what you were told?"

"I talked to Darnell. He told me. I'm sorry, Ma. I wanted to tell you that I was going there. Then I wanted to tell you I went. I had to go back and get something."

He had that thick sound to his voice as if tears were to come, but Juan was not going to shed any tears. He strengthened his tone. Tara was standing close to him looking up at him now. She put her hands on his shoulders. They were broad and very tense. Tara had not realized just how tall and firm he was. She gave him that reassuring mother's touch to relax him a bit.

"Juan, sit down," she said, calmly.

He obeyed quietly. After he was seated, she took a deep breath to gather her thoughts.

"Stop apologizing to me. I should apologize to you. I realize that I have kept you in the dark about a number of things. I can't say I was trying to protect you. I just didn't think you needed to know much about the past, and my past. I thought my job was to give you a good start. I'm sorry I put you in a situation where you felt you had to go all the way to Chicago to learn about your past. But I need to tell you a few things."

Tara took a seat beside him and took his hand gently. She didn't know how else to say it, so she spoke directly.

"Charles Baker is not your father and Charles did not rape me."

"I don't understand. Darnell said--" he started, but he stopped himself. His mother had never lied to him. He did not expect her to start doing so now.

"Darnell Baker was not truthful to you."

"He said Charles hurt you." Juan felt more comfortable substituting the word 'rape' with 'hurt.'

"Charles did not hurt me," Tara said, picking up on his cue. "He was nice to me--the only person in that house who was. He also helped me get away from that place. He helped me escape from Darnell. He gave me a few dollars towards my one-way bus ticket. When I left, I was a pregnant teen. I was pregnant with you."

There was silence as the meaning of her words sunk in. Juan's feelings of confusion and betrayal now turned to rage. However, he masked his rage because he wanted to know more.

"So, Darnell lied to me."

"If he told you Charles hurt me, then yes. He lied. That is typical Darnell. He lies. I see he hasn't changed. He was never one to take responsibility."

"What about Tim's murder? Charles Baker was the trigger man. What type of crazy coincidence is that?"

She shook her head. "I hadn't spoken to Charles in years. Tim's murder was the first time I had even seen him or thought about him in so long. It was crazy to see him after all those years under arrest. I don't think he recognized me. Charles was no saint, but he helped me. I can't speak to what he had become. I don't really know what happened inside him to kill for money."

"Ma, why did you keep me?" He had been wanting to ask her that question ever since he learned about the circumstances of his conception and birth. "Didn't you want to get rid of me when you found out you were pregnant?"

"No." She seemed surprised by his question. "You gave me a reason to keep trying. Before you, I had no one in this world to call family. Juan, we are family. You're my gift from God Himself. And look at you with this bankbook. Joshua Benson is going to finally answer for Tim. It will probably be the first time in his life he has had to answer for anything he's done. You helped me get through many lonely nights."

He nodded with comprehension and relief. He was thankful his mother did not just say it was the right thing to do. Tara stood up and looked at the bankbook again. She gathered it up in her hand and smiled at him. "I'll pass this over to the auditors and Detective Monroe. We got him. No--you got Joshua. Thank you."

"Ma, what about Darnell? When is he going to answer for what he did to you?"

"Juan, don't worry about that. God will take care of Darnell."

With that, she hugged him and walked away to put her tea cup in the dishwasher. Juan felt something shift in him. He was no longer angry and distressed. But his work was not done. Charles Baker died in prison for murder and, although Mrs. Baker did not agree, that is where he belonged. Darnell Baker belonged in jail as well. Darnell had raped his mother, a minor while she was in his care. Tara was through with that part of her life and would never bring a charge.

However, Juan had a burning desire to see Darnell pay for what he'd done. Juan began to conceive a plan at that moment. Darnell was going to pay, for sure. He thought he had once read that the statute of limitations for sexual assault in Illinois was 20 years--and he, Juan, was only 16 years old.

Chapter 56

That night Tara was transported back to the past in her dreams. She was a young girl again living in the Baker household in Chicago. The afternoon she dreamt about was like so many afternoons before it. She arrived home from school around 3:00 PM, anxious to start her homework. The teacher had asked for an essay about *Their Eyes Were Watching God*. Tara had enjoyed reading the book and she considered this assignment a treat as opposed to a task.

A boy who lived close to the Bakers was talking to her as she walked toward the house. He was a nice boy with a very handsome face. Although she did not realize it then, he liked her. However, Tara was too withdrawn and quiet to notice things like that. She chatted with him briefly, but her main objective was to get away from all the other kids and get into the house. Other kids teased, joked and asked questions. Sometimes their teasing, jokes and questions were burdensome to her, even those comments with no malicious intent. Hearing her classmates' constant complaints about their parents was a chore for Tara. At least they had parents to complain about. Tara preferred to keep their whining conversations short.

What she did not know is that she was being watched from the window of the house as she moved toward the front door. When she opened the front door that day, Darnell was on the couch, relaxing and smoking a cigarette. He was not usually home in the afternoon. His presence surprised and annoyed her, but it did not worry her. Usually she had the house to herself for a few hours before Darnell and Mrs. Baker arrived home.

"Hi," she said politely as she entered the door. Tara was already making her way past him to the hallway.

"Hey." He took another puff of his smoke. "How was school?"

"Fine."

"You like Freddy?" he asked with a hint of surprise in his voice. "I didn't think a boy like Freddy would be your type."

"Freddy?" She did not know who he was talking about at first. Then she realized he was talking about the nice boy. "Oh, Fred. No. I mean, he's nice, I guess, but that's it. I don't really know him."

"I could tell he likes you. He probably looking at those tight jeans and those nice round butt cheeks." He laughed.

Tara did not know how to respond, so she decided not to. She gave him an uncomfortable smile instead. Darnell looked at her and smiled. "I'm just joking with you. He's a nice boy. I know his dad. You want me to arrange something? That could be nice-- the two of you."

"No, thanks," she said. "Well, I am going to start on my homework."

"Uh, okay. Good. I like that. You got books. I hate dumb, pretty women."

She walked past him and went to her room. Tara put the lock on the door instinctively. She thought Darnell was an okay guy, but she did not like how he looked at her sometimes. She found the look downright creepy. She had already had a few experiences with uncomfortable touching by men when she was younger. They always seemed to do just enough to make themselves feel decent while making her feel violated. Tara cringed when older men flirted or made fresh remarks to her.

It was not long before there was a knock at her bedroom door.

"Tara, are you hungry?" Darnell called through the door.

She looked over and watched as the knob jiggled from his attempt to open the door. Her heart started beating a little faster. Her stomach growled. Normally, she would have fixed herself a snack, but she forfeited that today. "No," she called back. "I'm going to wait for dinner."

"You sure? Open the door. I am about to eat. It would be rude of me not to share with you. Do you mind joining me?"

"No I don't mind. It's just I need to get this homework done. It's an essay and it takes me a while to get my thoughts together," she lied.

"Okay. No problem," he called back. His voice carried disappointment.

She thought that was the end of it, but he knocked again. "Tara, open the door. You can do your homework after you eat."

This time his voice sounded more insistent. Tara debated whether she should just ignore him. Mrs. Baker should be home any moment, she thought.

"Uh, give me one sec," she called, trying to mask her annoyance.

She went over to the door and opened it. He was standing there with a smile. Darnell smelled like cigarette smoke, which Tara hated. He moved past her and entered the room.

"What are you doing?"

"What am I doing? I am coming into a room in my house. Is that all right with you? This is still my house."

"I suppose, but I thought we were going to the kitchen to eat."

"Tara, you want to eat in the kitchen. Would you like to go to a nice restaurant? I can take you to a great place. I can take you to lots of nice places."

"Not really. I need to finish my homework. Besides, if we're going out, we can just wait for Mrs. Baker, anyway. I'll do my homework while we wait."

Darnell was standing close behind her now. Tara was surprised when he grabbed her. She gasped, but did not lose her composure. He wrapped his arms around her waist, leaned forward and placed his lips against her ear.

"What are you doing?" she asked, in alarm.

"What does it feel like I'm doing?" he responded, whispering sensuously.

Tara tried to move out of his grip, but he tightened his hold on her. "Please --"

"Don't get excited," he cautioned. "Tara, I am not going to hurt you. Just relax. It's okay. You're with me."

"I don't want to do this," she said as he slipped his hand inside her shirt.

"But it's okay. You are such a sweet girl. I won't hurt you. I would never hurt you."

"No," she said, trying her best to pull away from him.

Darnell held her even tighter now and she was having trouble breathing. He hoisted her up so that her feet were off the ground. Tara could feel herself being pulled away from the door and over to the bed. As he walked away from the door, he kicked it closed.

"Please, Mr. Baker," she begged. "I can't breathe."

He loosened his grip a bit and Tara caught her breath. He watched her as she took a deep breath. Tara was deeply scared for the first time. He did not seem like himself. He was staring down at her with a look of determination. She felt tears start to well in her eyes, but she refused to let them flow. All she could think about was Mrs. Baker walking in the house—a rescue, yes, but the end of her welcome in this house.

Panic arose in her at the thought of having to deal with the aftermath of his game with her. She looked past him toward the door. Lord, I got to get out of here.

"Lie back," he commanded.

"Mr. Baker, stop!"

"Tara, I told you I won't hurt you."

"But this hurts," she complained, her voice shaking. "Mrs. Baker is going to come home. She's going to blame me. Please!"

"Tara, I will handle her. She's working late tonight. Don't worry about that. Just trust me. It won't hurt if you stay calm and lie back," he reasoned.

Tara knew she could not win against him on the basis of strength. But she knew she was faster than he was. If she could run around him, she could make it to the front door. There was no way he would run outside after her. Then she could just stay away until Mrs. Baker arrived home.

"Come on," he urged quietly. He had his hand in his pants. Tara was starting to realize the gravity of her situation. Darnell was not going to rub on her. He was going to rape her.

Every part of her body was alive with fear, but she was not about to submit to him without a fight. He had grown impatient, so he bent over to grab her legs. Tara used the opportunity to kick him in the face with all her might. Her kick was effective in that it pushed Darnell back. He groaned in pain. However, he recovered more quickly than she anticipated. He caught her around the waist again as she tried to run past him. Darnell hoisted her up again and slammed her on the floor.

Thankfully, she did not hit her head, but her back hurt terribly. He put his hand under her chin and started to squeezed lightly. "I will snap your little neck off, bury you in the backyard, and say you ran away. Who would even look for you Tara? Huh? Lie back."

The rest of the memory faded and Tara woke up with a start. Tears were in her eyes and she found herself crying uncontrollably. She pounded her pillow with her fists in frustration. Tara had never really cried or vented to anyone about her terrible ordeal. After that day, Tara stopped talking much altogether. She stayed to herself and tried to avoid coming home until the last minute. She stopped participating in school and doing homework.

When Charles Baker joined the household, Darnell was distracted for a while. His brother was a thorn in his side and the brothers were in constant conflict. Perhaps Charles only helped her in order to spite Darnell. Darnell had taken this liberty multiple times until she discovered she was pregnant. Mrs. Baker was openly and increasingly hostile toward her. Tara knew if she popped up pregnant, the stress would be unbearable for her and her child. That was when she realized homelessness would be better than living in a house with the Bakers.

Lord, I don't know. Sometimes I wonder why things were as they were. Suddenly, Tara felt a sensation of comfort engulf her. She lay back in the king bed and thought about Juan and Kacey. Both her children slept in the house with her name on the title. They were safe and sound in her care. Her despair eased.

"It's going to be all right," she assured herself. "I know it will."

Chapter 57

Joshua Benson was upset when he realized his gamble had not paid off. His lawyer informed him of the news as his client sat before him, adorned in an orange prison uniform. The clean-shaven Joshua who had appeared in the courtroom had now been replaced by a hairy, unkempt Joshua. His face had a mean look to it. He frequently looked over his shoulder with suspicion and disdain at the other inmates.

The prosecution had evidence of his payment to Charles Baker. His lawyer explained his options to him carefully. There was enough evidence to convict him. In fact, the Benson's old lawyer was prepared to also testify that Joshua had obtained information about his parents' will weeks before the murder. Motive was established as well as consideration for the contract killing. His life on the run for the past seven years did not help. Juries tend to believe that innocent men do not run.

His lawyer told him they would go to trial, without doubt. His recommendation was that Joshua plead guilty and allow the lawyer to focus on saving him from the death penalty. The state would be prepared to offer life in prison without the possibility of parole, but at least he would be alive.

Joshua was too much like his mother in some respects. The fact that he lost one gamble did not stop him from wanting to take another. He mocked the concern in his lawyer's eyes. There was no way he could see his life ending in such a despicable manner.

"The actual shooter did not get the death penalty. I won't either," he said in the arrogant Benson way. "My plea remains not guilty. And you need to focus on doing your job. Get me out of this."

"How am I going to get you out of this? I can advise you according to the law, but I can't make a miracle happen--I'm not Jesus Christ."

"You're the lawyer. Figure it out," Joshua said curtly. "That's what I am paying you for."

"About that," the lawyer followed up, clearing his throat. "Will you be able to pay?"

"I'll be able to pay. See, no matter what happens with this case, I plan to sue for the full portion of my inheritance. I am the natural son of George and Sheryl Benson. The money belongs to me and my descendants. I have the right to determine where it goes—and that doesn't include some orphaned, homeless girl who just happened to marry my so-called brother. Get me out of here. Stop focusing on this new evidence. File some motions--a change of venue--something. Challenge the money flow. There's got to be enough to make at least one juror doubt. Find it."

Chapter 58

Darnell was strolling with his dog when he saw Juan's parked car in front of the house. He was surprised to see it, but part of him was happy. Darnell wanted some type of relationship with Juan. The boy reminded him of himself—Darnell recalled a time when he had too had been handsome. Juan was a real go-getter and that made Darnell even prouder. Juan did not necessarily look like a Baker in the face, Darnell had to admit, but he had the body structure and muscles of a Baker man.

When he approached the car, he noticed Juan sitting in the front seat. Darnell had expected him to be in the house eating some of his mother's food already. When the young man noticed him, he eased out of the car. He didn't speak or greet him, though, so Darnell opened the conversation.

"You sitting out here? You want to come on in the house?" he said reaching to give him the manly one-arm hug men customarily provide one another.

"No. I was waiting to talk to you," Juan said, with a manly thud of the fist against Darnell's knuckles.

"Okay. Well, I was about to go in the house. I am sure Mama would love to see you. Everything going all right, young brother?" Darnell could tell he was bothered by something.

Juan shrugged. "I'm okay. If you don't mind I need to talk to you about something, but it's kind of delicate. I don't want your mother to hear it. You may not want your mother to hear it, either."

"Okay," he said. Darnell noticed he used the "your mother" phrasing instead of a more endearing term. "What about?"

Juan was standing closer to him now, but turned to walk down the street. Darnell dutifully followed him. "This is awkward. So I will just come right out with it."

"All right." Darnell stopped walking. They were now looking one another in the eye and stood toe to toe. Although Juan was younger, he did not cower from Darnell's stare.

"Would you take a DNA test to prove you're not my father?"

"What?" Darnell was shocked, although he knew he should not be.

"I talked to my mom. She says you're lying. Charles did not father me. You did. I am assuming you are prepared to deny this because that would mean that you were a married man in his 20's having nonconsensual sex with a girl who was around 15 years old. You were more than five years her senior in a supervisory role. I am sure that's sexual assault."

"Are you crazy?" Darnell shouted. "You don't come down here talking like that to me."

"You're calling my mom a liar?" Juan challenged. The younger man's fists were balled up suddenly and he held one higher than the other, indicating he was ready to strike. Darnell did not want to fight Juan and he certainly did not want to discuss this in the open.

Shame shrouded him at that moment. A neighbor had come out on her front porch. Darnell did not want a scene in the middle of the street, so he lowered his voice.

"Juan, calm down."

"Don't tell me to calm down. I want an answer. You lied to me."

"Juan, please listen to me."

"I am listening. Tell me the truth."

"Okay. okay. I may have omitted some facts."

"Omitted some facts? You said Charles was my father."

"I did not say that. I said Charles hurt your mother."

"Well, according to her, Charles helped her get away from you. You raped my mom."

"Hold on. little brother. I realize you're upset, but don't make me beat you like a man. And I will whip your narrow butt in this street. You don't come accusing me of crimes in my neighborhood."

"If you think you can beat me, come on. I don't scare easily." Juan bucked up and threw his body close enough to bump Darnell with it. "Tell me what I want to know."

Darnell looked at him. The level of rage Juan was displaying reminded him of how angry his brother Charles could get. He noticed that Juan was wearing a long jacket, but it was not really that cold outside. The young man kept putting his hand on the right side of his pocket. Did he have a gun? Darnell remembered his brother pulling a gun on him once. He certainly hoped that this supposed son of his would not do the same. He decided he wouldn't take a chance with a lethal encounter. He turned his back on Juan. "Get out of here. Don't ever come around here again."

"What? You think it's that easy? You going to talk to me today? You had so much to say the last time I saw you. Keep speaking now. Oh, since I know the truth and you can't hide what you are, you don't have anything to say anymore? You lying hypocrite! You're worse than a dog. I wish I could call you what you are, but my ma taught me better."

"Listen," Darnell said, turning around with venom. "Get out of here! You came for answers. Now you got them. If you come around here again, I'll make you and your whore mama sorry."

When he said that, Juan could see nothing but red. He lunged at Darnell, but the older man moved out of the way. Juan fell forward. Darnell laughed while looking down at him. "You can't fight me. Boy, I'll kill you out here. Go home to your mama."

Juan was up on his feet again. This time he caught Darnell with a back kick squarely in the stomach. The older man was bowed over and coughing as he held his stomach in pain. The younger's hands were up as if he was ready to attack again. He bounced around a little on his toes. But Darnell had no fight in him. The kick had knocked the wind out of him.

Juan prodded, "My ma put me in boxing and karate when I was very young. I been fighting all my life. You can't whip me. But I would love for you to try."

"Okay. Okay," Darnell said, coughing and still catching his breath. "I don't want to fight you. Just leave, Juan. I'm sorry, okay? I lied to you. I am what you think and worse. Just let this go. It's not worth it now."

"I want you to say it," Juan said again. "We have an audience now. People are looking. Tell the truth for once in your life."

Mrs. Baker had come outside now. She quickly moved to stand beside her son, glaring up at Juan with intense anger and hatred. "He don't have to confess nothing to you and no one else. Get out of here before I call the police. You and your trashy mama are nothing but trouble. You got breath in your body? You alive, right? What difference does it make how you got here? Get out of here!"

Juan looked at her in disgust. She had raised a rapist and murderer, both of whom this woman was prepared to defend. Juan shook his head, jumped in his car and drove off.

Chapter 59

The next day, Juan played the tape for Detective Monroe at the police station. The Detective looked at him without speaking. He liked Juan. He thought he was an extremely intelligent young man. He admired the way he tried to protect his mother, but he could not comprehend what the young man told him at that moment. The Bakers were dangerous people and Juan's dealings with them were risky, to say the least.

"Juan, that's not enough to prove that a crime took place years ago. It doesn't really prove anything. It's you and this man arguing. Besides you may do yourself more harm than good with that tape. You struck him first."

"He threatened me."

"He told you to leave and you were in his neighborhood."

"I was in his neighborhood. I was not on his property. If you listen, he invited me in the house and I did not go into the yard. He told me he'd beat me like a man."

"You're too smart for your own good," Detective Monroe replied, shaking his head. Now in his early 40s, the detective wished he could say he was as smart as the 16-year-old Juan. "Look I can appreciate your efforts, but he did not exactly say he raped your mother. You said that."

"No. I want this man brought to justice. I like you a lot, detective, but you all are too cautious. Everything is clear from this tape. He said he lied. He admitted that. He admitted that I came to him for answers and I got answers. He said he was what I said he was and worse. Can't you at least get one of your friends up that way to question him?"

"Juan, we're in the middle of wrapping up your stepfather's case. I don't want to do anything that might jeopardize that."

"It's been wrapped up. Besides your work there is done. You just need to testify. Joshua Benson is done. Now I need your help. This man raped my mother years ago and that is a criminal offense. I want the state to bring charges against him."

The detective sighed. "Juan, your mother is not bringing this accusation--"

"And she won't. You know her, detective. I am bringing it."

"Juan, you're right. I know your mother. She's been through a lot. You have, too. Let it go. It's not healthy for someone your age to be dealing with things like this. Does she even know you're here? You should be enjoying your teens and having fun."

"No. That's not the point. We got to stop letting people like this think that the people they are supposed to help are their property to do with as they wish. How many other young girls and boys are out there, feeling that no one will help them? Detective, we can't let people like this get away with this stuff. We can send a great message--it might be sixteen years later, but the law will catch up with you!"

"Juan, listen to me. If your mother came forward with her story, it would be different, maybe," he sighed. "The burden of proof is on the state in a criminal trial. You have to prove the case beyond a reasonable doubt."

After a brief silence, Detective Monroe spoke again. "Juan, I understand you are angry. But bringing one man to trial to get a few years in prison, and that's a maybe, is not going to help. Your mother is a prominent woman in the community. I agree that she could help a lot of people if she spoke up. I think that's where you need to start."

"My mother helps a lot of people already, Detective. I am looking for some help for her," Juan said. "Can't you at least have the Chicago police go by and question Darnell? Scare him or something! He'll crack with the right pressure."

"Juan, I can't use my influence like that. If your mother wishes to pursue, that's a different story. But then there is the proof--"

"That's my point! I am the proof. My mother had me when she was 16. Darnell was much older and she was a minor. If I can prove he's my father, he's done. Just like Joshua Benson, he's going to jail."

"Okay," Detective Monroe nodded. "He would go to jail under those circumstances. But what does that give you? What does it give your mother?"

"It gives her closure."

"Juan, I think she has closed that chapter of her life already. That's my point. She moved on, but somehow she didn't take you with her. Go home. Talk to your mother. She may not want to relive all this again."

Juan leaned back in the chair and banged the back of his head against the wall in frustration. He thought about Darnell. Then his mind drifted to his mother. Detective Monroe was now chatting on the phone with someone about another case.

So, he was supposed to let it go just like that?

Chapter 60

Juan left Detective Monroe's office and went straight home. His mother's car was there, but there was also another car parked in front of the house. He pulled in the garage and made his way inside quickly. For some reason, he was not surprised to see Darnell in his home, sitting in his mother's office. Tara was not in the office, however, and he could not hear her in the house.

"Where is my mother?" Juan asked with his fists balled again.

"Don't hit me, please." Darnell said. He was on his feet with his hands in a defensive position. Juan let his eyes settle on him. The older man looked sincere and contrite. He had put a few feet of distance between Juan and himself.

Juan felt something in him soften because of the sorry look in Darnell's eyes, but he did not want to give in to those feelings. Juan recounted again in his head what had transpired. Not only had Darnell abused his authority over his mother years ago, he had lied to him. It was unforgivable. Juan was not going to let some sense of misguided pity rope him into giving someone like Darnell a second chance.

"What are you doing here? Does my mother know you're here?"

"Yes, of course. I called before I came and she agreed to see me," Darnell answered, his voice trembling a bit.

"Get out of here. Why would you come here?" Juan demanded in frustration.

"Juan," Tara's voice sounded behind him. "Calm down. Mr. Baker said he had something he wanted to tell both of us. Now that you are home, he can tell us and he can leave after he has shared it."

"I don't want to hear anything from him," Juan repeated, keeping his eyes on Darnell.

"Juan, I think I would like to hear it. Can you listen if I can?" she asked.

Tara walked into the room passed Darnell. Darnell coughed, cleared his throat and took the seat Tara motioned him to take. He looked at her and was reminded of how pretty she was. The toughness she tried to exude when she was a teen was gone now. Before him sat a refined woman. She was not afraid of him or visibly bothered by his presence. Beside her was the male version for herself. Juan had the teen toughness she had, but it did not come from not knowing where the next meal would come from, as had been the case with his mother. Juan's toughness was from recent disappointments. Had this latest disappointment pushed him over the edge?

"Well, what do you want?" Juan asked shortly, after a few moments. "I can't say I want you around my mother or me any longer than you have to be. So say what you have come to say and leave."

"Juan," Tara said gently. "I am sure Mr. Baker understands this is not a social visit."

They were both looking at Darnell now. He had their full attention. Suddenly, Darnell felt even more nervous. He was crazy for coming here. After they heard what he had to say, they were sure to throw him out.

"Look," Darnell said shaking a bit. "I don't know why I came. I mean, I do know why I came. I know this is strange. Tara, I have wanted to tell you I'm sorry for years. I was wrong. I was really messed up in the head at the time. As a teen in our home, you needed me. You needed my wife. And I took advantage of you. I betrayed her. I have never forgiven myself."

He dropped his head as he spoke. Darnell was afraid that he would only see scorn in Tara's eyes. As he spoke, he remembered grabbing her violently. He could hear her crying underneath him while he put his hand over her mouth the first time. Once his hand had covered her mouth and nose. She could not breath while he forced her. After that, she would not cry. She would only lie stiff and in silence. He could remember the look in his wife's eyes when she realized what he had done. Instead of dealing with him, she vented her anger on Tara.

He looked up. "I have paid for it. My brother is gone. My wife left me. I barely have a relationship with my own son. And now I am going."

"What do you mean?" Tara asked. "Where are you going?"

"I'm dying."

"Are you serious?" Juan asked, with disbelief. "You didn't act like you were dying when I saw you on the street yesterday."

"Juan, please." Tara directed to him to be quiet. Then she turned her eyes to Darnell. "Darnell, I agreed to see you. Honestly, I am not sure why. But this is very serious. If you are not being truthful, I am going to have to ask you to go. My family has gone through a lot and is going through a lot. We can't take a--I have to just tell you--we can't take a con right now."

"It's not a con, Tara. I really am dying. I want to get my affairs in order. I wanted to ask for your forgiveness. Juan, I need to ask for you to forgive me, too."

"I see," Tara said. She looked at Darnell. In truth, she did not know what to make of this sudden revelation. He looked healthy to her. However, his request for forgiveness was independent of his health problems, or lack thereof.

"Darnell, so you came to purge your soul before you die?" Tara asked.

"Ma, you can't be serious," Juan protested. "You believe him?"

"Juan," Tara said, laying her hand on his forearm. "I have no reason not to believe him. So, Darnell is that what it is? You came here to purge your soul."

"Look. I know I don't deserve pity or compassion, but I have to do this."

"If you feel so bad, why don't you go down to the police station and turn yourself in for what you did to my mother? That will show you're really sorry."

"You want me in jail?" Darnell seemed surprised as if he had never considered that what he had done was criminal.

"In jail is where you belong. So, you see you and your brother are not that different after all." Juan felt his cheeks grow hotter.

"Juan, please--" Tara interrupted. "Darnell, I have moved on with my life. I had to for the sake of my child. He went and found you. I never wanted him to deal with this, or with you. Now here we all are, together. I am looking at you and I had sworn I would never look at you again. I am sorry you are sick. But if you are looking for me to give you some words of peace, I don't know that I can give you that right now."

"I understand, Tara," Darnell said. "I just want you to know that I been doing a lot of soul-searching. Those days have been bothering me a lot. And then Juan showed up. I knew this was my sign to take a chance and let you know I know I was wrong."

"Well, you can leave now," Juan said, deliberately trying to keep the mood full of friction. Darnell could be a disarming figure. Juan remembered that he had not seen through his con the first time he met him. Although Juan knew his mother was a shrewd judge of character, she was a Christian. She had a soft spot for the lost and contrite. Juan did not buy Darnell's ploy.

"There is one more thing I need to tell you both before I leave. I came to ask for forgiveness, but I came also for one other thing."

"What?" Tara asked him with raised eyebrows.

"I have a rare genetic disease. The doctors tell me they can try to treat me to try to prolong my life, but death is inevitable." He took a deep breath. "My son has been tested. It seems he has a form of the disease. The doctor recommended that I have all my children tested. I thought it was right for me to let you two know. I think you should get tested, Juan."

Juan was taken aback by Darnell's words. Darnell's dying made perfect sense to him. He had it coming, but his own death from some inherited disease seemed absurd to him. Before thoughts could swim more wildly in his head, Tara interjected.

"Get out," Tara said coldly.

"Tara!" He tried to plead.

"Get out of my house!" She was on her feet now. "How dare you come to my home to bring your doom and gloom and lies! If you are sick, that is your sickness. Juan is my son, not yours. He does not have anything from you!"

Juan was quiet. He watched his mother's anger explode. He also observed the look of shock on Darnell's face. In part, Juan was satisfied with his mother's reaction because he could see the power she was exerting over Darnell. The man had not expected this reaction. Perhaps he had come, thinking he would leave them both helpless after his confession. For Juan, the magnitude of what was being suggested seemed abstract, not concrete. Juan felt healthy. He played sports. He was young and he was not sick. Or was he?

"Tara, please," Darnell was on his feet now. "Look, I came here because I felt it was the right thing to do. Don't blame me."

"I don't know or care why you came here. But I tell you one thing. You can get out of here and go back to where you belong. Don't ever come near me or my family again."

Darnell stood and started to make his way out of the house. "Again, I'm sorry. You really should have Juan tested. For yourself, Juan. Get tested. If they catch it soon enough, you might have a chance."

Tara picked up a crystal vase and hurled it at his head. The vase burst into shards next to his head as he shuffled out of the door. "Get out!" Tara shouted.

Carla Brice-Talley *Tara's Touch*

Chapter 61

Darnell left the house feeling bitter. He was a divorced man in his fifties who lived with his mother, did not feel close to his son, and lost his wife years ago because he raped a foster teen. In some respects, he resented Juan's thoughts about him. It was not as if Tara was a baby when he met her. In fact, she was not a virgin when he took her.

He still did not know why he touched her. It frustrated him that he had done such a thing in his life, but he could not change it now. Asking forgiveness was a ridiculous proposition. He had no idea why he attempted such a fruitless exercise. When Charles had asked that Darnell come to see him, he refused to do so. Why would anyone provide him with any grace? Darnell did not believe he was worthy of forgiveness. Not even God should forgive him.

However, as he drove, he could not help but shake his head in disgust. What did either one of them have to complain about? Tara and Juan lived in a 5,000 square foot house filled with fine items. Tara was a successful business woman. Every aspect of her spoke of grooming, refinement and poise. Juan was a spoiled brat, although Darnell had to acknowledge that he was a confident, well-spoken, strong-willed young man. He had all the makings of someone destined for greatness. He was a real leader. What frustrated Darnell was that he had nothing to do with any of it. At this point in his life, he did not have one single accomplishment he could point to.

He had a dream a few nights ago. In his dream, he was justifying himself to someone. He was trying to tell the person that they should give him another chance. He wanted them to understand his point of view. He even remembered now his insistence in the dream that he was not a bad person. It was just that he had done a few bad things in his life.

A question kept lingering from the dream. "Is a man to be judged by one action for the rest of his life?"

Arriving home, Darnell found a comfortable chair, but no comfort there. His heart was pounding in his chest. Sweat popped on his brows. His mother had come into the living room and asked him if he was all right. As usual, Darnell lied and said, yes, he was all right.

His mother now out of the room, tears flowed down Darnell's face. He was a pitiful example of a man at this stage in his life. He had nothing to offer this world or anyone else.

Was he sick? For him, it didn't matter one way or the other. He just wanted to test Tara and Juan to see if they had any compassion for him. They did not. He had tested his ex-wife with the same tale. She had listened patiently, but then she told him she would pray for him and wished him well.

He did not even bother to tell his son from his marriage, because the teenager would only look at him with indifference.

He knew how to gather the sympathy he desired from people in his life. In his misery, he had a small epiphany: if a made-up tale of terminal illness wouldn't move people, his actual death would turn on the tap of love for him from those who had known him. They'd be sorry when he was gone.

Chapter 62

Mrs. Baker was the one to phone Juan about Darnell's death. On the other end of the line, she sounded angry and spoiling for a fight.

"Your father is dead," she spat.

"Excuse me?" Juan had asked. He did not think of Darnell as his father, so he had to think about it. However, he could hear the aged voice on the other end of the phone and he recognized the area code for Chicago from the caller ID.

"I said your father is dead. So, I hope you're satisfied now. I hope you have the peace in your life you were searching for."

He did not respond immediately.

Mrs. Baker continued. "Yeah. You came to our house. With you, you brought all that trouble from the past. It was dead and buried. Dina had left with her accusations. You came with that junk and now my boy is gone. I hope you are satisfied."

Juan had always been taught to respect his elders, but he could not hold back at this moment. Mrs. Baker was still mumbling on the other end of the phone. Suddenly Juan exploded.

"Just stop it! I didn't want him dead. But if he's dead, that's not my fault. By the way, your son was a rapist. Your other son was a murderer. Maybe you should stop blaming the world and look at yourself.

What could you have done better? So, I am satisfied. Thanks for the call, but I won't be attending the funeral."

With that Juan slammed the phone down. He felt surprisingly unmoved. Tara walked into the room.

"Juan, are you all right? Who was that?"

"What?" He turned around, as if surprised to see her.

"I heard you on the phone. Are you all right?"

"Oh, I am fine. Just some crazy telemarketer. They keep mixing me up with you." Juan put on his best face under the circumstances and gave her a shallow smile. Tara knew something was up, but she decided to let it go.

"Okay. Well, I did book an appointment with Doctor Lasing. Darnell is a liar, but I don't want to ignore anything about your health. If there is anything, we'll get the best care money can buy."

"Mama, I know I am fine."

"I know, too. Just want to make sure," she said, leaning forward and giving him a kiss on the cheek.

Juan decided he would not mention Darnell's death. It was his fault that his mother had to look the man in the face again. He was not even going to tempt her to feel even remotely compassionate or responsible for him.

Chapter 63

The People vs. Joshua Benson commenced six months later. Joshua stood trial for the murder of Tim Benson, a natural person. The trial went relatively quickly. The prosecution presented its case over three days. The defense tried to cast doubt over the course of two days. The bankbook was the most damning piece of evidence. When combined with the circumstantial evidence and Joshua's seven years on the run, the totality of the evidence convinced jurors beyond a reasonable doubt of his guilt. Their verdict pronounced him guilty of first degree murder with aggravating circumstances.

The penalty phase was the most unnerving aspect of the process for Tara. She did not necessarily see herself as a pro-death-penalty person, but her husband's life had been taken away in absolute evil and cold cruelty. She nevertheless sat in the court room and listened to the information presented.

Joshua had no one to speak for him. Mr. and Mrs. Benson were both dead. Mrs. Claire was also dead. Jose had never been a fan of Joshua's, so was not asked to testify for fear of what he might reveal. Tina was completely incoherent now. Ironically, Tim would have likely tried to say something in his brother's defense, but his brother had ended that possibility. Over Joshua's seven years on the run, there were no acts of rehabilitation or remorse that could be highlighted to demonstrate to the court that his life was worth saving.

Joshua Benson, as he sat helpless in court, was not unlike Tara in her teenage years. He had no one to help him and he was at the mercy of the system. Joshua was a man without a family and no real advocate.

Therefore, it would fall to Tara to advocate for him, against her strong feelings of revulsion for the man and his actions. He was guilty of killing her husband. But did she want him executed?

She was given an opportunity to speak at the sentencing phase. When she approached the podium, she could see Joshua's eyes fall on her. He seemed resolved to his fate and his face was blank. There was no hatred, mockery, or scorn in his eyes as in prior encounters. He looked soulless.

The members of the jury and the judge stared at her. The prosecution and the defense looked dutifully in her direction. Even Detective Monroe had put aside his busy schedule to be at the sentencing hearing.

Tara stated her name and respectfully addressed the court.

"Thank you for allowing me to make a statement. I have waited a long time for this. Over the last seven years, I have often thought about what I might say. Now that I have this opportunity, I want to use it in the right way. I am not here to talk about what Joshua Benson deserves or what my husband, Tim Benson, did not deserve. I am not even here to dwell on how much I miss my husband."

"I grew up hard. I often did not know where my next meal would come from. I never knew my mother or my father. I went for years not being connected to a family or having an identity that tied me to something greater than myself. Then I had a son. He helped me understand how important life is. Because of him, I know that life is greater than my individual thoughts and feelings. It is even greater than the actions I take. When I met Tim Benson, he enriched my life further. Because of him, I also have a beautiful daughter who also helps me find encouragement and joy. Tim, although he is not here today because of Joshua Benson's actions, would not want us to look at Joshua Benson as worthless and doomed to execution. Tim would ask that we look at Joshua Benson through a lens of compassion. Therefore, I am asking the court to consider granting Joshua Benson life in prison. My husband--the love of my life--and I were and are opposed to the death penalty. Thank you."

After Tara's simple statement, the court room fluttered a little with emotional expressions. But there was no dramatic reaction in response to her speech. Tara took her seat again and waited.

Joshua Benson was given a chance to speak. He did not apologize for Tim's murder and he did not address Tara directly. He addressed the court with a long, angry dialogue. He reiterated his plea of innocence and then bitterly said that his blood would be upon everyone in the room.

With that he was sentenced to death by lethal injection.

Tara stood and left the courtroom. She did not know how she felt. Although she had waited for justice for years, there was no satisfaction with this outcome. It was another unfortunate event she needed to put behind her. Tara decided then that she had done what her conscience demanded. She would not participate in any clemency hearings. If the execution were to happen, she would not attend. Joshua Benson had consumed enough of her life. It was time for her to move on.

She turned her thoughts to her children. Juan was a handsome boy destined for greatness. He had tracked down Darnell and he had secured the crucial bankbook evidence. He was resourceful and courageous. She did not see any limitations on what he could accomplish. She only hoped she could guide his natural intelligence and strength in the right direction. There was a lot of good he would do, not just for himself, but for others as well.

Kacey was a beautiful, innocent girl who lived a safe and secure life. Tara knew she had spent too much time protecting Kacey and not enough time pushing her toward her daughter's independent destiny. Kacey needed a sense of working toward something. Tara decided she would have her trust documents revised so that Kacey had to fulfill certain criteria, including college graduation, before she could inherit a substantial fortune.

Tara had finally turned a major corner in her life. As she stepped out of the courthouse and felt the bright rays of the sun on her face, she felt light and ready for new beginnings. There were no weights or burdens on her. The past was behind her. She knew in her heart that there were boundless possibilities for her and her children. She had a family that nothing could destroy. Finally, this was Tara's time.

Tara's Touch

Made in the USA
Middletown, DE
18 March 2019